The Marriage Lesson

VICTORIA ALEXANDER

The MARRIAGE LESSON

WHEELER
PUBLISHING, INC.
ROCKLAND, MA

★ AN AMERICAN COMPANY ★

Published in Large Print by arrangement with Avon Books, an imprint of HarperCollins Publishers Inc., in the United States and Canada.

Wheeler Large Print Book Series.

Set in 16 pt Plantin.

Library of Congress Cataloging-in-Publication Data

Alexander, Victoria.
    The marriage lesson / Victoria Alexander.
        p. (large print) cm.(Wheeler large print book series)
    ISBN 1-58724-131-5 (hardcover)
    1. Large type books. I. Title. II. Series

[PS3551.L357713 M37   2001]
813′.54—dc21   2001047438
                                                CIP

This book is dedicated with great affection
to Meg Ruley,
who lets me find my own way
through the dark forest
but always makes sure I come out alive.

Chapter 1

Spring 1819

"**B**last it all, I'm a marquess, not a bloody governess." Thomas Effington, the Marquess of Helmsley and future Duke of Roxborough, drained the glass of brandy he held in his hand and promptly poured another.

Randall, Viscount Beaumont, studied him over the rim of his own glass. "You've mentioned that already this evening. Several times, in fact."

"It bears repeating." Thomas sank into a wing chair identical to the one his friend occupied. Both were angled toward the massive oak desk that had well served the previous eight Dukes of Roxborough.

For a moment he considered suggesting they move to the sofa facing the fireplace at the far end of the long Effington House library. In spite of the fine spring day, the evening was cool and the warmth of the fire would be welcome. Still, these chairs were closer to the cabinet that housed his father's supply of spirits and their proximity was more important than mere creature comfort.

Thomas drew a long, appreciative swallow.

1

There was a great deal of warmth to be had right here. "I ask you, Rand, how can my family possibly expect me to find a bride—their idea, mind you, not mine—if I'm also expected to play nursemaid?"

"I'd scarce call it playing nursemaid. Or perhaps I've misunderstood." Rand glanced wryly at his drink. "It's entirely possible I've overlooked some of the finer details of your dilemma."

"It's quite simple." Thomas heaved a heartfelt sigh and launched into a recitation he thought he'd already given at least once tonight, although at the moment he was not entirely certain. "Last year my sister, Gillian, married Richard, the Earl of Shelbrooke. You know him, don't you?"

"I know *of* him."

"He promised his three youngest sisters—they've been raised in the country—a season in London, with all the stuff and nonsense such a thing entails to women. My mother—"

"Ah, yes, the Duchess of Roxborough," Rand said, "and a woman not to be trifled with, if rumor serves."

"None of the Effington women are to be trifled with. From my grandmother to my youngest cousins, they are stubborn and opinionated to the last." Thomas glared at his glass. "My mother had planned to take Richard's sisters under her wing personally and had gone so far as to arrange for a come-out ball for them. It seems my sister was something of a disappointment to her when she married her first husband after only one season. It was all my mother could do to keep from drooling at the very thought of steering not one but three young women through the rigors of a first season. And as an added bonus, I'd finally agreed to seriously look for a bride." He narrowed his eyes. "She was quite beside herself with glee at the thought of it all."

Rand snorted with ill-concealed amusement.

Thomas slumped deeper in his chair. "Unfortunately, my parents are no longer in England, and I've been forced into the temporary role of head of the family, with all the accompanying headaches and responsibilities."

"Pity. Are you up to it?"

"When it comes to handling estate concerns or family business or my own financial affairs, for that matter, I haven't a worry. Effington men may well spend their nights in questionable pursuits, but we are remarkably competent when it comes to the maintenance and increase of the family fortune. Runs in the blood." He grinned and raised his glass in a salute. "Even my more disreputable ancestors didn't squander whatever wealth they'd stolen."

Rand laughed and lifted his glass. "To the Effington ancestors, then." He took a sip. "A shame the Beaumonts can't say the same. Now, where have the duke and duchess gone?"

"America." Thomas grimaced. "Richard and Gillian inherited a great deal of property in that godforsaken land and for some absurd reason wanted to see it in person. While there, Richard had the nerve to get her with child."

"Damned inconsiderate of him."

"I thought so. And he calls himself my friend." Thomas pulled a long sip and considered the events of the last year. He'd been delighted when his dearest friend had fallen in love with his sister. And no one could have been more pleased than Thomas when the couple had been the beneficiary of a substantial inheritance. Now, however, he did wish Richard's timing had been better. "When my mother learned of Gillian's state, not more than a month ago, she insisted on going to be with her rather than having Gillian risk the voyage home. First grandchild, and all that."

"And the duke went with her?"

Thomas nodded. "He's never been to America and apparently has a much more adventurous streak than I'd ever credited him with."

"Bad piece of luck there. Still, correct me if I'm wrong, but I thought England was riddled with Effingtons. Surely there's some other relation, preferably female, who can shepherd these girls around for the season?"

"One would think, but this year they all seem to have scattered to the four corners of the earth. One branch of the family is hanging about old ruins somewhere—Greece, I believe. Richard's oldest sister and her husband are in Paris, and everyone else in the family is too taken up with their own affairs to lend any assistance whatsoever. In short, old man, I'm trapped. Sad-

4

dled with the responsibility of launching three girls onto the choppy seas of society." Thomas blew a long breath. "As well as fulfilling a promise to find a bride of my own this season."

"What on earth possessed you?"

"Oh, the usual reasons," Thomas said grimly. "I'm three and thirty. My father, my mother and even my sister delight in pointing out to me the need to provide an heir."

"Any prospects?"

"Not as of yet, but I do know what I want in a wife." He rested his head against the back of the chair and gazed toward the ceiling. "I want a woman who will be biddable and soft-spoken. A woman to whom I will be the moon and the stars. Who will acquiesce to my desires and not challenge my decisions."

Rand laughed. "In short, you want the complete opposite of the Effington women."

"Exactly."

"And how will you find such a paragon?"

"I don't know at the moment but it shouldn't be too difficult. Effington women are the exception not the rule. And while Effington men have always managed to keep them well in hand, I have no desire to spend the rest of my days in a battle of wills and wits. Still," he drained his brandy and got to his feet, "it's going to be bloody difficult to pursue anyone at all if I have to spend all my time watching over Richard's sisters." He stepped to the cabinet, grabbed the liquor decanter and returned to his seat. "In all good conscience, I have no choice. I received a letter from Richard last week in which he expressed every confidence that I would safeguard his sisters as he would. He said he was relieved they would be in my capable hands. And he thanked me for my efforts."

"You're right. You are trapped." Rand held out his glass and Thomas obligingly refilled it. "When do they arrive?"

"Oh, they've been here for a fortnight now." He filled his own glass, placed the decanter within easy reach on the table between them and took a healthy swallow.

"Really?" Rand raised a brow. "Yet I've seen you every night for at least that long at Whites or some other establishment. They don't seem to be much of a hindrance thus far."

"I've simply become quite adept at avoiding them. It hasn't been all that difficult during the day. They've been exceedingly busy with fittings and shopping and dancing lessons and God knows what else. They came complete with a chaperone, an iron-willed curmudgeon of an aunt. An extremely unpleasant, dragonlike creature who glares at me as if I were a well-known seducer of innocent young women." He shuddered. "That alone is reason enough to stay out of their paths.

"However, the ball my mother arranged is in three days' time. She even procured vouchers for Almacks for them."

Rand winced. "My sympathies. Still, if you are to pursue a bride of your own, wouldn't you be doing all this anyway?"

"No doubt, but at least I would be unfettered. So..." Thomas studied him for a moment, wondering if Rand had consumed enough liquor to be amenable to his proposal or if Thomas should add another dollop of brandy to his glass. "I have come up with a plan."

"Oh?"

"The true purpose of any season is to find a good match. Richard has provided his sisters with impressive dowries, and it shouldn't be all that difficult to find acceptable husbands. Quickly and with a minimum of fuss."

"Perhaps." Rand took a thoughtful sip and considered him carefully. "Unless, of course, they're as ugly as toads."

"Oh, they're not. Not at all," Thomas said quickly. "I have met them, although admittedly briefly, but all three are quite lovely.

"The oldest—her name is Merry-something, I believe—is a bit of a bluestocking, but still very attractive, even if she is nearly two and twenty. Rather unruly blond hair, and I think her eyes are blue behind her spectacles. I understand she's quite intelligent."

"No problem marrying off that one. There's quite a demand on the marriage mart for bespectacled, aging, intelligent bluestockings," Rand said wryly.

Thomas ignored him. "The next—I don't recall her name, either—is the prettiest of the lot and bound to be considered a diamond of the first water. The youngest is lovely as well. An excellent rider, I hear. Very fond of horses and the country. And Rand"— he forced a note of enthusiasm to his voice—

"she has a dog. A great furry beast of an animal any man would be proud to own. She brought him with her."

"Good for her." Rand's brow furrowed in suspicion. "Why are you telling me all this?"

"I was thinking, they haven't been introduced to society yet and at this point"—Thomas leaned forward—"you could have your pick of any of them."

"My *pick*?" Rand said slowly.

"Yes, your choice."

"Are you mad? What would I want with any of them?"

"Come, now, Rand," Thomas said in a placating tone. "Isn't it time *you* found yourself a wife? We are of a similar age and you, too, have the responsibility to provide an heir."

"I don't want a wife right now, thank you all the same." Mild amusement sounded in Rand's voice.

"Well, none of us really *wants* a wife, now, do we?" Thomas reached for the decanter to top off Rand's glass, but his friend waved him off. Pity. The man definitely needed more to drink. "But the time comes when we must live up to our responsibilities."

"Your time, perhaps, but not mine." Rand downed the rest of his drink, placed his glass beside the decanter and got to his feet. "However, it is past time for me to take my leave."

Thomas stood. "You disappoint me, Rand. I thought we were friends."

"We're not that close." Rand started for the door.

"If the situation were reversed, I'd happily marry one of them to help you," Thomas said staunchly and followed him, goblet still in hand.

Rand laughed. "Even you don't believe that."

"I knew I wouldn't be able to convince you. Still, I thought it was worth a try." Thomas heaved a sigh of resignation. "The very least you can do is help me find matches for them."

"As much as I would be willing to assist you, or at a minimum watch what will surely be a most entertaining endeavor, that, too, I must decline." Rand reached the door and pulled it open. "I'm afraid I've been called away and probably won't be back in London for some time. I could well miss the season altogether. You, old chap, are on your own."

"Are you certain you wouldn't at least like to meet them?" The marquess's hopeful voice echoed in the room.

Marianne Shelton stared at his distorted reflection in the brass andirons flanking the fireplace and choked back yet another of no less than a dozen scathing comments she'd thought of in the last few minutes.

Helmsley and his friend—she never did get a good look at him—left the room and the door closed firmly in their wake.

She breathed a long sigh of relief and stretched. Her cramped position on the sofa hadn't been uncomfortable when she'd reclined here to page through a book. She'd only come to the library at this late hour to find something interesting to read. She'd had no intention of staying, but she'd dozed off, only to awaken when Helmsley and his friend had come in. When she'd realized they had no idea of her presence, and further discovered exactly what they were discussing, she'd taken care not to move so much as a single muscle. She sat up, slid her glasses back to the bridge of her nose and rubbed the nape of her neck.

What an insufferable creature this marquess was. Speaking of her and her sisters as if they were nothing more than inconveniences to be disposed of as quickly as possible. It certainly wasn't their idea to inflict themselves on him. No, in point of fact his mother was to blame.

The original arrangement had been for Marianne, Jocelyn, Becky and Aunt Louella to reside with Richard and Gillian. But when the couple could not return for the season, and Aunt Louella had threatened to cancel their trip altogether, the duchess had written insisting they all stay at Effington House. Her Grace had even anticipated Aunt Louella's objections that it might well be considered improper for unmarried young women to stay under the same roof as a single gentleman, pointing out it was an exceeding large roof with a small army of servants who provided no lack of chaperones. She further noted they were all more or less family at any rate and what could be more appropriate, indeed, expected, than for family to stay with family?

Marianne was no more thrilled with the change in plans than Helmsley was, especially after hearing him tonight. She had to admit she did agree with him on one point: Richard did indeed have remarkably bad timing.

She got to her feet and stretched her arms high over her head. Well, Helmsley needn't worry himself about her. She had no intention of looking for a husband this season or any other. Her parents' marriage was not a shining example of wedded bliss.

Her mother had died when Marianne was six years old and she remembered her as kind and loving but weak in both body and spirit. While Marianne had been told her father had married her mother for love, she certainly never saw any evidence of it. At least not on his part.

After his wife's death, Marianne's father had had little to do with his children. Instead, he'd spent the remaining years of his life gambling, drinking and squandering the family fortune. It had been left to Richard to recover the family's resources and good name. It was still difficult to get used to the idea that after years of making do with little, they were once again financially sound.

Marianne reached her hands out to warm them before the fire and stared thoughtfully at the low-banked embers. No, what little she'd seen of marriage did not entice her in the least. The world held the prospect of far too many adventures to limit herself to the less-than-exciting idea of marriage. From Shake-speare to Miss Austen, the stories she'd read since she was old enough to turn a page were of grand adventures, peopled with coura-geous heroines and noble heroes. She wanted nothing less than to be such a heroine.

As for heroes—she shrugged—they had no more substance than the words that created them. Heroes were only to be found in books or dreams. And, except in very rare instances, so was love.

She picked up her book and stepped toward the door. Oh, she fully intended to enjoy all that the season and London had to offer, but her plans went well beyond that. After all, if she wasn't going to pursue marriage, she should pursue something. Something that would lead her to the independence she needed in order to pursue adventure. Some-thing that paid.

Marianne already had a definite notion of exactly what that something could be. She had no idea if she could manage it, but the more she thought about it, the more intriguing it became.

The door swung open and she froze.

Lord Helmsley strode into the room with a swagger in his step that spoke as much of an evening of carousing as any confidence of character. He headed to the desk and settled into the chair behind it, never so much as glancing in her direction, then placed a sheet of paper before him, dipped a pen into ink and scribbled as if possessed.

Marianne took the opportunity to study him. He was not an unattractive sort if one liked tall, dark-haired, broad-shouldered men with regular features. She'd had barely more than a passing introduction to him in spite of having lived under his roof for the last two weeks and had wondered if he was actively avoiding his guests. Tonight was the first time she'd heard him say more than a polite greeting, even if his words were not intended for her ears.

He paused and glanced up, his brow furrowed in thought. He stared directly at her yet didn't appear to see her. Was he that involved in what-ever he was writing? Or was he simply too ine-briated to focus? Of course, the long library was well lit only at either end and she stood in the shadowed midsection of the room. Whatever the reason, she didn't dare to so much as breathe.

An endless moment later his gaze returned to his work. Well, she had no intention of standing here like a statue all night. She drew a deep breath and started for the door.

"By God, you're real!" Helmsley rose to his feet. Marianne halted in midstep. It was far too much to hope that she could escape unde-tected. She braced herself and turned toward him. "Of course I'm real. What did you think?"

"I thought I'd made you up." He shook his head as if to clear it.

"Made me up?" The man created his own

people? Like…God? Good Lord, was he insane? She'd heard some members of the Effington family were considered a bit eccentric. A touch of madness would not be completely far-fetched. She inched toward the door. "Do you often see people you make up?"

"No, not often." He circled the desk and moved closer. "Never before, in fact. Who are you, anyway?"

"Who am I?" she said slowly. She'd be insulted that he didn't remember their meeting, brief as it was, if she weren't more concerned about his state of mind. Somewhere she'd read one should make allowances for those afflicted with insanity and treat them as carefully as one would a small child. "Who do you think I am?"

"I thought perhaps you were a vision conjured out of my imagination. Or an angel to escort me to heaven. Or perhaps a muse to help my feeble efforts." He grinned and she realized his features were more than regular. He was really rather handsome. For a madman.

"I can assure you, I am neither angel nor muse." She resisted the impulse to lunge for the door. It might be best not to startle him. Still, she wondered if anyone in the huge house was awake at this hour, if the need arose to scream for assistance.

"But you are indeed a vision." His gaze flickered over her in an assessing and intimate manner and she wished she had on something more substantial than her nightgown and wrapper. "Even if now I can see you are most definitely flesh and blood."

His madness may well be in question, but his rudeness was not. Nor was the gleam in his eye. She'd never seen desire before, but surely that was the look of it. Abruptly she realized madness was not his affliction at all. "And you, my lord, are most definitely drunk."

"Drunk?" He raised his chin in an annoyingly haughty manner and stared down his nose at her. "I most certainly am not drunk. I do not get drunk. I occasionally imbibe a bit more than is wise in my effort to live life to its fullest—"

"Its fullest tankard, no doubt."

"Hah. I know your type." He pointed an accusing finger at her. "You're one of those women who believes men should be respectable and responsible at all times and never have a bit of good fun."

"I am not." She laughed in spite of herself. "I was right all along. You are a lunatic. Worse, a tipsy lunatic."

"I am hardly a lunatic, tipsy or any other kind. Admittedly, I have had a fair amount to drink tonight, but not substantially more than usual."

"I wouldn't boast about it, if I were you."

"I am not you and I am not boasting. I am simply stating a fact. I am not in my cups and I am more than capable of doing whatever requires doing. Or whatever I wish to do, for that matter."

"Really? I doubt that. A moment ago you

weren't certain whether I was real or something you'd conjured out of thin air and shadow. Just what do you wish to do?"

"Nothing in particular at the moment." He stared at her and she noted that interesting gleam had returned to his eye. "Or rather, I might wish to make certain the vision who has intruded on my solitude is indeed real and not an apparition conjured by an inebriated mind."

"How would you determine that?"

"A kiss should suffice for proof." He stepped toward her. "To verify she is indeed flesh and blood."

"I can assure you—"

Before she could say another word, he strode to her and took her in his arms.

Her book slipped from her hand and she stared up at him, at once struck by how very much this was like a scene from a novel. A scene in which the dashing hero embraces the courageous heroine and kisses her senseless. She should probably be afraid but at the moment she felt rather courageous, and if nothing else, he was more than a little dashing. Excitement raced up her spine. She'd never had the opportunity to be kissed senseless before. Or kissed at all. Marianne stared into his eyes and smiled. "Very well."

"Very well?" He frowned down at her and his puzzled expression changed to one of horror. "Bloody hell." Without warning, he released her and stepped back. "You're that Merry-person!"

"Well, I hardly feel at all merry right now, although I was beginning to feel somewhat giddy." She tilted her head and grinned. "Aren't you going to kiss me?"

"No! Absolutely not! Never!" His eyes widened and he backed away from her as if she were plague-ridden.

"Never?" She drew her brows together and planted her hands on her hips. "How very impolite of you. Whyever not?"

"Because you're Merry...Merry—"

"I told you, I'm not at all merry, but I am getting a bit annoyed."

"No, blast it all, that's not what I meant." He blew a frustrated breath. "Your name is Merry. Merry something-or-other. What is your name, anyway?"

She rolled her eyes toward the ceiling. It was obviously too much to expect that a man who scarcely remembered her face would remember her name. "It's Marianne."

"You're Richard's sister." Helmsley groaned. "Good God, I almost ravished Richard's sister."

"You were going to ravish me?" Delight surged through her. "How exciting. I've never been ravished before."

"And you shall not be ravished now." He turned on his heel and stalked to a table bearing a decanter of brandy. He glanced around in obvious frustration.

"If you're looking for your glass, I believe you took it with you when you said good-bye to your friend."

"Then I shall get another." He headed toward the cabinet, but she reached it before him and blocked his way.

"Don't you think you've had quite enough?"

"My dear young woman, I have not had nearly enough."

She shrugged. "As you wish." She selected a glass and handed it to him, then took another for herself and followed him to the table.

He filled his glass and she held out hers. He glanced at it and his brows pulled together in disapproval. "I scarcely think—"

"For heaven's sakes, my lord. I am not a child." She snatched the decanter from his hand and poured a moderate amount into her glass. "I am well used to brandy and other spirits." It was a lie, of course. She'd had little more acquaintance with brandy than she had with kissing. She cast him a confident smile, raised the glass to her lips and drew a long swallow.

The intense flavor flooded her senses, the liquor burned in her throat and for an instant she wondered if she'd die horribly right there in front of him. She stifled the need to gasp and clamped her jaws tight, but she couldn't stop her eyes from watering.

"How is it?" he said innocently, but a laugh lurked in his eyes.

"Excellent," she lied.

"I think so." He swirled the brandy in his glass and tried to hide a smirk. "I quite like a brandy before bed."

"Or two or three, no doubt," she murmured and sank into a chair. She took another, much smaller sip and her glasses slid down her nose. Actually, it wasn't bad. A pleasant warmth spread through her. She smiled up at him and waved at the other chair. "Would you care to have a seat?"

"I believe I'd prefer to stay right here." He perched on the edge of the desk and considered her thoughtfully. "So you're Marianne."

"I believe we've established that." She sipped again. No, this wasn't bad at all. She pushed her glasses back into place and gazed up at him. "I'm the aging, intelligent bluestocking."

He winced. "You heard me?"

"I couldn't help it. I was on the sofa." She gestured at the far end of the room. She hadn't planned on letting him know she had overheard his conversation, but at the moment she couldn't resist confronting him. "You are rather rude, you know."

"I never would have said a word if I had known—"

"Piffle." She waved away his objection. "Regardless of what you say now, it's still what you think. However"—she took another swallow—"you are right."

"I am?" he said cautiously.

"Um-hmm." She nodded. "I am an aging intelligent bluestocking. And I quite like it."

"Do you, my Lady Marianne?"

"I do indeed, my Lord Helmsley."

"Why?"

"When one is viewed in such terms, one's behavior is far less confined. People are not

nearly as shocked when you do the unexpected, when you break the rules others abide
by."

He raised a brow. "And do you break a
great many rules?"

"Not yet, but I fully intend to." She raised
her glass to him. "And I shall begin by calling
you Thomas. It seems appropriate. After all,
you did nearly ravish me."

"Don't remind me. I didn't realize who
you were. Obviously the result of an over-
active imagination coupled with a poorly lit
room and, admittedly, the influence of a good
deal to drink. Although"—he narrowed his
eyes—"I am not drunk. Still, I would never take
such liberties with the sister of my dearest
friend."

"Why not? He's taken such liberties with your
sister."

"That's entirely different. My sister was a
widow when they met. You are an innocent
young woman straight from the country and
under my protection as well. Kissing you, or
anything else, is not acceptable."

"What a shame," she murmured. "Thomas,
would you care to know what else you were
right about?"

"I'm not sure," he said cautiously.

She leaned toward him, her glasses again skid-
ding down her nose. "I am quite attractive."

He laughed. "Indeed you are."

"But there is something you were wrong
about." She rose to her feet, stepped close to
him and pulled off her spectacles. "My eyes

are brown. Not a deep brown, mind you, but a not-unpleasant shade of medium brown. What do you think?" She fluttered her lashes. "Are my eyes pleasant?"

"Exceedingly pleasant." The corners of his lips quirked upward. His eyes were a dark blue and rather pleasant as well.

"I thought so." She grinned and replaced her spectacles, then turned, grabbed the decanter and refilled her glass. "And the color of my eyes isn't the only thing you don't know."

"Don't you think you've had enough?" he said mildly.

"Oh, no, my lord, you're the one who's had enough." She shook the decanter at him. "You are drunk." She replaced the decanter and shook her head. "Or mad. I haven't quite decided." She drew a healthy swallow and wondered why she hadn't experienced the wonder of brandy years ago.

She glanced around curiously. "This is really a wonderful room. I could happily spend my life in such a place." The side walls of the long library were covered with shelves of books reaching from the floor to the ceiling. She crossed the room and walked slowly past the rows of volumes, scanning the titles. "There are entire worlds here just waiting to be discovered. Have you read any of these?"

"A few. I admit I am no scholar, but I'm not a complete dolt." He paused. "You said there were things beyond the color of your eyes that I didn't know."

"I'm certain there are all manner of things you don't know," she said loftily.

"Probably, but I believe this may have been about you."

"Well..." She took a thoughtful sip. "To start with, your plan won't work."

"My plan?"

"Your plan to marry us all off as quickly as possible." She leaned back against a bookshelf and smirked.

"Is there anything I said tonight that you didn't hear?" he said wryly.

"I don't believe so. I heard your assessment of my sisters and myself. And Aunt Louella, of course." She laughed. "Rather accurate, actually. Oh, and then there was the offer you made to your friend to let him have his pick of us. Exceedingly generous of you."

"Damnation." Thomas had the grace to look properly chagrined. "I do apologize."

"As well you should." She raised a shoulder in a casual shrug. "This is a very large room, but voices do seem to carry well from one end to the other."

"I shall make a note of it for future reference. And remember to check the sofa for hidden visions as well." He drew his brows together. "Why won't my plan work?"

"Because, Thomas, I have no intention of marrying." She sipped at her brandy. "Marriage isn't the least bit adventurous or exciting and I have no desire for it whatsoever."

He snorted. "Nonsense. Every woman wants to marry."

"Not me." She stepped away from the shelves and waved in an expansive gesture toward the rows of volumes. "Look at these, Thomas. They're filled with quests and dangers and excitements. I wish to experience some of them for myself. I want to experience life itself. There's an entire world of things I've yet to do. I want to meet interesting people and have grand adventures and travel to exciting places like Venice and Cairo and, well, live what I have only read about. And I can't accomplish any of that if I shackle myself to a husband."

"Come, now, Marianne," he said in an altogether too condescending manner. "You cannot possibly—"

"Hah! I know your kind." She pointed her glass at him. "You're one of those men who believes women should be boring and proper at all times and never have a bit of fun."

"Not at all." He grinned in a decidedly wicked manner. "I am not opposed to women enjoying themselves. A certain kind of woman, that is. However"—a firm note sounded in his voice—"I do not extend that particular freedom to young women under my protection."

"You shall simply have to reconsider." She drained the last of her brandy and headed toward the decanter. "Since I neither want nor need your protection."

"Nonetheless, at the moment, thanks to your brother and my mother, that is my responsibility and I will not shirk it." He straightened and reached the decanter one step before her, removing it before she could grab it. "And also, at the moment, I'd say that's enough brandy for one night."

"I don't see why. It's really quite tasty." She stared at her empty glass. "Isn't it curious the way the more I drink, the less drunk you appear?"

"It often works that way." He took the glass from her hand and put it on the desk. "You, my dear lady, are foxed."

She lifted her chin and glared at him with all the indignation she could muster. "I most certainly am not. If anything, I'm merely a bit"—she giggled—"merry."

"So I see. Well, merry or not"—he grasped her shoulders and turned her to face the door—"it's past time you retired for the night."

He gave her a gentle push and she started for the door. Then she swiveled and stepped back to him. "I'll tell you something else you don't know. I've never had brandy before."

"No?" His eyes widened in feigned surprise. "Yet you handled it so well."

"I did, didn't I?" she said smugly.

"Good evening, Marianne." His tone was firm, but his eyes twinkled.

"Good evening, Thomas." Once again she started toward the door, and once again she returned to him.

He heaved a sigh. "What is it now?"

"I've never been kissed, either." She gazed up at him expectantly.

"And you're not going to be kissed now."

She waved toward the bookshelves. "They have no doubt been kissed."

"They who?" He studied her as if she were the one whose sanity was in question. "The books?"

"Don't be absurd. Heroines. *In* the books." She nodded emphatically. "Many of them have been kissed. And more than once."

"Perhaps. But this is not a story and you are not about to be kissed."

"As you wish." She sighed dramatically. "However, if you don't kiss me, I shall be forced to fling myself at every man I meet in hopes one will take pity on an aging, intelligent bluestocking, and I should think, given your attitude toward your responsibilities, that it would be most irresponsible—"

"Very well!" He grabbed her shoulders, pulled her close and planted a chaste kiss on her forehead. Then he released her so abruptly she was hard-pressed not to lose her balance. "There."

"There?" She glared up at him. "Not precisely what I had in mind."

"It shall have to do," he said haughtily.

"I'm sure others could do better."

"I doubt that."

"I don't. However, you leave me no choice but to find out at the first opportunity." She grinned. "Actually, I rather like the idea of throwing myself on the mercy of one gentleman after another for however long it should take, although I can't imagine it should take any time at all——because you did agree that I was attractive...very attractive, you said—until at last some kind soul is willing—"

"Blast it all, you are an annoying bit of baggage," Thomas snapped. Again he grabbed her, jerked her closer and planted his lips on hers in a kiss hard and firm.

For a moment, the shock of his touch held her still. His lips were nicely warmed and surprisingly soft and tasted deliciously of brandy. She tilted her head and the pressure of his mouth against hers relaxed.

One hand slipped from her shoulder to her back and pressed her tighter to him. She rested her hands against his chest. He slanted his mouth over hers and at once she wished this moment would last forever. Her breath met and mingled with his and she marveled at the intimate nature of what she'd always assumed was simple and not at all complicated.

He pulled away and stared down at her with an odd, cautious look in his eye.

"Oh, my." She exhaled a long breath. "That was...that was..."

He stepped back and cleared his throat. "Yes, well, I do hope that was satisfactory."

"Quite." A lovely warm glow washed through her. *More than satisfactory.* "Although—just to be certain, you understand—I think you should try again."

He stared at her for a long moment, his expression puzzled, as if he were trying to determine precisely what she meant.

"I think you should kiss me again," she said, with deliberate emphasis on each and every word. Perhaps the man was mad after all. Or simpleminded. Or maybe he just didn't want to kiss her again.

He shook his head slowly. "I think not."

"Why not?"

"Because you've had too much to drink, I've had too much to drink. You're Richard's sister. You're under my protection." He ran his hand through his hair and glowered. "How many more reasons do you need?"

"Those will serve." She grinned. "For the moment."

"Forever."

"We shall see, my lord," she said primly and headed toward the door, resisting the urge to glance at him over her shoulder. "We shall see."

Chapter 2

"The neckline should be lowered a bit." Jocelyn frowned down at the décolletage of her new ball gown. "Don't you agree?"

She stood on a hassock, elevated barely a few feet above the floor, yet high enough to allow her to gaze over the small assembly with the attitude of a queen surveying the peasants. A seamstress's assistant blessed with the patient soul of a saint was busy trying to pin Jocelyn's hem in place. Becky and Marianne together had taken less than half the time with their gowns as Jocelyn was taking with hers.

Marianne perched on the edge of a chair and paged through a book in an effort to force her attention on something other than the letter hidden among its pages and the need to speak to her sisters in private. Without their support, she couldn't possibly succeed in her plan.

Becky lounged on a nearby chaise and tried to stifle a yawn. "I think if it was any lower your bosoms would spring free of their own accord."

"Rebecca," Aunt Louella snapped.

"At least I have bosoms worthy of springing free," Jocelyn said loftily.

Aunt Louella narrowed her eyes. "Jocelyn."

"My bosoms are worthy of springing free." Becky frowned, staring down at her own bust. She drew a deep breath and slowly released it, then nodded as if satisfied. "More than worthy."

"That's quite enough from both of you. I've never heard such nonsense. You are well-bred young ladies and I expect you to behave as such." Aunt Louella's glare pinned first Jocelyn then Becky. "And well-bred young ladies do not discuss the worthiness of their bosoms."

"Of course, Aunt Louella. And I do apologize," Jocelyn said sweetly, "to you."

Becky opened her mouth to respond and Marianne shot her a quelling glance. Indecision washed over the younger girl's face, then she clamped her mouth shut, but rebellion still glittered in her eyes. Marianne groaned to herself; this was a truce at best, uneasy and more than likely brief.

She should have said something when the squabbling began. Since their older sister Emma had married last year, Marianne had been thrust into the role of peacemaker between the younger girls, a position she did not relish. Still, she should be grateful, since on those rare occasions when Jocelyn and Becky cooperated with each other they were a force to be reckoned with.

The dressmaker rocked back on her heels, studied Jocelyn's hem, then raised a questioning brow. Aunt Louella first frowned in consideration, then nodded her approval. "That will do. Now, then, I wish to speak with you about some of the patterns—"

"Why don't you take her in the other room?" Marianne said brightly and got to her feet. "That way you can discuss whatever you'd like without us hanging about and adding our opinions every two seconds."

"I quite like adding my opinion," Jocelyn said indignantly. "I think my opinion should be taken into consideration, given as the discussion is what I shall be wearing."

"As do I," Becky said with a frown. "Come, now, Marianne, you can't possibly think—"

"Oh, but I do." Marianne hooked her arm through her aunt's and steered her toward the door. "After all, Aunt Louella has experience and knowledge far beyond our own as to what is truly fashionable and it can only be to our benefit to allow her to guide us in such things."

Jocelyn and Becky traded glances and Marianne bit back a sigh.

Once again, alliances had shifted and foes were now allies. Still, there was never a question that when matters were of a serious nature the Shelton sisters would always form a united front. More often than not, that front was against Aunt Louella. Even with Jocelyn, who most among the girls had fallen prey to the elderly woman's stories of the glories of London and the joys of the social season, there was no question of her primary allegiance.

Not that Lady Louella Codling's heart wasn't in the right place. It had been ever since she'd moved in to take care of her dead sister's daughters a dozen years ago. But the woman brooked no nonsense and never so much as laughed more than once or twice a year. In addition, Aunt Louella had always hated the girls' father, the late Earl of Shelbrooke, not that Marianne could blame her, and until recently hadn't seemed to care much more for their brother, Richard.

Her aunt studied her for a moment. "Excellent idea." She nodded at the dressmaker and the woman followed them. Louella glanced back at the younger girls. "I shall send a maid to help you, Jocelyn."

"No." Marianne jerked opened the door. "I mean, it's not necessary. We can help her."

"Not me," Becky said under her breath.

30

"Very well." Aunt Louella turned to the seamstress. "You must thank Madame Renault for being so kind as to permit you to do these final fittings here rather than at her shop. I do hope..." They stepped through the door and Marianne closed it behind them.

"Kind?" Becky scoffed. "Given the scandalous amount of money we've spent, the woman should come and dress us on a daily basis." She grinned. "It is great fun, though, isn't it?"

"It is indeed." Marianne laughed. After living most of their lives having to watch each penny, the girls still weren't used to being able to purchase whatever they wished without worry. Only Jocelyn had taken to spending money without Marianne's twinge of guilt or Becky's sense of wonder. "Now, then," she said brightly, "let's talk."

"What do you want to talk about?" Idle curiosity sounded in Jocelyn's voice. She reached out and Marianne helped her off the stool.

Becky smirked. "Whatever it is, she was certainly eager to get rid of Aunt Louella first."

"I wasn't eager at all," Marianne lied. "I simply wanted to talk about...well...our lives and futures and our expectations. It's so much easier to speak freely without Aunt Louella here."

Once again, Jocelyn and Becky exchanged glances.

"Not if that's all you want to talk about,"

Becky said slowly. "I thought it was understood. The only purpose of a London season is to make good matches. It's our lot in life." She stood and reluctantly moved to assist Marianne. "We are, as Aunt Louella never fails to point out, well-bred young ladies with a responsibility to our family. And substantial dowries." Becky's words rang with all the sincerity of a memorized recitation.

Marianne stared at her. "But that is what you want, isn't it?"

Becky shrugged. "Eventually."

"I, for one, have no intention of wedding after my first season." Jocelyn turned to allow her sisters to undo the variety of pins, tapes and other fasteners that held her dress in place.

"What do you intend?" Until this moment Marianne had no idea Jocelyn had planned anything beyond snaring herself the most eligible bachelor to be had as quickly as possible. Obviously she hadn't paid nearly as much attention to her sisters as she should have.

"I intend to fully avail myself of the pleasures of the season; and more, I intend to be the toast of London. I shall attend each and every ball of note. I shall drive in the park during those hours when it is fashionable to do so." Jocelyn's face took on a dreamy, yet determined, expression. "I shall amass proposals of marriage as one gathers flowers in a field—"

Becky snorted.

Jocelyn ignored her. "—and shall, no doubt, break more than one heart. Although I will— Ouch!"

"Sorry," Becky said sweetly. "A pin slipped."

Jocelyn shot her a wicked glare. "As I was saying, I shall endeavor to be kind and gracious in my rejections and leave each and every discarded suitor thinking of me with fondness even in his disappointment."

"I may be ill," Becky said under her breath.

"I'm sure your thoughtfulness will be appreciated," Marianne said wryly.

The dress slipped off Jocelyn's shoulders and the girls helped her step out of it. "And at some point in time, when I have found a exceptional candidate with a considerable fortune, of course—"

"Of course." Marianne fought back a grin. She had heard Jocelyn's litany before but never with quite as much detail. Or perhaps she hadn't ever really listened. She laid the gown carefully across the chaise and handed Jocelyn a day dress.

"—and a lofty title." Jocelyn paused thoughtfully. "I should very much like to marry a prince, but that does seem somewhat farfetched, as they are exceedingly rare. A duke would be lovely, although there are rather too few of them. And most are terribly old."

"Thomas Effington will be a duke someday," Becky murmured, fastening Jocelyn's dress. "And I think he's quite attractive."

"If you like arrogant men who think they know everything and, further, think they know what's best for everyone," Marianne said without thinking.

Becky and Jocelyn stared with identical expressions of surprise.

"Why do you say that?" Becky said. "The man's scarcely said more than a few words to us since our arrival."

Jocelyn sniffed. "Rather rude, really."

"And doesn't that spell arrogant to you?" Marianne wasn't sure why she had no desire to tell anyone about her late-night encounter with the marquess or his brandy. Perhaps it was simply because it had been her very first adventure and she wasn't yet ready to share. "Besides, I know the man's type."

"You don't know anything about men," Jocelyn said with a haughty sniff.

"And you do?" Becky scoffed.

Jocelyn crossed her arms. "I certainly know more than she does. She's had no experience whatsoever that hasn't come from a book."

"And all yours comes from little more than the smitten son of the butcher in the village." Becky smiled in an overly sweet manner.

"A man is still a man regardless of his station, and a real man is far preferable to a fictitious one," Jocelyn said in a superior tone, then frowned. "Not that I had much of anything to do with him."

"Of course not." Becky nodded. "He has warts."

Jocelyn shrugged. "One has to have standards."

Becky laughed and Marianne joined her. The butcher's son's infatuation with Jocelyn had been a source of amusement for the girls for some time. A stranger listening to Jocelyn's high-flown ambitions would never suspect that even as she'd tried to dissuade the young man's suit, Jocelyn had never treated him unkindly. While in many ways Jocelyn thought only of herself, Marianne had never seen her deliberately hurtful.

"And what of your desires, Becky?" Marianne said, deftly changing the subject.

"Oh, I quite agree with Jocelyn." Becky collapsed back onto the chaise. "I, too, plan on savoring all that London has to offer: the routs, the soirees, the eligible men." She flashed Jocelyn a grin. "I have no desire to wed this year, either. I'd rather like to enjoy several seasons before I agree to marry."

"And what are your requirements in a match?" Jocelyn said, apparently as surprised by the genuine interest in her voice as her sisters.

"Well." A thoughtful frown furrowed Becky's forehead. "I'm not terribly concerned about a man's title, although I should like him to have a grand estate with a lovely manor house, perhaps even a castle, and incomparable stables with the finest horses in all of England." A wistful look crossed her face. "I should like him to be the kind of man who prefers to spend most of his time in the country. Who likes children and dogs—"

"Where is Henry, anyway?" Marianne glanced around the room, half expecting to see the wagging tail of the big, furry beast sticking out from beneath a desk or behind a sofa.

"In the kitchens, I suspect." Becky grinned. "He seems to have quite charmed the servants." Probably why, in spite of Aunt Louella's decree that Henry be kept out-of-doors, Becky managed to keep him in the house and by her side more often than not.

"Why this sudden interest in our plans?" Jocelyn sank down on the hassock and studied Marianne curiously.

"I was wondering the same thing," Becky said. "It's not as if we, especially Jocelyn, haven't talked about it all over and over again."

"Curiosity, nothing more than that. So," Marianne said carefully, "neither of you is in any great hurry to wed."

"Not this season. After all, Becky is but ten and seven and I am only a year older." Jocelyn studied her. "You, however, are one and twenty, practically on the shelf."

Becky nodded. "She's right, you know. It is past time you wed."

As confident as she was that her sisters would assist her, there was still the possibility of objections. She drew a deep breath. "I have no intention of marrying. I want to make my own way in the world."

"Why would you want to do that?" Jocelyn stared in disbelief.

"Marriage holds no appeal for me." Her sisters were far too young when their mother died to remember much of anything of their parents' marriage, and that was probably for the best. "I want to know what adventures life holds beyond the confining world of wedlock. And in order to do that I need to be independent. Financially independent."

"I see. And how do you propose to achieve this financial independence?" Becky eyed her as if she were afraid of the answer.

"Admittedly, my skills are minimal. All I've ever really done is read and study. Still, I thought...that is, I've considered..." She'd never said it out loud before, never told another soul, and for the barest moment wondered if indeed she could. If Emma was here... She sighed to herself.

She'd always been closer to Emma than anyone else. With barely a year between them, she and Emma had been natural allies, as were Jocelyn and Becky when the need arose. Now Marianne found herself without a confidante. The age difference between her and the younger girls had never seemed greater than today. She squared her shoulders. "I'm going to write for a living."

"Write what?" Jocelyn frowned. "You've never written anything but letters. I can't imagine it's possible to make your fortune in letter writing."

"Don't be ridiculous." Becky stared at her older sister thoughtfully. "You're going to write books, aren't you?"

"Perhaps eventually." The excitement Marianne had kept bridled all morning surged through her. "But not at first. I believe it takes rather a long time to write a book, and I admit I'm somewhat impatient. Frankly, I'm not entirely sure I can write an entire novel.

"However"—Marianne opened her book

and pulled out the letter she'd kept folded between the pages—"when we arrived in London, I sent an inquiry and a sample of my work to a gentleman who publishes a newspaper—"

"Good Lord, you sent something to the *Times*?" Jocelyn's eyes widened.

"It's not exactly the *Times*."

"The *Morning Chronicle*, then?" Becky said. "Or the *Observer*?"

"No, no, nothing quite so traditional." Marianne waved off the suggestions blithely. "I sent it to *Cadwallender's Weekly World Messenger*."

Becky stared. "What is a *Cadwallender's Weekly World Messenger*?"

"Is it a real newspaper? It doesn't sound like a real newspaper." Jocelyn frowned. "I've certainly never heard of it."

"Not that you would," Becky said dryly. "However, I've never heard of it, either."

"And you're so aware of current affairs." Jocelyn rolled her eyes toward the ceiling.

"I daresay I—"

"It's a very small publication," Marianne said quickly. "Not nearly as old as the *Times*, with a philosophy not quite as..."

"Legitimate?" Becky suggested.

"Stuffy. Besides, the *Messenger* only comes out on Sundays and I doubt many outside of London have ever heard of it. At any rate, I wrote to Mr. Cadwallender about the possibility of writing of my adventures—"

"What adventures?" Becky asked.

"Well, I haven't had any yet, but I fully intend to."

"What kind of adventures?" Jocelyn said cautiously.

"The adventures," Marianne paused dramatically, "of a country miss in London."

Again, the younger girls traded glances. Marianne ignored them and shook open the folded sheet with a flourish. "And I received Mr. Cadwallender's response this morning."

"And?" Jocelyn raised a brow.

"And he says he quite likes my writing and he further likes the idea of the adventures of a country girl in town. I propose to write the stories as a series of letters. As you've noted, I can write letters." She couldn't hide a triumphant smile. "I sent him the first."

Becky rose to her feet, plucked the letter from the older girl's hand and scanned it. "He also says his readers are not interested in ordinary, everyday occurrences." She frowned. "What exactly did you send him?"

At once Marianne's euphoria vanished. "That is a bit of a problem. I believe I wrote of the thrill at seeing the Tower of London for the first time. And the delight of a drive through Hyde Park. And the enjoyment to be had—"

Jocelyn groaned. "I know I would certainly wish to read that."

"You don't read anything that isn't a report of a soiree or the descriptions of the latest in fashion," Becky murmured. She studied the paper, then glanced up. "Forgive me for agreeing with Jocelyn once again, but your adventures thus far are exceedingly ordinary and the potential for anything more exciting, especially with Aunt Louella hovering over you, is rather slim."

"I know. I've been giving that a great deal of consideration." Marianne pulled off her glasses and tapped them against her palm. "Mr. Cadwallender thinks my proposal is intriguing, but he does say he would like to see another *adventure* before he decides whether or not to print my work. I suspect if he doesn't like what I send him he'll find someone else to write them. I'm not entirely sure how to make my experiences more exciting."

"You can stop writing about the sights, for one thing," Jocelyn said firmly.

"No doubt, but the problem still remains as to precisely how to entice Mr. Cadwallender's readership."

Becky shook her head. "Surely with all the books you've read you know better than anyone what makes a good story."

"Certainly I do. I just..." Marianne paced the room and tried to put her thoughts in order. "I don't want to make up stories. I want to write about *my* adventures."

"*You* haven't had any. Let me see that." Jocelyn stood, snatched the letter from Becky and skimmed it quickly. "There's nothing here that says your writing has to be entirely truthful."

"I wouldn't want to lie—"

"Nonsense. We're not talking about lying,

40

exactly, we're talking about..." Jocelyn thought for a moment. "Embellishing. Simply making whatever experiences you may have more interesting. It's merely a matter of perception."

Becky nodded in agreement. "It's the difference between saying a woman is fat and dowdy and saying she's voluptuous with the beauty of a harvest goddess."

"Exactly." Jocelyn grinned at the younger girl. "It all depends on one's point of view. Take your country miss—"

"Or rather, me," Marianne said.

"Yes, yes. She, or you, would be much more interesting..." Jocelyn paused, then her eyes lit. "If she was alone in the world. An orphan."

"But I'm not—"

"Of course you are," Becky said. "We all are by definition orphans. Our parents are both dead."

"Yes, but we're not exactly alone in the world. We have a titled brother with a respectable fortune," Marianne said wryly. "Scarcely the stuff to provoke sympathy."

Jocelyn ignored her. "An orphan raised in the country. Yes, that will do nicely. Very innocent and quite naïve."

"But I'm not—"

"Nonsense." Jocelyn waved away the objection. "You were raised in the country. It's not a lie, it's simply bending the truth a bit to make a better story."

"I suppose, but—"

"And if she's an orphan, she needs a guardian." Becky grinned wickedly.

"A guardian who has brought her to London to live under his protection." Jocelyn's smile matched Becky's. "In his house."

"This is absurd." Marianne laughed, but her mind raced.

While not entirely truthful, none of her sisters' suggestions were complete lies, either. After all, they were, in the strictest meaning of the word, orphans. And the Marquess of Helmsley was, for the moment, acting as a sort of guardian. And they were indeed living in his home....

"The guardian should be handsome," Becky said.

"And wealthy," Jocelyn added. "And titled."

"And arrogant," Marianne murmured.

"A rake, I should think." Jocelyn nodded. "Definitely something of a scoundrel."

"And he can ruin her!" Becky fairly shouted with excitement.

At once shocked silence fell in the room.

"What?" Becky's eyes widened innocently. "It's just a story. It's not like you're actually going to be ruined."

"Certainly not." Although if she truly wasn't planning on marriage, and she really wanted to write about her own adventures... Good Lord, what was she thinking? She pushed aside the outrageous thought.

"It would be nicely scandalous, though." Jocelyn's brows pulled together. "And it does seem to me people do love to read about scandal."

"Which means Mr. Cadwallender will love

42

it." Excitement surged through Marianne. "It will work. I know it will."

"However"—Jocelyn pinned her with a firm glance—"no one must know about this. It is one thing to write about scandal and quite another to be in the midst of it."

"Should your name appear in a paper, any paper"—Becky shuddered—"the consequences would be dire. No one will believe what you write isn't completely accurate. It would destroy your reputation and ours as well. As for Aunt Louella, she'd—"

"Not if Aunt Louella and everyone else doesn't find out. I have fully considered the secrecy this endeavor of mine requires. If you'll notice, the letter is addressed to Miss Smythe. I thought it best to conceal my identity from the outset. And it's not necessary to meet with Mr. Cadwallender on a regular basis. I'm confident most of our business can be conducted through letters, so the risk of discovery there will be minimal.

"I've already decided the adventures should be published anonymously. It will add more excitement for readers if the author is unknown."

"No one can resist a secret." Jocelyn grinned. "Or a scandal. And if Becky or I"—she glanced at the younger girl—"should have any interesting adventures of our own, you may use them for your stories. Besides, no one is going to know you're the author and if you don't use real names for any other characters—"

"I can use initials," Marianne said quickly.

"Let's see, the guardian could be Lord…" *H* for Helmsley? *E* for Effington? *R* for Roxborough? *T* for Thomas? The annoying man had so many names and titles he claimed half the alphabet. Lord…*who?* Marianne grinned. Of course. *Lord Who.* "He shall be Lord W. That will work."

"*W* for What's-his-name." Becky giggled.

"Or Wonderfully Wealthy." Jocelyn laughed.

"Or Wildly Wicked." Marianne nodded with satisfaction. "Perfect. Now all I have to do is actually write my first adventure." At once she knew exactly what that first adventure would be. She started toward the door. "If anyone wants me, I shall be in my room for the rest of the morning."

"Don't forget, the duchess's ball is in two days," Jocelyn called after her, "and we have a dancing lesson this afternoon. If you aren't prompt, Aunt Louella will—"

Marianne shut the door behind her, cutting off her sister's warning. Not that she had paid it more than scant attention, anyway. Right now her head was far too full of possible adventures for a country-bred orphan and her rakish guardian.

Adventures beginning with a bit of brandy and a forbidden kiss in the night.

Chapter 3

My Dear Cousin,

London is indeed the most exciting city in the world. I have scarce been here a fortnight and already I have received my first kiss!

The auspicious event occurred late in the evening when the rest of the household was asleep and I found myself alone with his lordship.

It is shameful to admit, but I was not in the least apprehensive, although in hindsight I should have been quite concerned, as I wore nothing but my nightclothes and the heady aroma of fine brandy....

The Absolutely True Adventures
of a Country Miss in London .

Thomas strode to the baluster overlooking the grand foyer and surveyed the scene beneath him with annoyance. His valet had warned him Effington House was already a veritable hive of activity in preparation for the ball, now only two days away. Still, Thomas wasn't entirely prepared for the sight that greeted him.

Below, servants scurried across the black and white check-patterned marble floor. Maids armed with cloths and dusters polished and waxed. Footmen carried chairs and tables. Everywhere he looked, there was activity of some sort in an impressive ballet of chaotic organization.

Not that Effington House hadn't seen its share of galas in the past, but his parents, or rather his mother, had always been here to oversee the arrangements. Luckily, she'd been deep in the throes of planning the event before deciding to leave the country. Invitations had been sent, menus compiled, flowers ordered and an orchestra already hired before his parents abandoned him for the wilds of America.

The duchess had done everything she could to ensure the ball was a success. After all, the event did carry her name, even if she wasn't present, and there were standards to be maintained. She'd left detailed instructions in the hands of the house steward. And had, as well, exchanged a flurry of letters with the girls' aunt, Lady Dragon, who probably had a real name, but he could not for the life of him remember it. She was now ostensibly overseeing the chaos here in addition to readying her nieces for their debut into society.

Still—Thomas uttered a silent oath—as the only Effington in residence, he was essentially responsible for the success or failure of the fete, a responsibility he'd neither asked for nor wanted. He hadn't the vaguest idea what, if anything, he should be doing, and thought it was probably best if he simply stayed out of the way. The staff was well trained and Thomas was confident they could carry it off without incident. Or, at least, he prayed they could.

At the moment, all he really wanted was to escape from this bedlam to the sanctity of his club. In barely more than forty-eight hours his life was as much as over.

Once he presided over this traditional offering of sweet young things to the gods of society, his evenings, and no doubt many of his afternoons, would be occupied with the duties of escort and protector.

Protector? He snorted to himself. The oldest needed nothing less than a jailer. All that nonsense she'd spouted last night about adventure and excitement and experiencing life. Well, she'd change her mind soon enough when presented with the right suitor. Thomas had already mentally compiled a list of possibilities and there were a considerable number of acceptable matches. He was not the only eligible bachelor in England under pressure to marry.

It shouldn't be all that difficult to find a decent match for Marianne, as long as she kept her mouth shut. She really was quite lovely, with that halo of blond curls rebelliously dancing around her head. He couldn't resist a smile. No wonder, in the dim light of the library, he'd thought she was a celestial vision. And when they'd kissed...

His smile faded. Blasted woman. Why had she insisted he kiss her? Of course, if he hadn't he had no doubt she would have carried out her threat to find someone who would. The best thing for her, for them *both,* was to get her wed as quickly as possible.

He straightened and started toward the broad double stairway that swept downward in a gracious curve to the ground floor. Thomas dodged a servant with an armful of linens and another carrying a silver tray and wondered if he'd make it out of the house in one piece.

"Lord Helmsley."

He flinched at the piercing voice and turned slowly, forcing a polite smile to his face. "Good day, Lady Dra—er, my lady." The older woman stood in the open doorway of the ballroom, a diminutive figure with the commanding, no-nonsense air of a general about her. "It appears preparations are well in hand for the festivities."

"Indeed they are." She sniffed as though the very idea that all was not under control was inconceivable. "I have no concerns about the duchess's ball whatsoever, although I do wish your mother could be with us. Nonetheless, I have tried to carry out her instructions and wishes to the best of my abilities."

"And admirably, too, I'm certain. I have no doubt this will be one of the highlights of the season. Now, then, if there is nothing else, I shall bid you good day." He nodded and stepped toward the stairs.

"Oh, but there *is* something else, my lord."

His heart sank. He'd known the moment he'd seen her she had more on her mind than a mere exchange of pleasantries. The determined glint in her eye gave her away. He drew a deep breath and turned back to her. "How may I help you?"

"If you would be so kind as to join us in the ballroom." She moved aside and waved him into the room.

He struggled to maintain his smile, silently bidding farewell to any hope of escape, and walked past her into the grand ballroom. The three Shelton sisters stood at the far end of the room by the pianoforte accompanied by a gentleman he didn't recognize, the sisters' furry beast of a dog lying under the instrument.

Lady Dragon started toward the girls, and he had no choice but to fall in beside her. "We are finishing a dancing lesson and it would be helpful if there was a new partner available."

"I am nothing if not helpful," he said under his breath, mentally adding dancing partner to the list of grievances he planned to present to his mother upon her return. He wasn't entirely certain what, if any, satisfaction he'd get from such a presentation; still, it did ease his irritation somewhat to acknowledge he was prepared.

Lady Dragon cast him a sharp glance. "I'm certain you understand it would not do to have them stumble about the floor like drunken sailors."

"Of course not," he murmured, pushing aside the unbidden but annoyingly delightful image of a tipsy Marianne.

They approached the group at the end of the

room and he noted for the first time the resemblance between the sisters.

All three were of a similar height, taller than he personally preferred but not overly so. Marianne was the fairest, her light blond hair a charming contrast to the eyes he now knew were brown behind her spectacles.

The girl beside her had hair a bit darker, more gold than blond, and squinted slightly at his approach. He wondered if she wore glasses as well.

And the last, and obviously youngest if the frankness of her gaze was any indication, had distinctly red hair. He wished he'd paid more attention to their names, but he'd been far too busy avoiding them, and the very thought of them, to pay heed to anything more than his quest to marry each off as efficiently and quickly as possible.

Lady Dragon pursed her lips. "Lord Helmsley, surely you remember my nieces, although I must say we have scarce seen hide nor hair of you since our arrival. I'm certain that has been nothing more than an oversight on your part."

"Indeed it has." He smiled in his most charming manner. "An oversight I shall do my best to remedy."

The trio studied him with a common expression of amusement mixed with challenge. There was something vaguely familiar about that look, but he couldn't quite place it. He ignored a faint sense of unease. Had Marianne told them of his plans? It little mattered, he supposed. After all, wasn't it the goal of every young woman to marry? Marianne was the exception—and he didn't quite believe her protests.

It was obviously in his best interest to learn as much about these ladies as possible. If he were to find them husbands, it would help to determine what type of men would suit. Well, he'd certainly never had any problem talking to attractive women, and they'd never hesitated to talk to him.

He stepped to the redhead and raised her hand to his lips. "My dear Lady...Lady..." He faltered and groaned to himself.

"Rebecca," the dragon said firmly.

"Becky," the redhead said, just as firmly. She stared at him as if he were an interesting insect for her examination. "Everyone calls me Becky."

"Do try not to confuse him." Marianne's tone was light. "Lord Helmsley has a bit of a problem with names."

"How would you know?" Becky said.

She shrugged. "I've no doubt heard it somewhere."

"However," he said quickly, "I shall have no problem whatsoever now remembering the names of my lovely guests." He turned to the next sister and took her hand. "And you?"

"Jocelyn." She too considered him carefully. He had the distinct impression she was assessing his merits and potential and wondered if he measured up to her standards. "Delightful to see you again, my lord."

"Yes, well, I have been remiss in my duties

and I will do my best to rectify that failing."
He kissed her hand. "Rest assured I will do
everything in my power to make it up to you
all now by being as attentive as possible."

She tilted her head and favored him with a
brilliant smile. Even as he returned it he realized neither she nor Becky would do anything they did not particularly wish to do. Up
to and including marriage.

Abruptly he realized why the look the sisters had shared was so familiar. He'd seen it
before on the face of every stubborn woman
in the Effington family. Very well. He was an
Effington man well used to dealing with
women exactly like these three. Marrying
them off might prove to be more of a task than
he'd originally thought but what fun would life
be without an occasional challenge? He was
certainly up to it. And at the moment, he
rather relished the idea of pitting his determination against these stubborn sisters. One
in particular.

He stepped to Marianne and cast her his most
devastating smile. The very one that had
served him so well in the past. The smile virtually guaranteed to melt the resistance of even
the most resilient woman. He took her hand
and raised it to his lips. His smile never faltered. His gaze caught hers.

"My dear Lady Marianne. I trust you are well
this morning?"

"Odd that he remembers *her* name," Jocelyn
said in a sidelong whisper to Becky just loud
enough for him to hear.

He ignored her, his gaze lingering on Marianne's.

"Quite." She stared back at him, her eyes twinkled with amusement. "And what of you, my lord? Did you sleep well? No unusual dreams or disturbing visions late in the night?"

"Odd perhaps but not in the least disturbing." He couldn't resist a grin. "Although I daresay I shan't be troubled in the future."

"Oh?" She raised a skeptical brow. "Then you intend to give up evenings of drunken revelry?"

"Not at all." He leaned closer and lowered his voice, his words meant for her ears alone. "I was not drunk and I intend to find you a husband as quickly as possible to take you in hand and keep you from accosting virtual strangers in libraries late at night."

"We shall see, my lord," she said softly, the corners of her mouth curving upward in a decidedly superior manner. "We shall see."

He'd dismissed her parting comment last night as being nothing more than the effect of the brandy, but today those same words carried a distinct challenge. A challenge he was more than willing to meet. And enjoy. And best. She withdrew her hand but her gaze lingered on his.

"This is the dancing master, Monsieur Sabatier." Lady Dragon nodded toward a fashionably dressed man who surveyed him with an expression of haughty superiority.

"Good day, my lord," the Frenchman said in a pronounced accent and bowed in a too courtly manner. "We are most grateful for your assistance. You do us a great honor." A polite smile hovered on his lips but a speculative gleam flashed in his eye.

"Monsieur Sabatier has done an excellent job." Lady Dragon nodded with approval.

"You are too kind, madame."

"I'm sure he has," Thomas murmured and studied the other man discreetly.

Although Monsieur Sabatier's clothes were the height of fashion, closer inspection showed they were well-worn, not unexpected given his means of making a living. The Frenchmen himself bore further scrutiny much better than his attire. It was obvious the breadth of his shoulders and fit of his jacket owed little to the skill of a tailor. His face was surprisingly handsome— too handsome, in Thomas's opinion, for someone entrusted with teaching young ladies to dance. Sabatier was not at all like any dancing master Thomas had ever met.

"This is their final lesson and yet I feel they still need a bit more practice," Lady Dragon said. "Unfortunately, Monsieur Sabatier's other obligations prohibit him from staying beyond today's allotted time."

"A thousand pardons, madame. I regret any inconvenience, but I have an appointment of some importance." Monsieur Sabatier smiled apologetically and Thomas could have sworn a collective sigh went up from the three younger women. He wasn't entirely certain Lady Dragon hadn't joined them.

"You have done more than expected, Monsieur." Lady Dragon returned his smile. "We are in your debt."

"It is my business, madame, mademoiselles." Monsieur Sabatier bowed slightly. "And my pleasure." He nodded at Thomas, then turned and strode down the long ballroom.

The gazes of all four females followed him as one.

Thomas cleared his throat. "Ladies?" Three, perhaps four, wistful expressions turned toward him. "The dance?"

"Ah, yes." Lady Dragon was once more a commanding presence, but for a moment he wondered if he hadn't had a glimpse of the girl she might have been. "It's the waltz I'm concerned with. I am not overly familiar with it. If you ask my nieces, they will tell you I am older than the earth beneath my feet and will swear to you my own days in London were spent when Elizabeth was queen. There was no waltz then. They will further inform you the earth itself will shake should I so much as crack a smile."

"And will it?" Thomas grinned.

"Yes." Lady Dragon stepped away and seated herself at the pianoforte. "I will play and you may begin with Lady Rebecca."

"Becky," the youngest said under her breath.

"Lady"—Thomas bit back a smile—"Becky." He swept a polished bow, indulging in the satisfaction of knowing it was every bit as good as Sabatier's. Perhaps better. "Will you honor me with this dance?"

"Of course, my lord." Becky bobbed a

curtsy, smiled and placed her hand on his arm.

He escorted her out onto the floor and took her in his arms. For a few moments they circled the room in silence.

He glanced at Becky and smiled. "I believe your aunt has underestimated you."

She looked up at him. "Do you?"

"Monsieur Sabatier has taught you well." Reluctantly, he acknowledged a touch of gratitude for the Frenchman's skill. If Thomas didn't have to pay constant attention to leading her through the steps, he could concentrate on much more important matters. "So tell me, my dear, are you looking forward to the season?"

"He really is a fine figure of a man." Jocelyn squinted at the dancers. She couldn't see well past a distance of about ten feet but vehemently refused to even consider wearing spectacles.

"Indeed he is." Marianne nodded. "Still, there is the problem of his character to consider. He is arrogant and quite annoying."

Jocelyn slanted her a suspicious look. "That's the second time today you've made such a comment. I find it difficult to believe you are simply making assumptions based on nothing more than his lack of attention to us. You've never been one to leap to misguided conclusions. Come, now, Marianne, what do you know about the man that we don't?"

Marianne sighed. "I simply had the opportunity to chat with him for a few minutes last night in the library."

"Did you?" Jocelyn raised a brow. "How very interesting. Almost as interesting as the fact that you would keep such a rendezvous secret."

"It wasn't exactly a secret. And it certainly wasn't a rendezvous." Marianne shrugged as if the encounter meant nothing. "I simply didn't think it merited mention."

Jocelyn snorted in disbelief. "You didn't think a late-night rendezvous—"

"A chance meeting."

"—with the heir to a dukedom, no less, was worth mentioning?" Jocelyn shook her head. "I don't believe you for a moment."

"Nonetheless, it's true."

"Um-hm." Jocelyn studied her curiously. "So what did he do to annoy you so?"

He refused to kiss me again. Marianne ignored the thought that was every bit as irritating as the man himself. And ignored as well how very much she enjoyed that kiss. "For one thing, he seems to be taking his responsibilities toward us as guardian or protector or whatever he is entirely too seriously. I daresay between him and Aunt Louella none of us will be able to so much as breathe without notice. For another, he is not at all happy to have us here—"

Jocelyn laughed. "That's scarcely surprising."

"And he has a plan to rid himself of us."

"What?" Jocelyn scoffed. "Does he plan

to bash us over the head and bury us all in the garden?"

"Worse," Marianne said grimly. "He plans to find us all husbands."

"The beast." Jocelyn paused and her brow furrowed. "Perhaps I've missed a significant point, but what is so terrible about that? Given his wealth, position and family, the man knows everyone who is anyone. Why, with his help we can all make exceptional marriages."

"Indeed we could. However, he wishes to marry us off as quickly as possible. Tomorrow would not be too soon for him." Marianne leaned closer in a confidential manner. "It appears our demands on his attention hinder his own efforts to find a bride."

"I see," Jocelyn said thoughtfully.

Marianne narrowed her eyes. "Exactly what do you see?"

"Well," Jocelyn words were measured, "if indeed he is looking for a bride, he has three eligible matches right under his roof."

"Oh? I suppose you're willing to step forward and sacrifice yourself on the altar of matrimony? After all, Helmsley will be the Duke of Roxborough one day. Precisely the kind of match you have always wanted." The words came out much sharper than Marianne had intended and she cringed at the sound of them. Why on earth was the thought of Jocelyn setting her cap for Thomas so disquieting?

Jocelyn paid no heed to her sister's tone and studied the dancers with narrowed eyes, as if that would somehow bring them into focus. "Don't be ridiculous. Duke or not, I was serious when I said I have no intention of marrying during my first season. To settle on Helmsley at this point would be akin to picking the first apple of the year without regard to the sweeter fruit to come."

"Still, that first apple can be quite tasty," Marianne said under her breath, recalling the intriguing flavor of brandy on warm male lips.

"No, I wasn't thinking of Helmsley for myself at all." Jocelyn cast her a sly smile. "I was thinking about you."

"Me?" Marianne started. "I have no desire to marry this season or any other. And certainly no desire to marry Helmsley."

"Oh, you needn't actually marry him," Jocelyn said blithely. "But if you occupy his time, he'll be far too busy to pay much notice to anything Becky or I do."

"I hate to spoil what is an impressive and obviously well thought out plan, but it won't work. I am not at all the type of woman he is looking for."

"Are you certain?"

I want a woman who will be biddable and soft-spoken. Marianne nodded and ignored a twinge of what might have been regret. "Quite."

"Pity." Jocelyn thought for a moment, then her expression brightened. "Very well then, you can still keep him busy trying to find a match for you and you alone."

"And why would he want to do that?"

"Why, we will make certain he understands we couldn't possibly marry before you since you're the oldest." Jocelyn smiled wickedly. "We'll tell him it's a family tradition. That it simply wouldn't be right if we married before you. It would be...rude."

"Oh, and we can't have that," Marianne said dryly.

"We'll make him believe that if he can marry you off, Becky and I will fall in line right behind you and he will be rid of us all."

"Lambs to the matrimonial slaughter?"

"Exactly." Jocelyn nodded with satisfaction.

"I see. However, I do have one question. I understand the benefits of your proposal for you and Becky, but," Marianne crossed her arms over her chest, "what, dear sister, are the benefits for me?"

"I would think that's obvious." Jocelyn's expression was smug.

"Obvious? I can't imagine..." She stared at Thomas, a tall, broad-shouldered, confident figure in perfect command of the steps.

"Think about it, Marianne. Whether you are carrying on a flirtation with Helmsley or the dozens of suitors he will no doubt throw at you—"

"I would have no end of amusing experiences from which to draw on for my stories. No end of...adventures," Marianne murmured. A man in perfect command of his life.

"Indeed. And isn't Helmsley in truth—"

"The kind of man I can write about," she said more to herself than her sister. A man in

60

perfect command of his world. *The kind of man I can—*

"And we will be free to enjoy the season without interference from anyone other than Aunt Louella." Jocelyn's tone jerked Marianne's attention from the unfinished thought. Mischief sounded in the younger girl's tone. "And we both know she cannot watch more than one of us at once."

The music drifted to a close and Thomas and Becky started toward them across the long ballroom.

Jocelyn leaned closer to Marianne, her voice low but insistent. "Well?"

A faint flush colored Becky's cheeks, from the exertion of the dance no doubt or perhaps Thomas's charms. It was he who fully captured Marianne's attention. He moved with a fluid, masculine grace, and the oddest sensation fluttered in her stomach.

"Think of the adventures." Jocelyn's voice carried a tempting note.

Becky said something to him and he laughed, a fascinating, male sound that resounded in her blood.

"And you do need adventures to write about," Jocelyn added.

Thomas and Becky drew closer.

"And I do want them to be *my* adventures," Marianne said softly. *Adventures with Thomas?* A thrill raced through her at the thought.

Thomas caught Marianne's eye and grinned and she noted once again that it was an extremely nice smile. The kind of smile a woman could lose her head over.

"Excellent, Becky." Aunt Louella's voice sounded behind them.

"I must say, Lady Louella, she has learned her lessons well." Thomas chuckled. "Why, we scarcely trod on one another's toes at all."

Becky laughed and bobbed a curtsy. "Thank you, my lord. I had an excellent partner."

"As well as an excellent teacher," Aunt Louella said. "Now, then, Marianne—"

"I believe it's my turn." Jocelyn stepped toward Thomas and cast him a dazzling smile. "My lord?"

"My pleasure." Thomas nodded and extended his arm. Jocelyn placed her hand on it and he escorted her onto the dance floor.

Marianne stared after them. What would be the harm? She had no intention of marrying anyone and she certainly wasn't what Thomas had in mind for a wife. Thomas's efforts to find her a match would surely be entertaining and it would provide endless possibilities for her writing. Why, hadn't he already unwittingly helped her write her first story? A story she had every confidence would soon appear on the pages of *Cadwallender's Weekly World Messenger*.

Besides, she wasn't at all averse to his company even if he was more than a little arrogant. Although he certainly was charming enough today. And there was always the possibility of another kiss. Or two. Or more.

She should have thought of it herself. After all, wasn't Thomas Lord W to her country miss?

Jocelyn glanced at Marianne over her shoulder and raised a questioning brow.

Marianne shrugged in feigned resignation and nodded. Jocelyn winked then turned her full attention to Thomas.

If it wasn't for the sense of anticipation bubbling up inside her, Marianne would almost feel sorry for him. His plan to marry them off quickly was doomed before it began. His efforts would surely provide her with all sorts of interesting experiences to spin into *The Adventures of a Country Miss in London*. In addition, the poor man wouldn't have so much as a minute to spare to search for a bride of his own.

It was curious, though. At the moment Marianne wasn't sure which result of Jocelyn's plot she relished more.

Chapter 4

...and every afternoon those members of society who wish to indulge in gossip and flirtation take themselves to Hyde Park, where they ride in carriages or on horseback or stroll the paths in a unique display of fashion and manners. It is a most impressive parade.

Lord W has taken me once and I do hope he does so again, for I quite enjoyed myself, although he was reticent to introduce me to anyone. For a moment I feared he was ashamed of my country-bred bearing. Then I noted the odd gleam in his eye, gone as fast as it had appeared.

Dear cousin, it was a look of possession such as I have never seen in man nor beast. Terror filled me at the sight; yet, I must admit, even in my fear, I was more than a little thrilled....

The Absolutely True Adventures
of a Country Miss in London

"It is exceedingly kind of you to take us to the park this afternoon." Marianne strolled at Thomas's side and slanted him a glance from beneath thick lashes. The younger girls walked a few steps in front of them. "Especially since it was only yesterday that you managed to fit us into your busy schedule at all."

"Yes, well, I can be exceedingly kind when the occasion calls for it," Thomas said with a grin. "Although admittedly it was scarcely a sacrifice to spend a few minutes waltzing with beautiful women. I daresay I will be the envy of every man in the park with the three of you by my side."

"Are you showing us off, then?" Marianne tilted her head. "Like wares to prospective buyers?"

"Not at all." Genuine indignation flooded him. "My intention in escorting you here was nothing of the sort."

"Only because you didn't think of it," she said primly.

"My dear lady, I..." His denial ground to a halt. Displaying them was an excellent idea and he should have thought of it. He ignored the realization and adopted his sincerest manner. "I simply think this is the least I can do to make up for the disgraceful lack of attention I have paid you and your sisters since your arrival." Even to his own ears it didn't ring true.

"Yes, it is. However, I do hope we have not inconvenienced you, pulling you from the comfort of hearth and home to brave the crowds of Hyde Park." The corners of her mouth quirked upward slightly as if she were holding back a smile.

At once he realized, regardless of her other charges, she knew exactly why he had proposed they join the parade of those wishing to see and be seen who frequented the park every afternoon. And it had little to do with his effort at being a gracious host.

"There is scarcely any difference today between the crowds here and those at Effington House," he said wryly.

The duchess's ball was tomorrow and it seemed the fevered pitch of work in the household had accelerated, if possible, in preparation for the grand event. Lord knew the Duke and Duchess of Roxborough had had any number of entertainments in the past, yet he couldn't remember ever seeing the household in such a frenzy. Perhaps it was due to the absence of his mother's personal attention. Admittedly it could well be that he'd simply never paid heed to such activity before.

Now, however, he was the official host, and the ultimate responsibility for the success or failure of the ball, and the launching of the Shelton sisters into society, would be laid at his feet. "I'm afraid I couldn't face another minute of it."

Besides, if he was to marry these girls off properly and quickly, this was the perfect opportunity to get to know them better without the protective gaze of Lady Dragon. He'd scarcely gained any useful information yesterday, although Jocelyn had let slip the younger girls' refusal to wed before their older sister. Marianne was obviously the key to his success. She'd been surprisingly quiet during their dance. Rather as if she were considering some matter of grave importance that had nothing to do with her partner at the moment. The idea that a young woman could be in his arms yet oblivious to his charms was disgruntling, to say the least. Particularly this young woman, since he'd been all too aware of her. The scent of her hair and the warmth of her hand in his and the quite enjoyable feel of her in his arms.

Today she seemed much more the talkative creature she'd appeared in the library and he had suggested abandoning their carriage for the footpaths precisely to be able to engage her in relatively private conversation. And admittedly, he rather liked not having to share her attention.

Marianne nodded toward a sedate, dark-haired beauty riding in an open carriage. "I think she looks like a distinct possibility."

"A possibility for what?"

"Why, for the kind of bride you're seeking, of course."

"How would you..." He grimaced. "Is there anything else I said in what I thought was a private conversation that you will use against me?"

She flashed him a smile and her eyes twinkled behind her spectacles. "You may depend on it, my lord."

He heaved an exaggerated sigh. "Very well, I surrender. Tell me why you think that young lady, the daughter of a marquess, I believe, would be a suitable bride."

Marianne studied the woman thoughtfully. "Well, she's perfectly attired in the latest stare of fashion, so she obviously has a respectable dowry. And she's not the tiniest bit mussed. That alone says a great deal about her character."

"Nonsense. I know any number of women who are faultlessly turned out yet not the least bit amenable."

"Perhaps, although strict adherence to the dictates of fashion certainly indicates a willingness to abide by other restrictions as well. Add to that her manner, which appears somewhat reserved, the way she smiles and acknowledges greetings, I mean. I suspect she'd be quite biddable and more than willing to acquiesce to your desires and your decisions."

"Do you think so?" He was amused in spite of hearing his own words thrown back at him.

"I do. I think she's exactly the type of woman who would make you...how did you phrase it?"

"I don't remember," he said firmly.

"Come, now, how could you forget? I know I can't. You said you wanted a woman to whom you will be the moon and the stars." She nodded. "Yes, I definitely think you should seek an introduction."

"Perhaps I will."

"I should be happy to inform you of any other prospects I might encounter."

"That would be most appreciated." He chuckled. "Now that we have identified a potential match for me, what of you? Do you see anyone you would consider?"

"I told you I have no intention of marrying."

"That's right. You wish to have adventures."

"And experience life."

"Of course." Under other circumstances, he might well find that declaration enticing and worth further exploration. But as the man charged for now with safeguarding Marianne and her sisters, he didn't like the implications of that phrase one bit.

"However, I have given your plan to find us all husbands a great deal of consideration."

"You have," he said cautiously.

She nodded. "Indeed I have."

"And?" He wasn't sure if he wanted to hear the answer.

"And I recognize adventures are in short supply for a woman in my position. I have no money of my own to speak of, at least not at the moment, so I am, again at the moment, trapped in a town in which the most exciting thing that could happen is a faux pas at a ball. I suppose there is the chance of some sort of scandal but surely that doesn't count as true adventure. Don't you agree?"

"Well, I—"

"Exactly." She nodded firmly. "After all, I scarcely think there is much possibility of running into pirates at the duchess's ball or marauding bands of Bedouins at Almacks or African cannibals at Vauxhall—"

"One never knows," he murmured.

"—therefore, since I can't expect adventures of any significance, I shall have to focus my efforts on experiencing life."

There was that annoying phrase again. He chose his words with care. "And what does that have to do with my plan?"

"Why, Thomas, it's obvious." She stared at him curiously, as if she couldn't believe he didn't understand what in the hell she was talking about. "I'm going to cooperate with you fully."

"You are?"

"Indeed I am." She nodded. "I shall embrace every introduction graciously. I shall flutter my lashes, and my fan and whatever else, at each potential suitor who crosses my path. I shall endeavor to be charming and witty and all any man could want. Why, I shall even attempt to gaze at these prospects as if they were the moon and the stars."

He snorted in disbelief then narrowed his eyes. "Why?"

"My goodness, do try to pay attention." Marianne sighed in exasperation. "The opportunity for adventure is minimal; however, the opportunity to experience life is endless."

"What?" He halted in midstride and glared. Surely she wasn't saying what he thought she was saying. "What on earth do you mean by that?"

"You needn't take that tone. Honestly, it's not as if I'm about to squander my virtue willy-nilly on the first man to come along." She thought for a moment. "Even though I do think virtue is an overrated quality."

"You do?" His voice had a stange, strangled quality about it.

70

"Indeed I do." She nodded vigorously. "If one is planning to marry I suppose it's important, but if one has no interest in marriage, it quite loses it's significance, don't you agree?"

"I most certainly do not," he said indignantly, wondering at the irony of him, of all people, discouraging such an attitude in a woman.

She studied him for a moment. "You know for a man with your rakish reputation you're a bit stuffy."

"Stuffy!" He drew himself up and stared down his nose at her. "I'll have you know I am not the least bit stuffy. In point of fact I am universally considered to be quite a rousing good time."

"You hide it well," she said mildly. "Except when you've had too much to drink, of course. I can see how then you might be considered just the tiniest bit fun."

"I do not... I have no need..." He clenched his jaw, took her elbow and steered her back into the flow of foot traffic. "We cannot stand here arguing about my nature—"

"I wasn't arguing—"

"—we shall attract no end of attention," he muttered. "The next thing you know all of London will be gossiping about the argument—"

"Really more of a discussion."

"—in public between the Marquess of Helmsley and an attractive young lady—"

"Attractive?" She glanced up at him, her brown eyes behind her glasses wide and enticing. At the moment he realized how very attractive she really was.

"Yes." He glared down at her. "Damn it all, attractive." Quite pretty and very appealing and more than a bit provocative.

She turned her gaze back to the walk before them and smiled a soft, private kind of smile. An urge to protect her that went far beyond the requirements of responsibility swept through him.

"Now, then." He pushed the feeling aside. "What precisely is your definition of *experience life*?"

"I'm not entirely certain." She raised a shoulder in an offhand shrug. "I shall have to figure it out as I go along. Although I do believe kissing you was a first step."

"There shall be no more kissing," he said with a no-nonsense tone that belied the realization that he would not be averse to kissing her again and again until she melted in his arms.

"Perhaps not with you."

Only with me. "Not with anyone." Damnation, he knew these sisters were going to be nothing but trouble, and this one dangerous as well, at least to him and his sense of honor. Getting them all off his hands and safely wed as soon as possible had never seemed a better idea. Marianne wanted to *experience life*, whatever that meant, and who knew what the other two had in mind.

Where were the other two? He glanced around with a mounting sense of unease. The footpaths were at their most crowded at this time of day; still he should be able to spot the girls.

A knot settled in his stomach. Blast it all, if he lost them there would be hell to pay. He scanned the drive filled with slow-moving carriages and finely bred cattle. Swiveled and searched the walkers behind him. Turned and studied the backs of those strolling in front of him. All the world was awash with bobbing hats and parasols, swishing skirts and muted voices. Each looking like every other. Why hadn't he paid attention to what the damned girls were wearing?

"Whatever are you doing?" Marianne said.

"Looking for your sisters," he snapped. "You may not have noticed but they've disappeared. Probably run off to experience life or execute some other fiendish plan designed for no better purpose than to muck up my life."

She laughed. "Nonsense. Why, they're right—"

"On foot today, Helmsley? Not your usual style." The arrogant drawl sounded off to the side behind him.

Thomas jerked around and bit back a groan. Lord Pennington grinned down at him from astride a fine piece of horseflesh. Beside him, on an equally excellent specimen, Lord Berkley mirrored the other man's smile.

"Pennington. Berkley." Thomas greeted them reluctantly. Both were known rakes and admittedly his friends; still, he wasn't particularly ready to expose his innocent charges to them.

"You spoke too soon, Pennington." Berkley's gaze shifted to a spot behind Thomas and admiration colored his voice. "This is much more impressive than Helmsley's usual style." Berkley slipped from his horse and stepped closer. "Well done, old man."

Thomas turned. Marianne, Jocelyn and Becky stood gazing at the newcomers, the same smile gracing all three faces. At once he saw them as the others must have. They were the perfect picture of feminine charm. Fresh, delightful and lovely. He frowned. Perhaps too lovely.

"Don't just stand there, Helmsley, introduce us." Pennington nudged him. He too had dismounted and both men now stood at Thomas's elbow.

"Yes, my lord." Marianne extended her hand to Pennington. "Please do." What on earth had happened to her voice? Surely it hadn't been quite that, well, sultry a moment ago. His frown deepened.

"Allow me to present the Ladies Marianne, Jocelyn and Becky Shelton," Thomas said reluctantly.

"Rebecca," Becky murmured.

Both men apparently felt compelled to kiss each and every offered hand in a flurry of greetings. A bit overdone to Thomas's thinking. And hadn't Pennington lingered a shade longer than necessary over Marianne's hand?

"On further consideration, I do believe a walk is an excellent idea. May we join you?" Berkley said.

"We'd be honored." Marianne favored Berkley with a smile that was entirely too inviting.

"If you would be so kind." Pennington absently thrust his horse's reins into Thomas's hands and moved to Marianne's side.

Thomas stared at them indignantly. "I say, Pennington—"

"Be a good chap, Helmsley." Berkley passed Thomas his own reins and stepped between Jocelyn and Becky, or rather Rebecca, and the group started off.

"I am not a blasted groom, you know," Thomas called after them.

"No one would possibly mistake you for a groom, my lord." Marianne paused and looked at him over her shoulder, her eyes wide with feigned innocence. "But you don't mind, do you?"

"How could he?" Jocelyn said in an airy manner. "He wants us to meet new people."

"How very thoughtful of you, my lord." Becky cast him an overly sweet smile.

Thomas stared in stunned disbelief. The others moved on and he had no choice but to follow, leading the horses and muttering to himself. "I bloody well do mind."

What on earth had happened to these girls? It was as if they'd become totally different creatures. They were country bred and not at all used to men of Pennington and Berkley's ilk. Yet one minute they were innocents straight from the schoolroom and the next they were sirens. Seductresses. Their flirtatious manner as polished as anything he'd seen in more experienced women. Not that he had ever particularly comprehended the female mind.

It was somewhat alarming the way Marianne and her sisters had taken to the art of flirtation. Thomas had always thought something of that nature had to be learned. Apparently it was instinctive. Rather like the calls of various birds during mating season. He could well understand why his friends wasted no time furthering their acquaintance. They were obviously enchanted.

And Thomas was leading their blasted horses!

Still, aside from his current position, was there anything really wrong with this? Didn't it all fall in nicely with his plans? Certainly Berkley and Pennington's reputations were no worse than most of the unmarried men he knew. In truth, no worse than his. Their titles were more than respectable, as were their fortunes. They were, in fact, considered excellent matches. Exactly what Thomas had had in mind.

His mood brightened. He certainly couldn't claim success yet, but this was a good start. Given the reaction of his friends, he wouldn't have any trouble marrying off the girls. Marrying off Marianne.

Feminine laughter floated in the breeze. Marianne's? She was certainly living up to her promise to cooperate with his plan in her desire to experience life. Annoyance drew his brows together. However, she needn't cooperate quite so enthusiastically. He wanted her wed not ruined.

He should be encouraged. If Pennington and

Berkley were any indication, the Shelton sisters would have the eligible bachelors of the ton fawning at their feet in no time. And surely there would be at least a few among them who could capture Marianne's affections and lure her to the altar. She'd change her mind about marriage soon enough if the right man offered for her. Yes indeed, he'd have her and her sisters off his hands in no time.

His plan would prevail. His obligation to ensure the girls had successful seasons would be discharged. After all, what greater accomplishment was there than to make a good match? And with luck, he would find the perfect bride for himself.

Lighthearted voices drifted back to him, oddly irritating, and he scowled. He should be elated at the certain knowledge that everything would work out exactly as he wanted it.

Then why wasn't he?

Thomas was unusually quiet on the ride home, a silent, somewhat forbidding figure. He stared out at the crowded streets as if he was alone in the carriage. While not exactly rude his manner was terse and the sisters chose to squeeze together on one side of the carriage for the brief ride rather than sacrifice one of their own to the fate of sitting beside him. Not that they paid him much notice.

Marianne leaned toward her sisters confidentially, her voice barely above a whisper. "Did you see that? Do you have any idea how we—"

"We had them both in the palm of our hands." Jocelyn's voice carried a touch of awe. "It was quite amazing."

Becky nodded. "Magic is what it was."

"Nonsense." Marianne truly believed in magic but this wasn't nearly ethereal enough to be magic. No, this was more down to earth than magic. "Still, somehow we did know exactly what to do."

"What to say." Becky fluttered her lashes. "How to smile."

"I don't recall ever being this charming with the butcher's son," Jocelyn said thoughtfully.

"That's because of the warts," Marianne murmured. "These gentleman had no warts."

"None at all." Jocelyn sighed. "They were both handsome and dashing—"

"And really quite," Becky grinned, "delicious."

Marianne nodded. "They were rather, weren't they?"

"Well if this is the type of gentleman Helmsley plans on introducing to us, I, for one, am looking forward to it," Jocelyn said firmly. "I find I much prefer delicious to warts."

A wave of giggles passed through the sisters.

"If you three insist on whispering and chortling all the way home..." Thomas turned and said something to the driver. "Then I shall ride up front with Greggs." The carriage shuddered to a halt. Thomas tipped his hat then exited the carriage and climbed up to sit beside Greggs.

Marianne stared for a moment. "What on earth has gotten into him?"

Jocelyn and Becky traded knowing glances.

Marianne raised a brow. "What?"

"I'd wager he's reexamining his plan." Jocelyn smiled smugly.

"Why would he want to do that? I would think he'd be pleased," Marianne said. "We've met extremely eligible suitors, exactly as he wants. His plan is going quite well."

"Perhaps too well," Becky paused, "especially in regards to you."

"To me?"

"We've seen the way he looks at you." Jocelyn smirked. "As if you're some kind of unknown confection and he isn't sure if you'll be the tastiest thing he's ever eaten or you'll—"

"Poison him," Becky said in an offhand manner.

"What a charming thought. Not the poisoning, of course, the rest of it." Marianne laughed. "It's also completely absurd. He wants nothing more than to be rid of the lot of us. And me probably most of all."

"I think he looked suspiciously like a man who is jealous and is trying to determine why. However, believe as you wish." Jocelyn shrugged in dismissal and promptly turned the conversation to the more interesting question of their new acquaintances. "Do you think they'll be at the ball tomorrow?"

"I daresay, everyone..."

Becky and Jocelyn chattered on but Marianne didn't find their conversation nearly as

79

intriguing as their suggestion. She settled back and stared at Thomas sitting stiff and board straight beside the driver.

It could be that Thomas was simply being overprotective. Marianne drew her brows together in annoyance. He was taking his responsibilities toward them far too seriously. In truth, Marianne was a grown woman and perfectly capable of making her own decisions, even if the rest of the world didn't think so. Beyond that, she and her sisters had Aunt Louella to look out for them and no one could ask for a more diligent chaperone.

Or it could be that he didn't appreciate being treated like a stable boy. Marianne stifled a grin. He had been rather indignant. Although, if he truly wanted to find them husbands, or rather to find her a husband, one would think encouragement was called for rather than irritation.

Her sisters' observations were utter nonsense, yet they did explain his withdrawn and somewhat sulky behavior.

Marianne had certainly been acutely aware of Thomas when they'd walked side by side today. And the memory of his arms around her as they'd danced did tend to surface with an unnerving frequency. And the kiss they'd shared lingered in the back of her mind.

Did it linger in his mind as well?

Nonsense. She brushed aside the ridiculous thought. Thomas was an experienced man. Little things like a single kiss or a mere dance or an innocent stroll would bear little more than passing notice from a rake like him.

No. Jocelyn and Becky were wrong. Thomas was probably feeling a little put upon and was therefore out of sorts. There was nothing more to it than that.

Besides, Marianne was not at all the kind of woman he was looking for. And even if she was interested in finding a husband, which she wasn't, Thomas Effington, the Marquess of Helmsley and future Duke of Roxborough, would not be her cup of tea at all. She wasn't entirely sure what kind of man would be but she did know he would have to be a man of adventure and excitement. Rakish reputation notwithstanding, Thomas did have a surprisingly stuffy streak and was not at all adventurous, even if admittedly his kiss was rather exciting and dancing with his body close to hers a touch intoxicating and even walking by his side oddly delightful.

No. Unexpected regret washed through her. She was not the woman for him and he was definitely not the man for her.

In that, if nothing else, they were agreed.

Chapter 5

...so I should perhaps, dear cousin, take a moment to describe Lord W to you. He is a fine figure of a man, tall and dark but prone to melancholy. He drinks a great deal and one wonders how he has achieved his notorious reputation as a rake with his surly manner.

I should be wise to be quite scared of him, for this is a man one knows instinctively is dangerous. Indeed, I would be quite frightened were it not for the way my heart flutters when he enters the room.

I can confess this to none but you, for it is surely wicked of me, but I am torn between fearing what may transpire between us and what may not....

The Absolutely True Adventures
of a Country Miss in London

"Are you quite all right?" Marianne's voice sounded from the doorway. Thomas hadn't seen her, or any of them, since they'd returned from the park hours ago. Precisely as he wished it. "We missed you at dinner, and I know you haven't joined us any other night, but I did rather think, now that we've broken the ice, so to speak, that you would—"

"I'm fine. Thank you," he said curtly, not

looking up from the barely legible scribblings on the desk before him. With luck his blunt manner would discourage her and she'd leave him alone. Exactly as he wanted it.

This afternoon had been extremely irritating to him and he'd spent much of the time since then trying to figure out why.

"What are you writing?" Her voice drew closer.

"Nothing of any significance." He pulled open a drawer, slipped the paper inside and closed it with a sharp click. He was not about to confide in Marianne, even though he suspected she would take his efforts seriously. Still, one never knew, and he was not in the mood to risk either criticism or laughter. He got to his feet, rested his hands on the desk and leaned forward. "Is there something I can help you with?"

"I just wanted to thank you for today." She reached the desk and perched on the edge of it. He straightened abruptly.

"Thank me? Whatever for?" She sat entirely too close to him. Why, he could reach out for her with no effort whatsoever. Pull her into his arms. Meet her lips with his...

"For taking us to the park. We had a lovely time."

"I took you to the park as much for my own reasons as to entertain you and your sisters."

She wore some sort of evening frock and he wondered with a touch of disappointment why, at this late hour, she hadn't changed to nightclothes. The modest but still fetching bit of frippery she'd had on the other night, for instance.

"Oh, I know that." She waved in an airy gesture. "But still you needn't have taken us. You could have escaped the bedlam by retiring to your club or a boxing saloon." She tilted her head and peered at him over her spectacles. "Do you box?"

"A bit."

Of course, she hadn't known she'd run into anyone that evening and now she could reasonably expect to find him in the library in the late hours. Certainly it would be most inappropriate for her to deliberately appear wearing something so personal and intimate as her nightclothes. Improper and enchanting.

"Rather nasty sport, isn't it."

Something that drifted around her with all the substance of an insignificant breeze.

"Isn't it?"

Something that revealed fetching curves and shadows when she stepped in front of the light.

"Thomas?" She waved her hand in front of his face. "Are you listening to me?"

"Of course," he murmured, wiping the vision from his mind. She narrowed her eyes. Surely she couldn't possibly know what he had been thinking. "Boxing," he cleared his throat, "is an excellent sport for both observers and participants."

She studied him for a moment then shrugged and changed the subject. "Do you have many

84

friends like Lord Pennington and Lord Berkley?"

"Enough," he muttered and picked up the brandy he'd nursed through the last hour.

She glanced at the glass and raised a brow.

He lifted his glass in a mock salute. "I warn you, I am in no mood to discuss my drinking habits."

"I didn't say a word," she said lightly. "We quite liked them, you know. Your friends, that is."

"I noticed." He swallowed the last of the brandy and wished for something stronger.

"And I believe they liked us."

"I noticed that as well." Something much stronger.

She plucked his glass from his hand, stood and strolled to the cabinet that housed the brandy. She pulled open the doors, refilled his glass and poured a second for herself. "You don't seem terribly happy about it. I should think a man who's goal in life is procuring husbands for the females who've invaded his home would be quite thrilled we attracted any attention whatsoever."

"I am ecstatic."

She stared at him for a moment then burst into laughter. "Come, now, Thomas." She handed him the glass. "Whatever is the matter?

"Nothing." She was absolutely right. He should have been pleased that the girls had been noticed. It would make his job much easier. What was wrong with him, anyway? Perhaps he simply wasn't used to this kind of responsibility. Surely there was nothing more to it than that. He hesitated then caught her gaze. "Is that what you want? Someone like Pennington or Berkley, I mean."

"What's wrong with them? To be honest, I scarce see a great deal of difference between them and you." She took a sip of the liquor. "Although they aren't nearly so ill-tempered and grumpy."

"Grumpy?" He tried not to smile. He didn't want to give her the satisfaction but the corners of his mouth turned upward in spite of his efforts.

"But, no, they are not what I want. Not that I want anyone, mind you. Remember, I have no desire to wed."

"No," he said under his breath, "you want to experience life."

"Indeed I do." She moved to one of the wing chairs and settled into it, cupping her hands around the glass. She gazed at him over the rim. "Even if I did wish to marry I should want someone a bit more exciting than your friends."

"More exciting?" He raised a brow. "Most women find them very exciting."

"Do they? Well perhaps exciting wasn't the right word." She thought for a moment. "Adventurous is a better word. Like the men here." She waved toward the rows of books lining the walls. "The men who fill the pages of the books I've read. Men who brave the rapids of the Amazon or explore the jungles of deepest Africa or search for the hidden treasures of Egyptian pharaohs."

"Damned hard to find explorers on the streets of London," he said mildly.

"I thought as much. I do believe adventurous heroes reside primarily in books and are exceedingly rare in real life. Should I ever meet one I would possibly change my mind about marriage. For now, however," she swirled the brandy in her glass, "in regards to my desire to experience life, it occurs to me both Pennington and Berkley would be more than willing to assist me in that endeavor."

"Assist you?" He circled the desk and leaned back against it to stare down at her. "Precisely what do you mean by assist you?"

"Well," she sipped thoughtfully, "just as an example you understand, you did say you wouldn't kiss me again."

"And I meant it." Even as he said the words he knew they were a lie.

"I believe either Pennington or Berkley would be willing to kiss me, and quite thoroughly, I suspect."

"No doubt. However," his eyes narrowed, "I cannot allow that."

"Allow?" She laughed. "I scarcely think you are in a position to allow anything."

"Oh, but I am. I am in charge here." He hardened his tone. "I have been given the responsibility for you and your sisters by your brother and I take that charge seriously. You are under my protection and—"

"Piffle." She smiled and took a drink.

"Piffle? What kind of response is 'piffle'?"

"Quite appropriate considering the nonsense

you've been spouting." Her voice was cool, her manner matter-of-fact. "I am of age. Regardless of any pledge you may have made to my brother, in truth, you have no legitimate say about what I can or cannot do and only the barest of familial relationship with my sisters."

"I have a moral responsibility." He groaned to himself. He didn't sound like Thomas Effington at all. He sounded like he remembered his grandfather sounding. He sounded, well, *stuffy*. And he couldn't seem to stop himself. "And while you are living under this roof there will be no kissing. Of anyone by anyone. I forbid it."

"Forbid it?" She placed her glass on the table and rose to her feet. "Don't be absurd." She stood barely a hand span away from him and locked her gaze with his. "I shall kiss whomever I want when I want. Pennington or Berkley, or even you, for that matter."

"Men like Pennington and Berkley are not known for their discretion. You could end up the center of scandal. Ruined. I will not allow that."

"And are you more discrete than your friends?"

"I like to think so, but this discussion is not about me."

"No, it's about me. However, as I have no intention of marrying, my reputation or lack of it scarcely matters." Her voice was light but defiance showed in her eyes. "I told you my thoughts on virtue. You must recall my saying—"

"Don't say it again."

"Very well. But I do want to experience life—"

With a growing horror he realized exactly what that phrase really meant.

"—and I need someone to, well, experience life with me. Teach me, I suppose."

Bloody hell.

"And if you forbid me to kiss anyone else—"

"Anyone at all." He clenched his jaw.

"Anyone *else*, then *you* should kiss me." The challenge in her eyes belied the prim note in her voice. They were toe to toe, nose to nose. She pulled off her spectacles and tossed them carefully onto the desk. "I think it's your responsibility."

"My responsibility? I daresay... I scarcely think...that is I..." He couldn't seem to get the right words out. By God, he was sputtering! He'd never sputtered before in his life. What had this infuriating woman done to him?

"Think of it as a lesson, Thomas." She leaned forward to brush her lips across his.

Desire battled with duty and he froze.

"A lesson..." her mouth murmured against his, "in life."

Her touch was tentative yet determined. Bold yet yielding. Innocent yet...inviting.

Her hands slipped around his neck and he forgot to breathe. He wanted her. Wanted this. He should push her away. Now. This minute before all thought of honor and responsibility was swept aside. Before desire overcame good sense.

She lifted her head and stared up at him. "If you'd prefer, Penn—"

"I most certainly do not." He tossed his glass aside, wrapped his arms around her and pressed his lips to hers.

Damnable woman. Very well, if she wanted a kiss he'd give her a kiss. If she wanted a lesson he'd be more than happy to be her teacher. Her only teacher. In this he was an expert. He was, he argued to himself, in fact, protecting her from other men. She was right; this was his responsibility. His duty. Besides, he was indeed in charge and this was an excellent way to make that point.

He angled his mouth across hers and deepened his kiss. Her lips opened slightly and his tongue met hers. Desire surged through him. He pulled her tighter against him and her body melted against his, molded to his. As natural, as right, as the beat of his heart.

She met his passion eagerly, with an innocent hunger that inflamed his senses. Her fingers tunneled through his hair. Her breasts pressed against his chest. Her breath was in rhythm with his own.

His hands caressed her back and lower across the lush curve of her buttocks. He gathered her tighter to him, the heat of her body searing him through his clothes and hers.

The long case clock at the far end of the library chimed the hour, its rich tone reverberating in the quiet night.

Thomas drew back and stared at her, his own

shock at the power of their kiss reflected in her eyes.

Still, it would not do to let her know. He forced a calm he did not feel. "I do hope that was to your satisfaction."

"It was well done, my lord." Her voice had a curious, breathy quality. "Quite well done."

He knew he should release her and step back. Yet he was unable to move. Unable to let her go.

"Well, I...um...that is I..." Marianne couldn't seem to find the right words, or any words at all for that matter. Now who was sputtering? He bit back a satisfied smile.

"It's late. You should retire for the night," he said gruffly, his arms still locked around her.

"Yes, yes, that's exactly what I should do." She made no move to leave.

"I think it would be best." He lowered his lips to hers.

"As do I," she whispered.

He kissed her with a light touch and fought the need for more. Reluctantly, he released her, leaned over and picked up her glasses from the desk. Gently, he set them on her nose and hooked the wires around her ears. "Good night, Marianne."

She stepped back. Her hair was more mussed than usual, her cheeks flushed, her eyes bright with passion and a bemused expression. "Good night, Thomas."

She turned and walked slowly to the door.

Her hips swayed slightly with each step and once again the ethereal vision she'd been on their first meeting in this room popped into his mind. It was a very good thing she hadn't appeared in her nightclothes tonight. Who knows what would have happened with so little between them?

She reached the door and turned. "Thomas?"

"Yes?"

"I daresay I shall enjoy experiencing life." She cast him a saucy smile then slipped out the doors.

A wave of foolish delight passed through him and he grinned in what he suspected was a most idiotic way. No, he knew full well what would have happened here tonight if she'd appeared in clothing flimsier and a great deal easier to remove than the gown she'd had on. As it was, another few minutes and he would have torn the dress from her obviously willing body and made love to her here on the library desk. If the chime of the clock hadn't dragged him back to his senses, he had no doubt what would have happened. What he wanted to happen.

What he wanted to happen?

Dear God, when had his desire to protect her changed to desire of another kind entirely? And what was he to do about it?

He moved to the high-backed chair behind the desk and sank into it, resting his elbows in front of him and burying his face in his hands.

Think, blast it, Thomas, think!

He wanted his best friend's sister. His best

friend's virginal sister. A young woman who had been entrusted to him by both her brother and his mother. His mother! She'd have his head on a platter if Richard didn't kill him first.

Of course, nothing of any consequence had really occurred with Marianne as of yet. He raised his head and stared unseeing across the room. Surely he could see to it that nothing did. How difficult would it be?

Certainly Marianne was stubborn, and he would not put it past her to seek out someone else to experience life with. Although if he continued with her *lessons in life* she would have no reason to look elsewhere. He would simply have to make sure they were not carried away by passion. He groaned aloud. He was wrong. It would be extremely difficult. Damn near impossible.

He had to concentrate all his effort on the task of finding her a husband as quickly as possible before it was too late. That, and nothing else, was in truth his responsibility.

He blew a long breath and ignored the troubling thought that finding her a husband was not as appealing as it had once been. Nor would it be easy. Still, he was resolved and there was nothing more to say on the subject. And nothing more he could do tonight.

For the moment, he would firmly set aside any further thoughts of stubborn, bespectacled temptresses and spend an hour or two doing what he really enjoyed. His secret vice as it were.

Thomas opened the desk drawer and removed

the sheet of paper he'd been working on before Marianne's arrival. He studied the scrawled handwriting before him and sighed. It was bloody awful.

Poetry was Thomas's private passion but he was smart enough to know his talents did not lie in putting verse to paper. In point of fact, his poetry reeked. He recognized that and, even if he didn't, the one or two people he'd allowed to see his work through the years had confirmed the inadequacy of his efforts. Still, he did enjoy it and he harbored a secret hope deep within him that one day he would write something that would make ladies fall at his feet and strong men weep with the power of his words.

He picked up a pen and stared at the paper before him. He wanted to write of the kiss he'd shared with Marianne. It was inspirational and unforgettable. Regardless of what happened in the future, the power of that kiss should be recognized, if only in bad poetry.

Especially since he was determined nothing of that nature would pass between them again. Precisely as it should be. Precisely as he wanted it.

Marianne closed the library doors behind her and headed to the bedchamber allotted her. She climbed the stairs and strode down the corridor with an even, steady step as if nothing of major importance had happened in her life and she didn't have the urgent desire to run while giggling insanely.

She stepped into her room, calmly closed the door, then collapsed back against it and drew a deep breath.

How could she have been so forward? So brazen? She'd practically demanded he kiss her. No, she *did* demand he kiss her. Why, she'd actually threatened the man that if he didn't kiss her she'd find someone who would. Again.

She groaned and crossed the room to her bed, flinging herself across it. He probably thought she was nothing more than a tart. And hadn't she done everything possible to encourage that belief? Especially given the way they'd kissed.

She rolled over and stared up at the coffered ceiling, candlelight flickering across the raised, intricate pattern. The first time they'd kissed it had been quite pleasant, but tonight—heat flushed up her face—tonight was different. Tonight was, well, *more*.

Surely this couldn't be love. This yearning of one person for another? This odd stirring of the blood? Thrilling and exciting but with no sentimental emotions involved? After all, she was not the type of woman he wanted and he certainly was not the kind of man she would ever be interested in. Of course, he was handsome. And he could be quite charming. And he certainly knew how to kiss, but there was nothing more to it than that. There couldn't be. Could there?

Not that she hadn't implied she was interested in much, much more with all that nonsense about experiencing life. How could she?

And why not? She sat up abruptly. Why not indeed? She truly did want to know more of life than she'd experienced thus far, and weren't the relations between men and women part of life? She was serious when she'd given Thomas her views on virtue. Preserving it was a waste if one was not interested in marriage. Marianne's family had had far too many lean years to accept waste easily. Besides, men had no such compunction about saving themselves for marriage. Why should women have to live by different standards?

Not that she intended to drag Thomas to her bed this very minute, if ever. But lessons in life with him needn't stop, and should they go beyond a kiss...she flushed at the thought. It would be a grand adventure and it certainly would provide excellent material for her country miss stories. The better the stories sold, the better she'd be paid, and she'd be one step closer to being independent. Besides, if she were ruined, her brother might see his way clear to handing over her dowry.

Then her adventures could truly begin.

And she'd have the future Duke of Roxborough to thank.

Chapter 6

...must tell you some of my impressions of London, yet they have little to do with the sights. Make no mistake, it is indeed a remarkable city, yet I think it is its residents that make it so distinct.

Those who inhabit the fashionable world are as alike as peas in deportment and appearance. One must wear one's hat just so, or tie a cravat in the latest style, or don the approved-of color for this year. And one is unfailingly polite and proper at all times.

It is the members of the merchant class who maintain an individuality of manner that is at once relaxed and to the point. It comes, I suspect, from living in a city where the streets are crowded and one's every breath is shared with one's neighbor.

Still, under certain conditions, the bluntness of their nature can be quite appealing....

The Absolutely True Adventures
of a Country Miss in London

"Good day," Marianne called out to no one in particular and stepped cautiously into the small shop and an entirely foreign world. This was allegedly the home of *Cadwallender's Weekly World Messenger.*

"I'm looking for Mr. Cadwallender?" Marianne called again, hoping to be heard above the clamor that was obviously part and parcel of the printing business.

A huge machine she assumed was a printing press dominated the main room. What space was left was crowded with any number of items she couldn't possibly identify and a few she could make a guess at. Stacks of paper, both blank and printed, leaned against the walls. Print blocks were heaped in piles or laid in racks. The air was thick with the scents of ink and oil and who knew what else. It was exceedingly hot and she fanned herself with the papers she held in one hand.

A layer of grime covered much of everything, although, on closer inspection, Marianne discovered it wasn't only dirt. Fine sprays of ink coated every surface. She ran a gloved finger along the edge of a wooden desk and studied it. She wrinkled her nose. It was definitely ink with more than a touch of dust.

"Mr. Cadwallender," she called again. Surely, given all this noise, he was here somewhere. She stepped closer to the press. "Is anyone here?"

A short, older gentleman popped his head out from behind the massive machine. Great furry brows drew together and he glared. "What do you want, missy?"

Her heart sank. Mr. Cadwallender was nothing like she thought he'd be from his letter. He didn't seem the type who would be at all inclined to like her work—or her, for that matter.

"Come on, then. Spit it out, girl. State your business."

She straightened her shoulders and clutched the papers in her hand tighter. She hadn't managed to slip out of the house unnoticed, locate a hired carriage and travel all the way to Great St. Andrews Street to give up now. Granted, it was an adventure of a sort, but also risky and far too fraught with the fear of discovery to be enjoyable.

She stepped toward him and favored him with her brightest smile. "Good day, Mr. Cadwallender. I'm delighted to finally meet—"

"Hold on, there." He craned his head and bellowed, "Ephraim!" He nodded at her then disappeared behind the machinery.

Apparently that wasn't Mr. Cadwallender. She breathed a sigh of relief. Surely he couldn't be any worse than the grizzled elf she'd just talked to. She did wish he'd appear though. She'd asked the carriage to wait and she needed to return to Effington House as quickly as possible. The duchess's ball was tonight and she counted on the frenzied state of the household to mask her disappearance. Still, she preferred not to run unnecessary risks. The last thing she needed was her absence noted.

She sighed and studied the machine. It towered over her, a complicated array of huge rollers and an astounding variety of gears, pulleys and levers.

"She's beautiful, isn't she?" a deep voice sounded beside her.

She turned to find herself eye level with a

man's chest. Her gaze traveled upward to a determined profile and eyes that gazed at the contrivance in front of him with something akin to love.

"She?" Marianne said curiously.

He grinned a lopsided grin and looked down at her. "Ships are always shes. Why not a printing press?"

"She's as cantankerous as a woman, I give you that," the elf muttered, stepping around them.

"Don't mind him." He turned back to study the press. "So what do you think of her?"

"Me?" She looked at the contraption. "It's—"

"She."

"She's quite..." she groped for the right word, "impressive."

"That she is. She's steam-powered, you know. The newest thing and my own design." He ran a hand along the metal frame. No, he caressed the frame with the affection of a lover. "She can print a thousand pages an hour."

"Really?" Surprise sounded in her voice. "I had no idea. That is impressive."

He nodded with satisfaction and turned toward her. "Now, then, how may I help you?"

"Help me?" For a moment she'd forgotten why she'd come. She stared at a muscled chest barely concealed by a thin, well-worn shirt scandalously open at the throat. She'd never seen a man this revealingly attired before. Most improper but interesting nonetheless.

"Miss?"

Her gaze jerked to his and heat washed up her face.

He smiled down at her. "Not that I'm at all averse to visits by attractive ladies, but do you have business with me? I'm Ephraim Cadwallender and for all intents and purposes this is my place."

"You are Mr. Cadwallender?" As much as she hadn't expected him to look like an elf, she didn't expect someone quite so imposing. "Of *Cadwallender's Weekly World Messenger*?"

"At your service." He bowed slightly. "And you?"

"Miss Smythe. I wrote to you?"

"Of course." His gaze flicked over her and at once she realized he knew it was not her real name. "Of the not-so-adventurous *Adventures of a Country Miss*?"

She bristled and handed him her writing. "It's rather more adventurous now, I should think."

"We shall see." He started toward the back of the shop. "Come into my office while I look at this."

The office was a small room dominated by a large desk butted against one wall, and not much else in the way of furnishings save a couple of wooden chairs and a tall precarious bookshelf. It was as cluttered as the main room and just as stifling.

He sat down at the desk and gestured to the other chair. It, too, was buried under mounds of papers. Apparently if she wanted to sit, she'd have to clear it off herself: Cadwallender was already perusing her work. She sighed and delicately picked up the stacks of papers—billings, they looked like—and plopped them on the floor in one of the few bare spots she could find. Then she dusted herself off, perched on the edge of the chair and waited.

Cadwallender skimmed the pages she'd given him, his dark hair, a bit longer than was fashionable, falling over his forehead. He let out a long low whistle. "Is this all true?"

"Does it matter?" she said without thinking. "Not that it isn't true, but, as I discussed in my letter, I wish to remain anonymous, and—"

"It's of no consequence, really. Truth or fiction, what you have here is quite intriguing." He studied her for a moment. "This country girl of yours, then, is it you?"

She hesitated for a moment. "Yes, of course it's me. These are my adventures. My experiences." *More or less.*

He raised a brow. "I don't particularly care one way or the other as long as the stories are good. And I like what you have here. It's exactly the type of thing my readers want. I don't suppose there's the possibility of a murder in your adventures?"

She started. "I scarcely think so."

"Pity." He shrugged. "Readers like a good murder as much as they like a good scandal. Probably more."

"I shall keep that in mind," she said primly.

He leaned back in his chair and considered her thoughtfully. "I should tell you, Miss

Smythe, that while I have a handful of people who write for me on occasion and a number of others who provide me with information, I do most of the writing for the *Messenger* myself. I also set the type, run the press and sell advertising."

"Do go on." She held her breath. Was this his way of letting her down? Rejecting her?

"I'm telling you this so that you understand, while I will compensate for your work, I cannot pay you well."

"I didn't expect—"

"However, the *Messenger* continues to grow in circulation every week and if this does as well as I think it will"—he tapped a finger on her story—"you will profit."

"I can ask for nothing more." She struggled to keep her voice businesslike and tried not to grin with the sheer euphoria of knowing he would print her stories.

They chatted for a few minutes more about payment—not a great deal, as he had warned, but it was something, at any rate. And something she earned herself. There was a lovely warm feeling about knowing she had taken her first real step toward independence.

"If that's all, then"—he got to his feet—"I shall get this in tomorrow's issue."

"So soon?" She stood and stared up at him.

"Absolutely. I want the readers of London to start following the adventures of a country miss—the true adventures of a country miss—without delay."

"Excellent." She extended her hand and he

took it. "Now, I have a carriage waiting and I—"

"Wesley," he said abruptly.

"Wesley?"

"Yes. Lord Wesley. He's rather a fine figure of a man. Is he your Lord W?"

"No, he most certainly is not." She tried to pull her hand back, but he held it fast.

"Wymore, then?" He nodded. "He's known to be melancholy."

"No."

"Windham?"

"No!" She laughed. "And I daresay I would not tell you if it was. It quite defeats the entire purpose of anonymity."

"I suppose. Although, as your publisher..." A teasing light shone in his eye.

"Mr. Cadwallender." Marianne firmly pulled her hand from his. "I must be on my way."

"I foresee a long and profitable relationship, Miss Smythe. May I see you out?"

"I can find my way, thank you." She stepped to the door and pulled it open, then turned back to him. "I was wondering..."

"Yes?"

"Have you ever explored a jungle in Africa, Mr. Cadwallender?"

"No." He grinned. "But then, the opportunity has never presented itself."

"Pity." She flashed him a smile. "Good day, Mr. Cadwallender."

"Blast, blast, blast!" Thomas glared at himself in the cheval mirror in his chambers. "Banks!"

The valet appeared behind him. "Yes, my lord."

"Would you do something with this bloody thing." Thomas thrust the now-limp cravat at the servant.

"Of course, my lord." Banks dropped the offending neckpiece onto a nearby chair. A freshly starched cravat was draped over his arm.

Thomas turned to face him. Why he continued to frustrate himself over something as silly as tying a cravat was beyond him. His valet had even had tiny gold Roxborough crests embroidered in the middle of the bottom edge of the neckcloths to help Thomas position them correctly. It made absolutely no difference.

Banks managed the chore with a minimum of effort and a barely concealed smile. It was a constant source of amusement to the valet that His Lordship could not tie a cravat in the intricate folds dictated for formal wear.

"Thank you, Banks." Thomas turned back toward the mirror and Banks helped him on with his white brocade waistcoat and finally his coat, a blue so dark it was nearly black.

"What do you think, Banks?" Thomas surveyed himself in the mirror with a critical eye. "Will I do?"

"The ladies will swoon and the gentlemen will choke with envy, my lord," Banks said matter-of-factly.

"Thank you, Banks." Thomas grinned. The valet had impeccable taste and he was right. The man smiling back in the mirror was the epitome of fashion and wore an air of supreme confidence. Handsome. Dashing. A man of the world.

"It's time, my lord."

Thomas grimaced. He'd never arrived at a ball on time in his life, but Lady Dragon insisted propriety dictated he and the girls, as host and guests of honor, be on hand from the first to greet the arrivals. He might as well get it over with.

He cast one more glance in the mirror, adjusted his cuffs and started for the door. "It's going to be an interesting evening, Banks."

"Isn't it always, my lord?"

Tonight, however, was different. He headed toward the ballroom. Tonight marked the Shelton sisters' official entry into society. And their entry into the marriage market—whether they liked it or not. He chuckled to himself. They'd be wed before they knew it.

There was something about knowing one looked one's best that bolstered the confidence of a man, and Thomas was extremely confident tonight. He'd even compiled a list of potential suitors, excluding Pennington and Berkley, of course. In fact, when he thought about it, he realized most of his friends weren't among those he considered appropriate matches.

The thought pulled him up short. What was the matter with him? When had he discarded the philosophy that any man, so long as he breathed regularly and walked upright, for *appropriate*? If this was what the fathers of girls went through, Thomas vowed never to sire anything but sons.

He reached the first floor and glanced around. Footmen in full livery were already stationed beside the front entry below him in the grand foyer as well as at the foot of the stairs. Two more flanked the doors leading into the ballroom. The floors sparkled, the marble gleamed, the chandeliers glittered. Effington House was as perfectly turned out as he was.

"Good evening, my lord." Lady Dragon descended the stairs to the first-floor gallery.

"My lady." Thomas caught her hand and brought it to his lips. "You are looking exceptionally lovely tonight."

"Don't bam me, boy," she said sharply, but she was obviously pleased by the compliment.

"I never lie to beautiful women," he lied, although in truth the older woman did look surprisingly handsome.

She'd discarded the overly proper and rather drab clothes she habitually wore for a fashionably styled gown in a deep claret color. A matching turban of silk and feathers was wrapped around her head. With a start he realized she was probably no older than his mother, and no one had ever accused the Duchess of Roxborough of being dowdy or plain. Perhaps the title of Lady Dragon should be retired.

He leaned closer and spoke softly into her ear. "You should take care, my lady, or you will quite outshine your charges."

"And you should take care, my lord, or I will be forced to smile, and I have done so once this year already." The twinkle in her eye belied her words. "We would not want the earth to shake on such a festive night."

She withdrew her hand and her gaze shifted to a point behind him. Something that might indeed have been a smile lifted the corners of her mouth. "Good evening, my dears."

Thomas turned and tried not to gape.

If he'd thought Jocelyn and Becky were lovely before, they were radiant now.

Jocelyn was an angel from the heavens. An inviting confection in a filmy white gown dusted with gold that floated around her. White and gold ribbons threaded through her honey-colored hair.

Becky, beside her, was an earthbound temptress in a pale green concoction that deepened the emerald of her eyes and complemented the mahogany hue of her hair. And molded a figure he'd never realized was so enticing.

"Ladies." He bowed. "I am overwhelmed."

The sisters exchanged satisfied smiles.

"Good evening, Aunt Louella," Jocelyn said and extended her hand. "Lord Helmsley."

"My lady. You are ravishing this evening."

He bent over her hand and at once noticed the low cut of her bodice. The extremely low cut of her bodice. Fashionable or not, how could her aunt have allowed such a thing?

He forced a smile to his face, straightened and turned to Becky, noting her bodice was no higher than her sister's. He took her hand and raised it to his lips, trying to keep his gaze at eye level. "And you, my dear, are exquisite."

"Thank you, my lord," she said with a grin.

"Where is your sister?" Lady Louella frowned and glanced up the stairs. "I don't believe I've seen her all day. I do hope she's not going to be late."

"She's still in her room," Jocelyn said absently, arranging the folds of her skirt.

"Perhaps I should go—" Lady Louella started for the stairway.

"I'm certain she'll be down shortly," Becky said quickly. "Why don't you and I and Jocelyn go into the ballroom?" She took her aunt's arm and led her toward the wide open doors. "The guests will be arriving at any minute and no doubt you'll want to make sure everything here is in order."

"You don't mind waiting for Marianne, do you?" Jocelyn smiled up at him with an innocence that would have melted any shred of resistance in another man but immediately put him on guard. The last time the girls had asked him if he minded something, he'd ended up leading horses through the park.

"Not at all," he said wryly.

Thomas watched the trio enter the ballroom, then turned and strolled to the balustrade. He rested his forearms on the marble, clasped his hands and leaned forward, surveying the scene with a sense of pride and satisfaction in total disregard of the knowledge that he'd had nothing to do with it all.

"Damn fine job," he said under his breath.

Aside from his responsibility for the Shelton sisters, it wasn't all that dreadful to be the temporary head of the family. He would be eventually, anyway. Not that he wished his father ill. Unlike some of his friends, he liked his father. They got on well together and Thomas would miss the duke's guidance and counsel and, most of all, friendship when the time came.

The duke had ignored Thomas's escapades through the years, while gradually increasing his son's responsibilities in regard to the estates and family fortune. He'd encouraged Thomas's own interests, including his occasional investments, most of them successful, and dabbling in real estate. Thomas was the owner of several business properties in the city that turned a tidy profit, and while he did have a man to attend to such things, Thomas put forth every effort to be a fair and conscientious landlord.

He resisted the urge to check on the hour and glanced at the stairway. His breath caught. Time itself seemed to stop.

Once again a vision held him entranced.

Marianne made her way carefully down the steps, holding her dress up just enough to reveal a pair of nicely turned ankles. Her dress was the color of fine champagne. Her blonde curls, as independent as the girl herself, had been caught up on top of her head in a wild cascade of gold and light. How could he ever have thought Jocelyn the prettiest of the lot?

He stared, stunned.

Marianne reached the landing and looked up. "Good evening, Thomas."

"Good evening." He could barely choke out the words. How could he have missed what was right under his nose? He prided himself on the recognition and appreciation of beauty whether it be in horseflesh or poetry or women. Had his resentment of her intrusion into his life completely blinded him? Oh certainly, he'd considered her attractive, very attractive, before, but tonight she was more than any man could ever want.

"Is anything amiss?" Marianne glanced down at her dress. The fabric caressed her form like a lover's hand. The color emphasized the creamy glow of her skin. "Will I do, do you think?"

"It's rather daring, isn't it?" he blurted without thinking. He hadn't wanted to say that at all. He'd wanted to tell her she was dazzling. A goddess. A dream come true.

Her bodice dipped perilously low, revealing the delectable swell of her breasts. Altogether too delectable. He drew his brows together. "I shouldn't think your aunt would permit you to appear in public in something so scandalous."

"Nonsense." She glanced down at her gown. "It's simply the fashion today and perfectly respectable. You needn't be so—"

"I am not stuffy," he said sharply.

"I wasn't going to say stuffy." She smiled sweetly. "I was going to say stiff."

"The difference escapes me."

"They are remarkably similar and both are apt descriptions." She narrowed her eyes. "Perhaps you would not find my bodice as bothersome if you would cease staring at it."

A hot flush swept up his face. "I was not...I am not..."

"You're sputtering, Thomas." She studied him with an amused gleam in her eye. "I noticed it the other night. Do you sputter often?"

"I don't sputter."

"Oh, but I'm certain—"

"Or rather, I had never in my life sputtered," he caught her hand and drew it to his lips, "until I met you." His gaze never left hers. "You make me sputter."

His words hung in the air between them. For a long moment, they stared at one another. Desire so fierce it stole his breath swept through him.

"Do I?" Her eyes were wide with...what?

"You do indeed." He forced a lighthearted note to his voice and released her hand. "And I am certain that dress will make any number of men here tonight sputter.

"I shall make a bargain with you." She laid her hand on his sleeve. "If you would be so kind as to escort me into the ballroom, I shall do my best not to draw attention to my bodice."

"How thoughtful of you." He covered her hand with his own and started toward the doors. With Marianne at his side, here in his own home, he had the oddest sensation of all being right with the world.

"It's rather endearing, you know."

"What?"

"The way you sputter."

"I don't sputter," he said firmly. At least not with anyone but her. She made him sputter and forget what he wanted to say and no doubt his own name as well. Who knew what else she had in store for him?

He was right when he'd told Banks it was going to be an interesting evening. He smiled in spite of himself.

A very interesting evening.

Chapter 7

...for I am to attend a ball! It shall be my first and I am quite beside myself with anticipation.

Lord W has seen to it that I have acquired a number of new gowns. They are the first stare of fashion and made of the finest fabrics I have ever encountered. They are also exceedingly daring. When I first ventured to try one on I thought I should die of embarrassment. The Frenchwoman who made them assured me they are chaste compared with those worn by others. It is most immodest of me to admit that I am not displeased by my appearance. I wonder if Lord W will notice....

The Absolutely True Adventures of a Country Miss in London

The evening was as perfect as anything she'd ever read about in a book.

The ballroom was a fantasy of light and color. Marianne would not have been surprised to see fairies flitting about, their movements in time with the orchestra's music. Huge flower-filled urns sat in every available nook and niche. Swags of silk festooned doorways and windows and balconies. Broad ribbons fluttered from columns and sconces. And all was done in a riot of spring colors: pinks and greens, yellows and pale blues.

But the ballroom paled in comparison to its occupants. Lovely ladies in jewels and feathers and silks flirted with gentleman clad in deep colors and wearing intricately tied cravats. The room was a kaleidoscope of colors and movement, sights and sound. Laughter vied with music in an effort to be heard.

Marianne wished she could write it all down here and now. It would prove most useful for her country miss.

"My lady, I was hoping you would honor me with this dance." A young gentleman no taller than she, and quite a bit rounder, stood before her. A pleasant-enough man, she supposed, and one of those Thomas had made a point to introduce her to.

She cast him with a regretful smile. "I fear I shall have to decline for the moment. I have danced every dance thus far and I am in dire need of a respite."

"Then may I fetch you a refreshment?" he said eagerly, his face aglow at the thought of currying her favor.

"That would be most appreciated."

He bowed, then disappeared into the crush of guests. Marianne brushed aside a twinge of guilt and headed toward the open doors leading to the terrace. She did hate to deceive the poor man, but it was exceedingly warm. She wanted nothing more at the moment than fresh air and a chance to catch her breath.

The terrace was decked with ribbons and flowers and lit by elaborate candelabra. Here and there groups of twos or threes laughed and flirted.

Marianne stayed in the shadows, unwilling now to engage in even the easiest conversation. She wanted a few minutes to reflect on the night's events.

She made her way to the far end of the terrace, where the candlelight failed to reach and the only illumination was provided by the stars in the heavens.

She rested her hands on the stone balustrade

and gazed out over the Effington gardens. The garden paths were lit by lanterns that danced in the slight breeze like moments of pure magic. She closed her eyes and reveled in the fresh, cool air.

It had indeed been a magical evening so far. As expected, Jocelyn was the undisputed queen of the ball. Still, Marianne and Becky had closely rivaled their sister in terms of the attention bestowed upon them. It was a heady feeling to be sought after by all manner of gentlemen. She hadn't lied when she'd said she needed a reprieve from the festivities.

"I daresay it can be somewhat overwhelming." A familiar chuckle sounded in the deeper shadows to her left.

"But certainly you are used to such revelry," she said lightly, paying no heed to the rush of pleasure brought by his presence.

Thomas stepped into sight, a dim figure in shades of gray. "I must admit, I rarely stay at a ball for its entire duration."

She laughed. "Then this must be quite a challenge for you."

"That it is. I make it a rule never to attend a function of this nature for more than an hour or two. By this point in the evening I am usually on my way to a club or occasionally a gaming hell."

"You gamble?" She kept her voice as level as possible but a cold fear touched her.

He swore under his breath. "I am sorry, Marianne, I should not have mentioned it."

"It's of no consequence," she said lightly.

It wasn't really. Just because her father had gambled away the family's fortune and honor and left his daughters destitute was no reason to paint Thomas with the same brush. Still, she couldn't help a twinge of dismay.

"Of course it is, and I should have realized it." He blew a long breath. "I want you to know, I see gaming for precisely what it is: an enjoyable way to while away a few hours. I have never lost more than I can afford and, win or lose, I know precisely when to walk away."

"You needn't explain. It's really none of my business. After all, we are merely guests here. When the season ends, we shall be on our way." A faint twinge of sadness touched her at the thought of leaving Effington House and its inhabitants.

Thomas hesitated as if choosing his words. "I believe I shall miss you." He cleared his throat. "All of you, that is."

"Piffle," she said, ignoring a touch of disappointment at his last comment. "You want nothing more than to have us gone as soon as possible. You would marry us off tomorrow if the opportunity presented itself."

"Oh, not tomorrow." His words were solemn, but she could hear the grin in his voice. "The day after, perhaps."

"Well, you'll never succeed if you insist on limiting your prospects to the caliber of gentleman you foisted on us tonight."

"What was wrong with them?" he asked cautiously.

"Come, now, Thomas, you know perfectly

well what was wrong with them." She blew a frustrated breath. "They were very pleasant, quite well mannered and eminently respectable. However, to a man they also were dull and tedious and not nearly as interesting as someone like Pennington or Berkley."

"I noted you showed no hesitation in dancing with Pennington and Berkley." His voice was grim.

"Absolutely not. They are both extremely charming and I quite enjoy their company. Not like those you have so eagerly introduced me to. They are one and all stiff and stuffy." She poked him in the chest. "Exactly like you."

He grabbed her hand. "I will tell you once again, I am not stuffy." He pulled her hand to his mouth and placed a kiss in her gloved palm. A delighted shiver ran through her. "I am, in fact, nearly as disreputable as Pennington and Berkley.

"I am generally considered to be as much a rake as my friends, although I have redeeming qualities." His eyes glittered in the starlight and fear, or perhaps anticipation, raced through her. He stepped back into the deeper shadows and drew her into his arms. "I do not shirk my responsibilities. I live by my word. The mothers of marriageable daughters view me as ripe for reforming."

"Thomas, I—"

"It is not easy to maintain the image of a respectable rake." He nuzzled the side of her jaw and she forgot to breathe. Dear Lord, what was he doing? "I have always walked a fine line between that which society will forgive and scandal. It's a matter of control."

He lowered his head and brushed his lips across hers. "Control, my dear."

"Thomas, I—"

"I have a reputation I have worked long and hard to acquire and I am rather pleased with it." His head dipped lower and his lips caressed her throat. Heat spread from his touch and pooled in her stomach. She closed her eyes, conscious only of his voice and his touch. "I have honed skills even your books fail to mention."

His mouth traveled lower. His hand cupped her breast and his thumb rubbed back and forth over her fabric-covered nipple. She gasped with surprise and pleasure.

"I know how to worship a woman, Marianne."

Her breath came faster and her chest heaved. *Dear Lord, don't let him stop.* He slipped her bodice down to reveal her breasts. Cool air teased overly sensitive flesh.

"To make her feel sensations she has never felt."

His mouth covered her breast and heat flamed within her. She gripped his shoulders to keep from crying out. With teeth and tongue, he tasted and teased until her knees threatened to buckle beneath her.

"To make her desire what she has never known."

His mouth trailed to the valley between her breasts and he whispered against her skin, "And leave her wanting more."

Without warning, he straightened. "And that, my dear, is a lesson in the behavior of rakes like Pennington and Berkley and myself."

She struggled to catch her breath against a sharp stab of frustration and a strange sense of loss.

He adjusted her bodice, his voice cool, his manner collected. "And precisely why I do not consider them suitable for you."

"Thomas, I...you..."

"Now who is sputtering?"

At once anger swept away disappointment. She clenched her teeth. "You are something of a beast, my lord."

He chuckled. "Exactly."

"Who suits me and who does not is not for you to decide."

"It is precisely for me to decide," he said in that overbearing manner she detested. No doubt he would begin that lecture on his responsibility to her brother again. "I have been given—"

"Oh, do shut up!" She whirled around and started off then turned back. Before he could say a word, she threw her arms around him, planted her lips on his and pressed her body against him.

He froze and for a moment she was afraid he'd push her away. She opened her mouth and traced the line of his lips with her tongue. And his so-called control vanished.

His arms wrapped around her, slipping down her back to cup her buttocks and hold her firmly against him. Her breasts crushed against his chest. She could feel his arousal through the layers of fabric between them. His lips met and matched her eagerness, her hunger. It was a kiss as glorious as the last.

She steeled herself against the sea of sensation threatening to drag her under and pulled back, her lips lingering lightly on his. "And that, my lord, is a lesson for you."

"A lesson?" He stilled. "What lesson would that be?"

She pushed out of his arms and stepped back. "A lesson in the risks of underestimating your opponent. I may well be less experienced than the women you are used to dealing with but I would wager that I am also more intelligent than most.

"I shall advise you one more time. I shall dance with, or kiss, whom I want when I want. Be that Pennington or Berkley or—" She grabbed the edges of his jacket, pulled his mouth to hers and kissed him firmly. "You, you pompous ass." She released him, pushed her glasses back up to the bridge of her nose and nodded. "Good evening, my lord."

She turned and started back to the ballroom half expecting him to grab her and stop her. Or call out. Or come after her. But no footsteps sounded behind her. And why on earth was that so annoying?

Of course he wouldn't follow her. That would draw attention to them both and he couldn't have that. No, it would be scandalous if the Marquess of Helmsley and a woman who, like it or not, was ostensibly under his protection were discovered pawing at each other in the dark.

She kept to the shadows, avoiding those who still gathered in the illuminated areas of the terrace, and slipped back into the ballroom. With Thomas's watchful eye on her she might well have the chance to dance with the Penningtons and Berkleys, not to mention the Helmsleys, of the ton but she had no doubt he'd never allow her to escape his scrutiny long enough to do anything else. She'd already realized rakes provided the only interesting adventure within the limits of the world allowed her. If she didn't have the opportunity for adventures she'd have nothing to write about. And if she didn't write she wouldn't get paid and she'd never be able to leave England in search of real adventure.

She scanned the throng for a moment and noted three of the gentlemen Thomas had presented had spotted her and were now heading toward her from three different directions. She plastered a smile on her face and steeled herself for their endlessly dull company.

Any lingering doubts she might have had vanished. If she was going to experience life, she needed a rake. And there was obviously only one rake within reach.

The pompous ass.

The last guests had finally taken their leave barely an hour before dawn, The ballroom was empty, all but a few lights extinguished. If the debris were any indication, the ball would be counted a success. Thomas had told the house steward to let the servants leave the cleaning until morning and remembered to thank him for all he'd done.

To Thomas's poetic mind, the room looked like the sad aftermath of a love affair: bedraggled and untidy, with only the memories left behind. He shook his head at the fanciful thought.

He wasn't sure what had made him return to the ballroom. He'd originally gone to the library, intending to write a verse or two, but nothing came to mind and he'd found himself wandering back here. Now he admitted that wasn't entirely true. There was a great deal on his mind that could be summed up in one word.

Marianne.

He sat on the steps leading into the ballroom and propped his chin on his fist. After their encounter, she'd spent the rest of the night actively avoiding him. It certainly wasn't much of a challenge. He couldn't have gotten near her if he'd tried. All evening she'd been surrounded by eager males, those he approved of and far too many of those he didn't. He could have sworn she'd danced every dance. And not one with him.

Whatever possessed him to pull that stunt on the terrace? He'd wanted to make a point, of course, and thought he had, until that last moment when she'd kissed him. And bloody hell, he'd kissed her back. And wanted to keep kissing her. To caress her silken skin. To taste her—

"Do I owe you an apology?" Marianne stood in the doorway.

He got to his feet and ignored a sense of pleasure at seeing her. "No more than I owe one to you."

She still wore the gown she'd had on for the ball, and even after the long evening he was not immune to its effect on him. Or was it the woman inside the dress? She walked down the steps to join him. "I would say the match is a draw."

"As much as I hate to admit it, for once we agree." He chuckled. "Although no man wishes to know he cannot best a mere woman." Even as he said the words, he knew they were a mistake.

She studied him for a moment. "Perhaps you need to stop considering women as *mere.*"

"At least I need to stop considering you as mere." No, she was more than a match for any man. "Agreed." He extended his hand. "A truce, then?"

"A truce." She nodded and took his hand. She'd discarded her gloves and her hand was warm and soft in his. A shock ran through him at her touch.

Her gaze met his and at once the air was charged with tension. He stared at her for a long moment.

"Why are you here?" he said quietly.

"I'm not entirely sure." Her voice was low and throaty, as if she'd spent much of the evening laughing. He pushed aside the annoying knowledge that she had not spent that time with him. "I suppose I didn't want to leave things as they were between us. I know you're just trying to do what you believe is best."

"We pompous asses are like that."

"Really?" She raised a brow. "I shall have to take care, then. I'm certain there are any number of pompous asses among those gentlemen you introduced to us tonight. I daresay, most of them would—"

"Enough." He laughed. "I thought we had agreed to a truce."

She grinned. "An uneasy truce at best."

He still held her hand and had no desire to release it. She made no effort to pull free. At once it struck him how very nice it was to stand here with her hand in his.

She tilted her head and considered him. "We never did dance together tonight and, after all, we did practice." She smiled. "Another lesson, of sorts."

"Then I have been remiss in my responsibilities." He stepped back and swept a low bow. "My lady, would you do me the great honor of joining me for this dance?"

"The musicians have all gone. There's nothing to dance to."

"Isn't there?" He cocked his head as if listening. "I'm certain I hear the strains of a waltz."

"Do you?"

"Can't you hear it?" He stepped closer. "I distinctly hear the sounds of violins. And listen."

"What?"

He nodded solemnly. "It's a flute. Definitely a flute."

She laughed. "Thomas, you are a madman."

"Ah, but there are few things more enjoyable than a dance with a madman. Now, then..."

"Very well, although I do try not to dance with madmen."

"This will be an exception, then."

She placed her free hand lightly on his shoulder. "I still don't hear anything."

He pulled her a bit closer than propriety dictated.

"You will," he said confidently and started off. The next moment they circled the floor in time to music only he could hear. They had not a single misstep; she followed his lead flawlessly. He had noted during their brief lesson how easily she fit into his arms. How effortlessly her body meshed with his. He'd disregarded it then. Now... "Do you hear it, Marianne? The melody?"

"I don't know. Perhaps, but I can't be sure." She gazed up at him with a tolerant smile. "How does it sound?"

"Magnificent. The musicians are highly accomplished. No, wait." He frowned and shook his head. "The cellist struck an discordant note, but..." He paused, then nodded. "Yes, he seems to have recovered nicely."

"Did he?" she said with amusement.

"Ah, yes. They play together as if they were made for each other." *Just as we dance together.*

"Do they? And the tune they play?"

"Exquisite. A melody redolent of light-hearted summer days and star-spattered nights. Of love poems and moonlight and magic."

"Magic," she whispered.

He stared down into her eyes. His steps slowed and they drifted to a halt. For a long moment they stood unmoving, as if waiting for a new dance to begin. Or a word to be said. Or a declaration to be made.

"I should retire or the sun will be up before I have been to bed," she said but made no move to leave.

"As should I." He had no desire to let her out of his arms. To say good night. To go to his bed. Alone.

She stepped back. "Good evening." She laughed lightly, the stange, uncomfortable laugh of someone who is ill at ease. "Or rather, good morning."

"Good morning."

"Thomas." She hesitated. "I should thank you for this evening."

"I had nothing to do with it."

"Nonetheless, this is your home and we are guests and—"

"It was my pleasure."

She smiled, and a strange feeling swept through him. As if her smile were a gift, rather personal and intimate. She turned and left the ballroom. He stared after her. A gift of affection or friendship—or something more? He swallowed hard.

He wanted to go after her. Take her in his arms. Take her to his bed. Without thinking, he started toward the door. He wanted her. More than he could remember wanting any woman.

Realization slammed into him and stopped him in his tracks.

What was he doing? This girl was under his protection. His responsibility. Damn it all, she was his best friend's sister! Anything that occurred between them would be a betrayal of Richard's trust. And hadn't he already betrayed that trust? He'd already gone much further with her than prudence dictated.

Thomas ran his hand through his hair. There could never be anything of a serious nature between them. She was not the woman for him—not the kind of woman he wanted for a wife. She was independent and headstrong. She'd insist on having her voice heard and her opinion matter. She'd question every decision he made, every step he took. And she'd never look at him as if he were the moon and the stars.

Whatever was between them, whatever sizzled in the air when they were alone together, was nothing more than pure lust. He could handle lust. It was, as he'd told her tonight, simply a matter of control.

He had to redouble his efforts to find her a husband. He had to do much more than introduce her to a few men at a ball. One way or another, he would find her a match, even if it took parading every bachelor in the city in front of her day and night.

She'd been at no loss for attention tonight; how difficult could it be to find one man she'd deem acceptable? One man who would make her forget about adventurers and explorers and men who were found only in books? One man she'd be willing to give up her dreams for?

Bloody hell, it didn't sound easy at all. But he'd manage it. Because he knew as surely as he'd ever known anything, if he didn't get her married and out of his life, and soon, it would be too late.

She'd be ruined or heartbroken or both. And he wouldn't fare any better.

Chapter 8

...dwell for a moment on the nature of men. They are odd and unusual creatures, prone to comments both rash and incomprehensible. I daresay I shall never understand them.

I do not know if Lord W is typical of his gender or unique in disposition. One moment he is quite reserved, as if I am beneath his notice, and the next he looks at me as if to devour me whole. A prospect I am surprised to discover rather intrigues me.

It may well be that proximity has alleviated my fears and indeed replaced them with a certain amount of courage, for I do not find Lord W as intimidating as I did upon my arrival. Admittedly he is both arrogant and disdainful.

Yet I find him extremely compelling....

The Absolutely True Adventures of a Country Miss in London

"I daresay, my lord, there are many people who enjoy Lord Byron's work," Marianne said thoughtfully.

"Yes, but can you truly separate the man from his words?" Lord Pennington shrugged. "I find his actions less than honorable and therefore I cannot approve of his work."

"Really?" She raised a brow. "To hear Lord Helmsley talk, you are cut from the same cloth as Lord Byron."

He laughed. "Helmsley is scarcely one to speak. His reputation is no better than mine."

"So I've heard," she murmured.

Pennington continued expounding on his assessment of Lord Byron's life and work. He was surprisingly astute. Still, Marianne's attention wandered.

Only the Effington House parlor was grand enough to hold today's gathering. And even it appeared overstuffed with the many gentlemen who'd arrived late in the afternoon to call on her and her sisters. The number of bouquets filling the room was three times that of its occupants.

The flowers had started arriving before noon, each offering accompanied with a note claiming the sender had quite been swept away by her presence last night or by Jocelyn's or Becky's. A few notes mentioned all three sisters. Obviously those senders weren't as particular.

Jocelyn's laughter rang out from the other side of the room where a tight knot of men was clustered, one or two literally at her feet. Becky sat in another corner with a smaller complement of admirers. Aunt Louella oversaw the scene with the air of a guardian lion, although Marianne was confident she was pleased by this homage to her charges.

Thomas was noticeably absent. After last night, Marianne had thought...well, perhaps it didn't matter what she'd thought. And now was not the time to dwell on it.

At the moment, she chatted with Pennington alone and was quite enjoying their conversation. He was far more intelligent than she'd expected, even if his views seemed rather at odds with his nature. Stuffy, even. Was she doomed to only meet rakes who were stuffy beneath their disreputable veneer? A *respectable rake*, Thomas had called himself. She smiled.

"I was not aware I was that amusing," Pennington said.

"Nonsense, my lord. I have no doubt you are well aware of your ability to amuse, and anything else."

He stared for a moment, then laughed. "And you, my dear lady, are delightful."

"You two are having entirely too much fun. May I?" Berkley pulled up a chair and plopped into it without waiting for an answer. "It's far too crowded near your sisters. I can't get so much as a word in on my own behalf, so I thought I'd join you."

"My lord, you will quite turn my head with such compliments," she said wryly.

Berkley's eyes widened. "Oh, I daresay, I didn't mean...that is, I never intended...blast it all." He huffed. "It's your own fault, you know. Yours and his."

"Indeed?" Pennington lifted a disinterested brow. "And how is it my fault or the fault of this lovely lady?"

"For one thing, your conversation is deadly. All about poets and authors and books." He snorted. "Damned boring, if you ask me. Might as well talk about politics."

She traded an amused glance with Pennington. "And what would you suggest we talk about?"

"Well, you know. What everyone else is talking about. Nothing of significance, really. Gossip more than anything, I suppose." He thought for a moment, then brightened. "I say, I know something."

"I hazard to guess," Pennington said.

"I read the most intriguing thing today." Berkley's voice rang with eagerness. "I can't remember the name of it, but it was most amusing and a touch wicked and it purports to be true. What was it?" His brows drew together.

"So the amusing aspect was in the content and not that you actually read something?" Pennington asked.

Marianne laughed. The insults between the two had an effortless feel and she suspected they were indeed good friends.

Berkley narrowed his eyes and sat a little straighter. "I'll have you know I read a great deal. The *Times,* of course, and the *Observer* and the *Messenger*—"

"The *Messenger?*" Marianne said. "What *Messenger?*"

"*Cadwallender's Weekly World Messenger.* It's extremely entertaining." He snapped his fingers. "Now I remember. That's where I read it."

"Where you read what?" Pennington's tone was mild, as if he didn't care one way or the other.

Marianne held her breath.

"*The Absolutely True Adventures of a Country Miss in London,*" Berkley said with a flourish.

"Absolutely true?" She managed to keep her voice unconcerned, but her stomach leapt.

Berkley nodded. "That's what it's called, and it certainly sounds true. Today's was the first installment. It's about an orphan who comes to London."

"I can't imagine the activities of an orphan, absolutely true or otherwise, to be of any interest," Pennington said.

"This isn't just any orphan." Berkley leaned closer. "This is a beautiful bit of baggage in the guardianship of a sinister lord."

"How do you know she's beautiful?" Marianne said without thinking.

"How do you know he's sinister?" Pennington asked at the same time.

"She writes the stories herself," Berkley said. "Letters to a cousin—"

"Do orphans have cousins?" Pennington murmured.

Berkley ignored him. "You can tell what she's like from her writing." He nodded sagely. "She's a tiny bit of a thing and as innocent as the day she was born."

"You can tell all that?" Pennington scoffed. "It's been my experience that there is typically a great discrepancy between beautiful women on paper and beautiful women in person."

"Not this time," Berkley said staunchly.

As much as Marianne wished to steer the subject to something much safer, she wanted more to hear everything Berkley thought about the *Adventures*. She forced a casual note to her voice. "Why do you say her guardian is sinister?"

He shook his head sadly. "He'll ruin her, poor thing. A man like that, he'd never marry her."

"Does it matter?" Marianne said. "I mean, if the story itself is interesting—"

"Of course it matters." Indignation colored his voice. "It's the honorable thing to do in a case like this."

Marianne pressed on. "What if she doesn't wish to marry?"

Berkley looked at her in amazement. "All women want to marry. It's what women do."

She opened her mouth to protest, but Pennington cut her off, showing interest for the first time. "What makes you think he'll ruin her? Didn't you say this was just the first installment?"

"I can tell from the way he looks at her." Berkley sat back and crossed his arms over his chest. "Mark my words, Lord W will have his way with her."

"Lord W?" Pennington grinned. "Who is Lord W?"

Berkley shrugged. "Haven't a clue. The thing is written anonymously."

"It shouldn't be too difficult to figure out." Pennington drew his brows together thoughtfully. "If it is true, of course."

"Oh, it's true," Berkley said.

"Absolutely true," Marianne said under her breath.

"After all," Pennington continued, "how many Lord W's could there be with sweet young innocents in their care?"

"Nonsense," Marianne said quickly. "If the stories are anonymous, Lord W could be anyone." She brushed aside a twinge of panic and plunged ahead. "Why, if you think about it, Lord Helmsley is more or less acting as guardian for us at the moment. He could be Lord W, and Jocelyn, Becky or I could be the country miss."

Berkley snorted. "Not bloody likely."

Pennington studied her curiously but directed his words to his friend. "Why not?"

"Because the country miss has no sisters."

135

Berkley grinned with triumph. "Besides, Helmsley would never—"

"Helmsley would never what?"

Marianne glanced up. Thomas stood looking down at them with a polite smile. She'd been too absorbed in the conversation to notice his arrival.

"Berkley was about to give you a great deal of credit." Pennington's mild tone belied the assessing look in his eye. "He doesn't believe you would ruin an innocent in your keeping."

Surprise crossed Thomas's face. "Thank you, Berkley. I never knew you thought so highly of me."

"I don't." Berkley laughed. "I just don't think you are Lord W, that's all."

Thomas frowned. "Who is Lord W?"

"Precisely what we are speculating on," Pennington said. "He is the unknown lord in the anonymous but purportedly absolutely true adventures of a beautiful orphan in London. It's a story running in *Cadwallender's Weekly World Messenger*."

"Never heard of it." Thomas shrugged in dismissal.

"I'd wager you will." Berkley chuckled. "I'd bet my entire fortune the whole city will be talking about *The Absolutely True Adventures of a Country Miss* in no time."

"And then Lord W, if there is a Lord W, had better take care," Pennington said.

"Why?" Marianne asked.

"Because, my dear"—Pennington cast her a knowing smile—"at that point we won't be

136

the only ones curious as to the identity of Lord W and his country miss."

Would this afternoon ever end? Thomas leaned idly on the mantel and tried not to glare at the assembly that had invaded his home. Home? Hah! At the moment the parlor looked more like a mad flower vendor had abandoned his wares. Had every man at last night's ball sent flowers to the Shelton sisters? It certainly appeared so. Not that he wouldn't have done the same thing if an intriguing young woman had caught his eye. He should be pleased at the attention they were receiving. With luck, it brought them one step closer to the altar. Then why was it all so bloody annoying?

Jocelyn and Becky were both surrounded by potential suitors. Of course, they would refuse to wed until their older sister did. And as for that sister...

He scowled in Marianne's direction. She was still chatting with Pennington and Berkley, and from the looks of it having rather a good time. Was she that taken with the likes of men like them? Admittedly, he had always enjoyed their company, but that was entirely different. Men expected loyalty and companionship from one another and wanted little else. Thomas had few doubts what these two wanted from any woman, and Marianne was no exception.

He recognized virtually every man here.

Many of them he considered friends and they were no more disreputable than he was. Abruptly he realized, reformable or not, he would hesitate to put himself on a list of acceptable prospects.

Where were the men he'd deemed suitable? Not a one of those he had so painstakingly selected and introduced to Marianne had deigned to call on her. Perhaps they were just biding their time. Waiting for the opportune moment. His scowl deepened. If one of them didn't move quickly, that moment would slip by and Marianne would be off *experiencing life* with Pennington or Berkley or someone else equally unacceptable.

Marianne glanced up and her gaze met his. He glared back and she laughed. The blasted woman laughed! She murmured something to Pennington and Berkley and all three got to their feet. Marianne headed toward him.

What did she want with him now?

"Delightful afternoon, don't you think so, my lord?" Amusement colored her voice.

"Not in the least." He narrowed his eyes. "My home is cluttered with flowers and"—he waved at the gathering—"crowded with vagrants."

"I'd scarce call them vagrants." She leaned closer in a confidential manner. "Now smile, or everyone will think you're quite inhospitable and in an extremely disagreeable mood."

"I prefer to be inhospitable and I am in a disagreeable mood," he muttered but adopted a stiff smile nonetheless.

"Oh, that's much better. You look positively jovial."

He clenched his teeth. "I have nothing to be jovial about. You have broken your promise."

She laughed. "What promise is that?"

"You promised to cooperate in my efforts to find you a husband."

"And I've lived up to it."

"Obviously not well enough." He sniffed. "Not a single man here is one I consider appropriate for you." He knew how, well, stuffy he sounded, but he didn't care.

A spark flared in her brown eyes. "What is it, Thomas?" she said in a low voice for him alone to hear. "Was I not charming enough? Did I not I flirt enough? Or hang on every uttered male word as if it were pure poetry? I'll have you know"—she gestured at the room—"a good portion of these flowers were addressed to me. Several from some of the very gentlemen who are here now."

"Pennington and Berkley, no doubt."

"Among others." She glared up at him. "At any rate, I'd say that indicates cooperation."

"Well, I do not. I'd say... I think...or rather it..."

"You're sputtering, and it's not nearly as charming as I had once thought." She swept off to join the others.

He stared after her and struggled to keep what passed for a smile on his face. By God, he'd get her wed or die trying.

"You do not appear to be enjoying yourself, my lord." Lady Louella joined him.

He'd been too intent on Marianne to notice the older lady's approach. "On the contrary. I—"

She lifted a brow.

He chuckled. "Very well. You have seen through me."

"It was not difficult." She pressed her lips together and he wondered if she was holding back a smile. "What precisely do you find so annoying about this gathering?"

Without thinking his gaze slipped to Marianne. "I am simply not pleased by the caliber of gentlemen who have seen fit to call."

"Nonsense, my lord. They are all from respectable families and, unless I am mistaken, are for the most part financially sound." She studied the crowd for a moment. "I understood, as well, most of them are companions of yours."

"And in that lies the problem." He nodded toward a gentleman beside Jocelyn. "Lord Markworth drinks entirely too much."

"As do you."

He ignored her, warming to this litany of his friends' sins. "And Lord Kenniston is passionate about racing his phaeton when any opportunity arises."

"And you do not?"

"Pennington's and Berkley's escapades are legendary."

"And yours are not?"

He glanced down his nose at her. "My dear lady, I am not immune to your point. I am exactly like this lot."

"Isn't this a case, then, of the pot calling the kettle black?"

"Admittedly, I am a pot." He blew a frustrated breath. "However, it is for that very reason that I know precisely what these kettles are all about."

"You do not give them, or yourself, enough credit."

"Or I give us all too much." He paused and considered her. "Tell me this, my lady, would you want one of this group—or me, for that matter—as a match for one of your nieces?"

She studied him for a long moment, as if balancing his deficits against his attributes. She nodded slowly. "Yes, Lord Helmsley, I believe I would."

"Why?"

"Any number of reasons." She ticked them off on her fingers. "You come from a good family. You have a respectable title and the finances to assure they would want for nothing."

"I sound too good to be true."

"I doubt that."

"And what of affection? Love? Doesn't that enter into it?"

"It's been my experience that love is fleeting. My sister married for love, although, granted, a title and position came along with it." She shifted her gaze to her nieces. "But their father was a very weak man, unable to live up to his responsibilities. Unable to live up to the expectations of that love and all that goes with it."

He studied her curiously. "Have you ever been in love, my lady?"

Her forehead furrowed in a frown. "That, my boy, is an impertinent question and extremely personal."

"Please except my apology. I had no intention—"

She waved aside his comment. "If I say no, then I am to be pitied for having lived my life without love. If I say I loved once and he died or, worse, left me, again I am to be pitied. I am satisfied with my life and have no desire for pity."

"I didn't mean—"

"Of course you didn't." She paused, and he wondered if she was indeed remembering a lost love.

He wasn't certain why he'd asked her about love in the first place. He'd never particularly considered it one way or the other. At least not when it came to matches for himself or the girls. Love didn't play a role in the practicalities of selecting a mate. And he had always considered himself a practical man.

"However, I suspect, when love is true"—her words were measured—"it can be a very powerful force."

"No doubt," he murmured. He thought Richard and Gillian had that kind of love. And perhaps his parents as well. Come to think of it, most of the matches in his own family had been for love and most were successful and happy.

He'd been in love, of course. No less than

a dozen times in his younger days, though none of it had turned out well. With age he'd grown cautious, and perhaps a little jaded and disillusioned. Now he wanted to select a wife for more sensible reasons than mere emotion. Odd, for a poet to be so pessimistic about that which all poets write.

"Do they want love, do you think?" Again his gaze settled on Marianne.

"They are sisters, but what they want, or rather what they think they want, is decidedly different from one to the next. I know them far better than they suspect." She nodded at Jocelyn. "Jocelyn wants wealth and position. She is preoccupied with appearance to the point that she refuses to consider spectacles, even though she cannot see clearly beyond a score of feet or so. But while I have seen her thoughtless, I have never known her to be deliberately unkind.

"Rebecca's wants are simple. A good man with an excellent stable, of course, and children." Lady Louella looked at the girl with an expression that might well have been fondness. "And of the three, Rebecca is the one most concerned with love.

"As for Marianne, she is perhaps the most complicated." Lady Louella studied Marianne for a moment. "She was very young when her mother died, but not so young that she doesn't remember her." The lady sighed. "My sister was a wonderful woman but with never an opinion or thought of her own. She was as weak as her husband. If she had been stronger, their lives together would have been different. And perhaps the lot of her daughters would have been better after her death."

Thomas was well aware of the family's history. How Marianne's father had gambled away everything and left his son and daughters struggling to make ends meet. He could not imagine a childhood in such circumstances. At once he understood Marianne's longing for independence and adventure. What could be more different from a bare existence in the English countryside than the excitement she'd only found thus far in books? And why shouldn't she want to taste that excitement for herself?

"Marianne has always been a dreamer. But she is also headstrong and opinionated. While not always qualities one would wish in a woman, I think they will serve her well. She will not allow any man, husband or otherwise, to destroy her life." There was a touch of pride in the older woman's voice.

Thomas smiled. "I daresay I needn't ask who she takes after."

Louella's chin lifted. "She will need a man who accepts his responsibilities. A man she can depend on. A man whose feet are planted firmly on the ground." Her lips curved upward slightly in a fair imitation of a smile. "Because hers will never be."

"Exactly what I thought," Thomas murmured.

A few moments later he excused himself and headed for the library. The type of man who could capture Marianne's hand was the type of man who was more than likely to ruin her instead. Men like his friends. Admittedly exciting and prone to adventure. Granted, adventure of a scandalous nature but adventure nonetheless.

In spite of her protests, it was obvious she was intrigued by Pennington and Berkley. Of course, they'd never explored the Amazon but they did have an air of adventure about them. Exactly the quality that would catch her eye. Exactly the wrong kind of man for her. And exactly what he wanted to avoid.

Thomas closed the library doors behind him and sat down at the desk. He opened a drawer and pulled out a few pieces of stationary, hesitated, then grabbed a thick stack of the writing paper. Who knew how many tries it would take to get this right?

If he couldn't, or rather wouldn't, entice her with men of the qualities she desired, he'd have to concentrate on quantity. Sheer numbers would wear down her resistance. And sooner or later, preferably sooner, she'd accept an offering of marriage.

Off the top of his head, he could think of at least half a dozen gentlemen that would suit. Dull and tedious she'd called them. Respectable, responsible and without an adventurous thought in their heads in Thomas's thinking. He should probably double that number, or triple it. He trimmed a pen and leaned back to think.

Exactly how did he want to phrase this?

He didn't want to be crass yet he did want to make certain the gentlemen he had in mind were well aware of the benefits of marriage to Marianne. No, he shouldn't actually say marriage; he wouldn't want to scare anyone off. But he could casually mention her impressive dowry and how an allegiance with her would mean connections with the Earl of Shelbrooke and the Duke of Roxborough.

He would also urge discretion. Marianne knew he wished to find her a husband but if she ever found out the lengths he was willing to go to...he shuddered at the thought.

He'd have his notes delivered at once and by the end of the week, the Effington House parlor would be filled with any number of proper suitors for Marianne. She would select one and then his duties toward her would be at an end. She would be out of his life. He brushed aside a twinge of regret.

Oh, certainly he would see her socially now and again or at the occasional family gathering. But she would be wed and so, by that time, would he. To a nice biddable woman who would never defy his wishes or question his judgment or argue with his decisions. To a woman who would never cause him a moment's concern.

Dull and tedious.

A woman who would never make him sputter.

Chapter 9

...Lord W has been particularly secretive of late.

In those hours long after the household has retired for the night, he can be found in his library. I have chanced upon him there unnoticed.

It is a strange thing, to observe a man when he is not aware of such scrutiny. There is a quiet gentleness about Lord W when he is confident in his solitude that belies the tempestuous nature I have been privy to thus far. There is much more to the man than I, and indeed the world, have suspected.

The knowledge triggers an odd ache deep within my heart....

The Absolutely True Adventures of a Country Miss in London

Marianne quietly opened the library door and slipped inside. Thomas sat behind his desk, intent on whatever he was writing.

She hadn't had the chance to speak with him privately in more than a week.

She'd come down to the library on previous nights hoping to find Thomas, but to no avail. Either he was retiring early or, more likely, was out carousing.

He'd escorted them to Lord Attwater's soiree and Lady Millbanks's rout, and so on, nearly every night. He'd no sooner introduce them to their hostess then disappear, although she had the feeling he was never far from reach. Not unexpected, given his overprotective nature.

His presence would have been pointless, at any rate. Jocelyn, of course, was always surrounded by admirers. Becky was only slightly less occupied. Even Marianne drew a surprising amount of attention. Not at all bad for an aging, intelligent bluestocking, even if the men she attracted were cut from the same cloth. An exceedingly dull cloth. She'd never considered herself particularly vain, yet the caliber of gentlemen seeking her out was annoying and humbling. It only reinforced her resolve *not* to hunt for a husband.

Marianne had discovered she rather missed Thomas. And missed, as well, the kisses they'd shared. If this was the result of their alleged truce, she wanted no part of it. It was past time to take matters into her own hands— if she was to have anything at all interesting to write about.

Another installment of *The Absolutely True Adventures of a Country Miss in London* had come out, and indeed it was the talk of the ton. Rumor and gossip was rife as to the true identity of Lord W and his innocent charge. It was at once thrilling and terrifying. She quite enjoyed hearing her stories discussed, even as she didn't dare dwell on the consequences if she were discovered.

Marianne drew a deep breath and crossed the room to the brandy cabinet. Out of the corner of her eye, she watched Thomas note her approach, but she paid him no heed. She opened the cabinet, selected a glass and filled it, then wandered over to a bookshelf and perused the titles.

"Looking for something in particular?"

"Not really." She took a sip of the brandy and continued to stare at the volumes before her. "Something amusing, perhaps."

"May I make a suggestion?"

"No, thank you. I'm quite capable of choosing a book on my own. After all, I know my likes and dislikes better than anyone." She slanted him a pointed glance. He'd gotten to his feet. "Please, do go on with whatever it was you were doing. Just ignore me." She smiled sweetly. "You seem to have become quite adept at that."

He glared for a moment, then took his seat, muttering under his breath.

"Did you say something?" She moved closer.

"No," he snapped.

"You needn't be so surly."

"I am not surly," he said in a manner that she'd be hard-pressed to describe as any-thing but surly.

She snorted with disbelief.

"I'm not. I'm simply"—he glanced at the paper before him—"preoccupied."

"With what?" She leaned forward over the desk to try to catch a glimpse of whatever he was writing.

"Nothing." He splayed his hands over the paper in a defensive manner, as if he'd been caught breaking a law or doing something exceedingly naughty. Curiosity surged through her.

She circled the desk to stand behind him. "Nonsense, it's not nothing if you're so concerned about it."

"I'm not concerned." His voice was casual, but he hunched his shoulders to shield whatever it was he had.

"Come, now, Thomas." She placed her free hand on his arm and leaned forward. He tensed beneath her touch. She smiled with satisfaction and bent close to whisper in his ear. "Tell me what you're doing." She nibbled at his earlobe just for good measure.

"Bloody hell." He jumped to his feet and stood back. "What are *you* doing?"

"I simply thought, as we hadn't had a lesson for a while—"

"There will be no more lessons," he thundered.

She laughed. "Of course there will. Now, then." She snatched the paper off the desk before he could make a move. "What is this?"

"Give it to me." He held out his hand in a commanding manner.

She handed him her brandy.

"You know perfectly well this is not what I want." He drained the drink and slapped the glass down on the desk. "Now hand it over."

She shook her head and hid the paper behind her back. "Not until you tell me what it is."

He clenched his teeth and approached her. "Give it to me right now."

She moved back and fluttered her lashes at him. "What will you give me for it?"

He narrowed his eyes. "What do you want?"

"Another lesson."

"Absolutely not."

Stubborn beast. "Very well, then. I suppose a kiss alone will suffice."

He glared at her as if she'd asked for something that would cost him his life or his fortune. "No."

She waved the page at him. "Yes."

"N—" He huffed a short breath. "If you insist."

"Indeed I—"

He grabbed her shoulders, jerked her to him and planted his lips on hers in a kiss resolute and far and away too brief. "There. Now give me my paper."

"I don't think so," she said, her voice a touch breathless.

"Why not?"

She paused, thoroughly enjoying his look of annoyance, and tried not to laugh. "I don't think it was up to your usual standards."

"Marianne," he growled.

"Or mine, either, for that matter." She shook her head in exaggerated regret. "No, I believe you'll have to do better."

For a moment she thought he was going to do just that. Instead he shrugged. "Very well, read the blasted thing, for all I care."

She shook the paper out with a flourish

and scanned it. "Your handwriting is barely legible."

"If you can't read it—" He made a grab for it, but she moved out of his reach.

"Oh, I can read it." She studied the sheet, then glanced up at him. "What exactly is it?"

"It's poetry."

She drew her brows together and read his words again. "I don't think so."

"It is," he said through clenched teeth. "I wrote it. It's poetry. It rhymes."

"Not much of it," she murmured.

"I'm still working on it." He snatched the page from her hand, crumpled it into a ball and threw it onto the desk. "I know it's not good."

"Not good?"

"Very well, it reeks. More than likely it always will. I've written since my school days and it does not seem to get any better. It is a complete waste of time. However"—his eyes shone with grim determination and challenge, as if he dared her to argue—"I don't particularly care. I will not give it up."

"Really? You've never struck me as a man who tolerates failure in anything. Even poetry. Why continue?"

"Because it's how I express myself," he said loftily.

"Oh?" She tried not to smile.

"Because it has no practical application whatsoever." He blew a long breath. "Because it's the work of Thomas Effington and has nothing to do with the Marquess of Helmsley or the future Duke of Roxborough. Because, even if it's the worst thing ever written in the history of mankind, I enjoy it."

She considered him thoughtfully. She'd never in a hundred lifetimes guess Thomas Effington wrote poetry, and never suspect he'd indulge in anything he didn't do splendidly, regardless of how much he enjoyed it. It spoke rather well of the man. What else didn't she know about him?

"Then you should certainly continue." She stepped around the desk, sat on a stool and picked up the crushed poem. "How long did you say you've been writing poetry?"

"Forever." He watched her cautiously.

She smoothed out the paper and studied it. "What are you doing?

"I've written a bit myself." But not like this. Her writing did seem to make sense, whereas his was an incomprehensible mix of vaguely connected phrases and cryptic thoughts.

"Really?" Suspicion sounded in his voice. "Poetry?"

"More a journal of sorts," she said absently. "You do realize *behind* does not rhyme with *shine*?"

"Of course. I told you I wasn't finished." He repeated the two words under his breath.

"Whereas *gout* does rhyme with *pout*; however, I'm not entirely certain that's the image you want to evoke."

"I was just seeing if it worked."

"Of course." She stifled a smile and looked up at him. "Perhaps I could be of some assistance. Help you to express yourself."

He crossed his arms over his chest. "I know how to express myself, thank you very much."

She lifted a brow. "*Gout* and *pout*?"

He studied her carefully, in the manner of a man trying to decide if he was viewing his savior or his executioner. Finally he sighed in resignation. "What would you suggest?"

"Well..." She stared down at his scrawled script. She had no idea where to begin. "Well..." she said again.

He came around behind her and leaned forward to peer over her shoulder, bracing one hand beside the page and the other on the back of her chair. She was acutely aware of his proximity. His breath near her ear. The rise and fall of his chest at her back. His presence surrounded her, engulfed her. She was practically within his embrace.

A curious sense of yearning washed over her. For a moment she wanted nothing more than to melt back against him. To surrender herself with no thought of a point to be made. Or a battle of wits to be won. Or a lesson to be learned. Simply Thomas's arms around her. His lips on hers. His flesh hot against her own. His—

"Will that work better, then, do you think?" Thomas's enthusiastic words wrenched her from her thoughts.

"No doubt," she murmured without so much as the tiniest clue as to what he was talking about. He shifted to grab a pen and his shoulder brushed against hers. Her heart pounded in her chest at the contact. He dipped his pen in the inkwell and scribbled on the paper, apparently unconcerned at the closeness of their positions.

"There. That's much improved." Thomas's attention was focused on the page and he continued to write, nodding and muttering as much to himself as to her.

She paid scant attention, too intrigued by her newfound awareness of him to concentrate on the futile goal of rewriting bad poetry. Yesterday, this morning, even a few minutes ago she would have said Thomas Effington was nothing more to her than a means to an end. A convenient rake with which to explore the limits of her world and experience life. And yes, with every passing day that idea included the more physical aspects of life. After all, she had no intention of marrying and no expectation of love.

But what was it she was feeling now with his body close to hers? As exciting as their intimate encounter in the garden had been, it was simply, and quite delightfully, lust. She'd thoroughly enjoyed it and indeed could scarcely wait for more.

This was different. Precisely how it was different she wasn't sure, but it was somehow...what? More? Definitely more. There was an odd ache inside her. A sort of flutter somewhere below her stomach. A sweet, sad, tremulous feeling as if she were waiting for something grand to happen.

Maybe the difference came hand in hand with learning Thomas's secret. Oh, not a notable

secret as secrets go, but still in all, a significant secret, if only to him. The secret not so
much in the writing of his verse but in his accep-
tance of the knowledge that he did not do it
well.

"And I think if I used *sunset* instead of..."

She nodded absently, wondering why the
eagerness in his voice was now so endearing.
The passion in the stroke of his pen now so
compelling.

"If, perhaps, I tried..."

She stared at his profile, fierce with con-
centration. If she turned and shifted just a bit,
her lips would be close to his. She could kiss
him, and then...

"Then I could say..."

She resisted the urge to reach out and brush
his hair away from his forehead. She wanted
to touch him, hold him, press her lips to his.

She wanted to run.

Instead she sat immobile, mesmerized by
nothing more than the look on his face.

And the growing realization that this
pompous ass might not be nearly as pompous
as she'd thought. He might, in fact, be something of an adventure in and of himself.

"I rather like it." Thomas cast her a questioning look. "Don't you?"

She stared into his eyes, dark and blue and
forever. She swallowed hard. "It's...better."

He laughed and straightened. "It is definitely
better. Much, much better. Oh, it will never
compete with Byron's or Keats's or Shelley's,
but I daresay it's no longer as dreadful as it was."

He picked up his glass, hesitated, then took hers as well and stepped to the liquor cabinet.

"No, it's not dreadful at all."

She watched him fill their glasses and wondered at this newfound, and rather urgent, desire to be with him. Alone. To find out more about this man who'd suddenly become important to her. An idea popped into her head. An idea he probably wouldn't like one bit. She drew a breath for courage. "I would certainly be willing to lend you my further assistance should you desire it."

He frowned and shook his head. "That's quite kind of you, but you see, there are fewer than a handful of people who know of this secret vice of mine and I prefer to keep this particular aspect of my character private."

"Oh, I quite understand, and I would never tell anyone," she said quickly. "I'm very good at keeping secrets."

"Even so..." Indecision crossed his face.

She pressed ahead. "We could meet here, after everyone else is in bed. No one need know."

"Late-night meetings? Alone?" He shook his head. "Highly improper, Marianne. I daresay—"

"Come, now, Thomas. It's not like we haven't met here before late at night."

"Unexpected encounters are one thing. Planned liaisons are something altogether different," he said in that stuffy manner that set her teeth on edge. "We have your reputation to consider."

"Piffle. I don't care one whit for my reputation."

"I do."

"Very well." She studied him for a moment. "You are here in the library most evenings, are you not?"

"Yes," he said cautiously.

"And if I should happen to wander in, looking for a book, perhaps..."

"Perhaps what?"

"Why, it would be most impolite of me not to offer my help."

"I don't think—"

"I shall make a deal with you," she said quickly, sensing victory. "We shall make a trade. Your lessons for mine. Lessons in poetry for—"

"Lessons in life?" He snorted. "I think not."

"Pity." She shrugged. "I'm certain there must be a gentleman or two available who would be more than willing...." She frowned. "Not that I seem to be inundated with that type of gentleman; still, I can't imagine even the most proper and boring man would find it too difficult—"

"Enough," he snapped. She loved it when he got that edgy, trapped look in his eye. She could practically see him weigh the pros and cons of her suggestion in his mind. And see as well his realization that she'd given him little choice. "Agreed. I shall continue your... lessons." He said the word as if it left a bad taste in his mouth.

"You needn't glare at me like that. I am not a trollop."

"I intend to make sure you do not become one." He blew a defeated breath. "However, if I am to go along with your absurd proposal—"

"Threat." She fluttered her lashes in exaggerated flirtation. "It was a threat."

"Indeed," he said wryly. "You must give me your promise not to accost other unsuspecting men."

She laughed. "You have my word."

"That is no doubt the best I can hope for." His tone was grudging and she wondered if he was as inconvenienced as he sounded or as intrigued by her as she was with him. Or perhaps he too was scared. No, surely not. Marianne doubted there was anything beyond the public ridicule of his poetry that frightened Thomas.

"I suppose, at the very least, this way I can be certain of what you are up to and whom you are up to it with."

"Do you think so?" She grinned wickedly. "You are exceedingly confident, my lord."

"In this, indeed I am." A determined glint showed in his eye. "Until I have you safely wed, I shall not let you out of my sight."

"As you wish."

He narrowed his eyes. She widened hers innocently. Her confidence matched his. She didn't doubt she could evade his notice whenever she needed to pay a visit to Cadwallender. After all, she had her sisters to help.

As for the rest of it, she'd already decided to concentrate her attention on him and explore the adventures to be had with a respectable rake.

And explore as well the turn her feelings had taken and precisely what they meant.

Three weeks later, Marianne sat on the library sofa staring thoughtfully at the fire, a glass of brandy in her hand. Thomas studied her and wondered, not for the first time, how they'd gotten to this point.

It had quickly become a habit, and a surprisingly enjoyable habit at that. Each night after they'd returned from whatever social event had claimed their presence, Thomas retired to the library as, he argued to himself, had always been his custom. And later, when she was confident the others in the household were firmly in their beds, Marianne would join him. She never said but he suspected she enjoyed the vague element of danger in their meetings. Should they be caught, marriage between them would be inevitable regardless of their own feelings in the matter. She, no doubt, placed these nights in the category of adventure.

She would offer suggestions as to the improvement of his poetry but equally as often they spoke of other matters; books they'd both read or artists they liked or the latest political conflict or the current scandal. Usually, their discussions took place over a glass or two of brandy. Marianne had quite taken to the liquor and only occasionally now showed its effects. He steadfastly refused to consider what a pity that was.

Thomas enjoyed those moments when their views were in accord but found he relished the differences between them as well. She had a sharp wit and a fine mind and arguing with her was as entertaining and challenging as anything in his life had ever been. And in those moments when they shared little else they shared a great deal of laughter.

And always a kiss or two.

He'd reluctantly gone along with the ridiculous idea of her lessons, telling himself it kept her out of the clutches of less honorable men than he. In point of fact, what he was really doing was keeping her safe. But with each evening that passed in her presence, it was more and more difficult to maintain his restraint, his control. More and more difficult to remember his plan and the reasons behind it. More and more difficult to consider exactly what would happen if—when—he succeeded.

And more and more he felt like the worst kind of traitor.

"You are exceedingly quiet this evening." Marianne tilted her head and considered him, a slight smile playing on her lips. "Whatever is on your mind?"

"We've become friends, haven't we?" he said without thinking.

"I suppose we have."

"I have never had a female friend."

She laughed. "I never imagined you had. However, I have never had a male friend before, so we are well matched."

"It's rather odd, you know." He settled back deeper in his chair and cupped his hands around his glass. "It's as if we have known each other forever. I feel I can discuss anything with you."

She quirked a brow. "You say that as if it's appalling to admit."

He chuckled. "Not appalling, just surprising. I simply never expected to be able to talk to a woman—"

"As if she were as intelligent as any man of your acquaintance and not an empty-headed twit who would accept your every word as if it were law." She smiled sweetly. "And gaze at you as if you were the sun and the stars in the process."

"Yes, quite." He laughed, more to cover his chagrin than anything else. He deserved her sarcasm. Had, in truth, earned it. "I admit, there is something to be said for a woman who knows her own mind. At least in your case."

Her eyes widened. "Why, thank you, my lord. I am not merely shocked but flattered. And since I can scarce hope for anything more momentous to occur tonight"—she swallowed the last of her brandy and rose to her feet—"I shall take my leave."

He started to stand.

"No, don't get up." She stepped toward him. "There is a certain amount of leniency regarding proper manners allowed between two friends in the late hours of the night."

"But what of your lesson?" The teasing note in his voice belied the realization that he looked forward to kissing her each night with a fair amount of anticipation and an ever-growing impatience.

"Oh, I believe I have learned more than I ever expected tonight." She bent forward and placed her fingers under his chin. "Much, much more."

"Have you?" His gaze met hers. Her brown eyes behind her glasses caught the light from the fire and glowed a rich, seductive amber. For a long moment she stared at him, a slightly puzzled expression on her face.

He caught her hand and pulled it to his lips. "Now tell me, what is on your mind?"

"My mind?" She shook her head, then leaned close and brushed her lips across his. "I very much fear I no longer know."

She straightened, turned and left the room before he could say a word. Not that he knew what to say.

What on earth had she meant by that? If ever a woman knew precisely what was on her mind and exactly what she wanted and what she didn't it was Marianne Shelton. She did want adventure. She didn't want marriage. And she bloody well wanted to experience life.

And he'd thought, he was under the impression at least—oh hell, he'd hoped he was the one she'd decided to experience life with.

Still, they'd gone no farther than kissing and he had to admit that was as much her doing as his own. In the past few weeks, while her embrace had been no less enthusiastic, he'd noted a vague, tentative quality. As if she was no longer sure of the course she'd set herself. Or their encounters had become something...well...more. Whatever that meant.

He got to his feet, brandy in hand, and paced the room. Damnation, she was an annoying chit.

He'd thought he'd wanted her married and off his hands. But the idea did not hold the same appeal it once had. Indeed, he'd set his plan in motion with those ridiculous notes and it now seemed to proceed under its own power whether he wanted it to or not. Like a rock rolling down a hill. Or an avalanche.

He'd thought he wanted to find his own bride. Someone completely different from Marianne. Now he wondered if the unnamed paragon he'd set his sights on wasn't as dull and boring as the gentlemen he'd pointed in Marianne's direction. Would he find that perfect bride every bit as tedious as Marianne found the perfect matches he'd selected for her?

And he'd thought their late-night meetings and their lessons were to keep her out of the hands of less honorable men than he.

Was he wrong? About all of it?

Damn, his head was more and more muddled and she was the one who had muddled it.

He had no idea what she wanted now. Worse, he had no idea what he wanted either.

Chapter 10

...still, I cannot forget the kiss we shared, although I suspect Lord W prefers not to think of it. No matter what his other faults may be, his honor will not allow him to take advantage of an innocent placed in his keeping. My virtue is quite safe.

Yet every moment I spend in his presence I wonder if the true value of virtue indeed lies in keeping it. I fear I have feelings for him that can no longer be denied. He is in my thoughts every minute and, worse, in my dreams every night.

I suspect he has feelings for me as well, yet whether his desires are of the flesh or of the heart, I cannot tell.

And, I confess, more and more I long to see the passion in his eyes replace the nobility of his manner....

The Absolutely True Adventures of a Country Miss in London

Lady Cutshall's rout was much like every other event Thomas had escorted the Shelton ladies to. The ballroom was stuffy and over-crowded. The music could barely be heard above the clamor of the throng. The refreshments were attractively arranged but lacking in flavor. He had long suspected the same morsels, tidied up and dusted off, were simply circulated from one party to the next throughout the season. All in all, it was a usual event with the usual attendees and, as usual, only one thing occupied his mind.

Marianne.

Thomas stood near the doors opened to Lady Cutshall's terrace, one of the few spots where the air wasn't stagnant, and engaged in amicable conversation with Pennington and Berkley. He divided his attention evenly between responding to their idle chatter and keeping an eye on Marianne.

Pennington said something about an ongoing dispute between two of the ton's reigning hostesses. Thomas murmured a reply. Berkley heaved a heartfelt sigh.

As always, Marianne scarcely had a moment to herself. She was continually besieged by one extremely proper gentleman or another. All of them eminently suitable. All of them perfectly acceptable to Thomas. All of them quite dull and more than a little tedious.

He tried, and failed, to stifle a grin. Marianne skillfully fended off one eager suitor after another with a natural grace and easy manner. The discarded gentlemen probably didn't even realize they'd been rejected. No wonder they didn't stay away for long. He shouldn't find it all so amusing—and wondered idly if perhaps he wouldn't if any of the men had even the remotest chance of capturing her affection—but he couldn't help himself.

Pennington made an observation on the quality of the champagne in his glass. Thomas nodded in agreement. Berkley sighed again.

Of course, Marianne's attraction no doubt had as much to do with the benefits of an alliance with her as her charms. Thomas's grin faded.

It was the height of stupidity to have sent those notes encouraging the attention of these men. What could he have been thinking? Or, indeed, was he thinking at all? If he hadn't been so arrogant, he would have realized any match he thought was suitable wouldn't appeal to Marianne. The men he'd so carefully selected hadn't a prayer of winning her hand. His plan to find her a husband was doomed to failure from the beginning. Oddly enough, that no longer bothered him.

Pennington commented on a couple that had just stepped onto the terrace. Thomas responded absently. And Berkley sighed.

Thomas drew his brows together in mild concern. Berkley looked anything but happy. Thomas leaned toward Pennington. "What on earth is the matter with him?"

"He's in love," Pennington said with a resigned air.

Thomas lifted a brow. "Again?"

"For the last time," Berkley said staunchly.

Thomas tried not to smile. He'd heard Berkley's declarations of love on occasions too numerous to mention. And nearly all of them were for the last time. "And who is the lucky lady?"

Pennington and Berkley traded glances. "Well, I haven't exactly met her yet."

"I see. One of those smitten-from-afar type of things."

"He's never seen her, either." Pennington snorted. "He doesn't even know her name."

"No?" Thomas raised a brow. Even for Berkley, who routinely fell in love at the barest flutter of a fan, this was uncommon. "Then can you be sure her affections are not engaged elsewhere?"

"I'm sure," Berkley said grimly.

Pennington rolled his eyes heavenward. "Have you by any chance read the *Adventures of a Country Miss in London?*"

"Who hasn't?" These so-called adventures were the talk of the ton. Thomas had picked up *Cadwallender's* out of mild curiosity but had found his attention caught by the amusing and somewhat provocative stories. Now he, too, followed the weekly installments as well as the ongoing speculation as to the true identity of the innocent miss and the mysterious Lord W. "There are wagers in every betting book in every club in London as to when Lord W will have his way with her."

Berkley's expression darkened. "He bloody well better leave her alone."

"Come, now, Berkley, admit it. It's most entertaining." Thomas laughed. "The suspense of not knowing if, or more likely when, the wicked lord will ruin his sweet young charge is half the fun."

"Not for me." Berkley's voice was grim.

Thomas studied him curiously. "Come, now, old man, it's nothing more than an amusing story. It's obviously fiction."

"It is not." Berkley glared. "It's true. Absolutely true." He stared down his nose at Thomas, not entirely effective, since he was a good few inches shorter. "It's in print!"

"You believe everything you read?" Thomas said slowly.

"He always has and I daresay he always will. I've tried to tell him, but he refuses to listen to me." It was Pennington's turn to heave a long-suffering sigh. "I always knew it would mean trouble someday."

"Trouble?" Thomas said in confusion.

"You still don't understand, do you?" Pennington leaned close to Thomas as if he were about to impart a state secret. "The last great love of my friend's life is the country miss."

"The country miss?" Thomas shook his head, puzzled, then abruptly realized exactly what Pennington was saying. Surely he wasn't serious. "The country miss of the infamous *Absolutely True Adventures?*"

"None other," Pennington said.

Berkley's face was a picture of the misery of unrequited love.

Thomas choked back a laugh. It would not do to show amusement; his friend's torment was all too apparent. Still, it wasn't easy to maintain a straight face. Thomas's words were strangled and a tad higher-pitched than normal. "Berkley. Er, Reginald." He glanced at Pennington for help.

Pennington raised his glass in resignation and downed the last of his champagne.

"Reggie," Thomas began in a hopeful voice. "I strongly suspect the *Absolutely True Adventures* are not at all true. Why, the writer is probably the wife of the printer, with a dozen children. Or a wizened old man, with a knack for storytelling."

"A gnome, actually," Pennington murmured.

"She's not a gnome," Berkley said indignantly.

"Well, there's a gnome who works at Cadwallender's." Pennington craned his neck, peered across the room, then crooked a finger to summon a waiter. "Beastly, cranky old goat."

"He's not the country miss," Berkley said under his breath.

"You've been to see Cadwallender, then?" Thomas asked.

"Twice." A waiter bearing a tray of champagne stopped and Pennington exchanged his empty glass for a full one. "Berkley insisted."

Berkley took a glass and Thomas followed suit. "And did you discover she is nothing more than the figment of an overstimulated imagination?"

"We discovered nothing. Cadwallender wasn't there." Pennington shrugged. "And the gnome was reticent to tell us much of anything."

"She's not a figment." Berkley drained his glass. "And I shall not rest until I find her."

He turned on his heel and stalked off through the open door and into the night.

Thomas stared after him. "I gather he has no intention of giving up."

"None whatsoever."

"It speaks well of the man, I suppose. His determination, that is." Thomas turned to Pennington. "I daresay, I've never seen him so resolved over a woman, any woman, particularly one whose existence is in question."

"Perhaps therein lies the secret." Pennington sipped thoughtfully. "I have known Berkley most of my life, and while it may not appear so, he has a distinctly romantic nature. I think, in his mind's eye, he sees himself as a knight on a white charger rescuing fair damsels in distress."

"Yes, well, there's something to be said for damsels who need rescuing." Thomas's gaze strayed back to Marianne. She would never need rescuing. And wasn't there something to be said for that as well?

"While I personally have no desire to rescue anyone, I find myself rather intrigued by the question of who this young woman is."

Thomas studied him. "So you think she's real?"

"I'm not sure why, but I do indeed. Perhaps I've simply listened to Berkley for too long." He smiled ruefully. "Or perhaps I may well be a bit of a romantic myself. Or perhaps it's the mystery that intrigues me." Pennington's gaze swept the ballroom. "She could be anyone, you know. With just the twist of a fact here and the bend of a truth there, many of these young women in attendance tonight could be the lady in question."

"Come, now, Pennington, that's absurd."

"Is it?" Pennington nodded at Marianne, who was about to take her place for a country dance. "Lady Marianne herself suggested she might be the country miss."

Thomas laughed. "And would that then make me the lascivious Lord W?"

Pennington eyed him thoughtfully. "Indeed it would."

Thomas started. "Surely you aren't serious."

"Probably not." Pennington's gaze shifted back to Marianne. "Besides, it would break Berkley's heart. He is determined to save her and I suspect Lady Marianne would never tolerate rescuing."

Or matchmaking. Thomas ignored a twinge of guilt. "I pity the man who tries." He raised his glass in a toast. "So what's the next step for our besotted knight-errant?"

"He still wants to talk to Cadwallender. I expect we'll go back to his shop until we find him in. In the meantime, he is looking into every lord in London with a *W* in his name." Pennington chuckled. "I anticipate he'll move into the *V*'s next."

"Regardless of the outcome, it does sound like an amusing venture." Thomas chuckled. "Please keep me apprised as to his progress. I'm as curious as anyone to discover the identity of the country miss. However, I must

172

admit I do not share your conviction that she does in fact exist."

"We shall see, Helmsley. We shall see."

"I can certainly understand your point," Marianne murmured and tried to concentrate on the conversation at hand, which would be a great deal easier if it was even mildly interesting.

Lord Moxley puffed up with pride as if her vague agreement were a wholehearted endorsement of whatever insignificant point he was espousing. Something regarding the social necessity of engaging the proper tailor and the lack of well-trained valets currently available.

"My lady, I have a matter of some importance to discuss." He took her arm and tucked it in his elbow. He stared up at her with a gaze that could only be called adoring. It was distinctly disquieting. "Would you be so kind as to accompany me to a place a bit more private? Perhaps a parlor?" He attempted to steer her toward the ballroom doors.

Lord Moxley was several inches shorter than she and, given the plumpness of his form, obviously did not partake of regular exercise. Marianne was confident she could fend him off, but she had no desire to let things progress to that point. She would prefer to escape his presence completely. "My lord, that wouldn't be at all proper." Deftly, she guided him toward the open doors to the terrace. "However, I should enjoy a refreshing breath of air." There were any number of people on the terrace and as long as they stayed in the lit areas there should be no problem.

In spite of her attitude about her reputation, if she were to be compromised she would prefer it to be by a man of her own height, one whose stature was significantly greater than his girth.

She noted Thomas lounging in another ballroom doorway, watching their departure. Good. Even if Lord Moxley wasn't the type of man she'd be at all interested in, it did no harm to allow Thomas to think she enjoyed the man's company. Short and stout and boring though he may be. Even so, Thomas's smile was a bit too amused, as if he knew full well short, stout and boring did not appeal to her.

"Now, then, my lord." She halted near a brace of candles where even the least indiscretion would be well illuminated—no doubt the reason few other couples lingered near the spot. She smiled pleasantly. "What did you wish to discuss?"

"My lady." He took her hand and an uneasy feeling settled in the pit of her stomach. "Marianne. I should like...that is, I would be delighted...or rather..." He drew a deep breath. "Would you do me the great honor of becoming my wife?"

"What?" She snatched her hand from his. "Don't be absurd."

"Absurd?" His face fell.

At once she regretted her words. He was a nice enough man, even if he wasn't for her. "I am sorry. I didn't mean *absurd*. You simply caught me by surprise."

"I do apologize." His expression brightened and he stepped closer. "I know I should be asking your brother for your hand, but as he is not here, I thought I would settle everything between us and then speak to Lord Helmsley."

She moved back. "Lord Helmsley has nothing to say about it. This is my decision and I scarcely think we've known each other long enough to even consider marriage."

"That is absurd." Moxley snorted. "Most couples of my acquaintance don't know each other well at all until after they're wed." Again he stepped closer.

"My lord." She thrust out her hand to stop him. The only way to dissuade him was obviously with the truth. "I am flattered by your offer, but I must decline. You see, I have no intention of marrying."

He brushed away her comment. "Nonsense. Every woman alive wishes to wed."

"Not I."

He studied her for a long moment. "I realize I am not as handsome as others I could name—"

"Oh, no, it's nothing—"

"However, my title is old and distinguished." He frowned. "You do realize I'm the fourth Viscount Moxley, do you not?"

"Actually, I hadn't, but—"

"My income is respectable, although not overly impressive."

"That isn't at all—"

"Then there is no impediment to a match between us." He beamed with confidence. "We shall be quite comfortable, with my adequate fortune coupled with your dowry—"

"My dowry?" she said slowly. "What do you know of my dowry?"

"Well, I know it's impressive." Moxley smirked. "Damned impressive."

She stared at him with growing annoyance. No doubt gossip accounted for his knowledge. "I would not rely on the veracity of idle rumor for my information if I were you, my lord."

Surprise widened his eyes. "Of course not. That would be foolish, particularly when it comes to something as important as marriage." He paused for a moment, as if debating the wisdom of his next words. "I can assure you my information comes from a highly reputable source who has only your best interest at heart. I'm certain he would prefer his involvement in our courtship—"

"There is no courtship."

"—remain secret, particularly now that it has blossomed to romance—"

"There has been no blossoming," she said indignantly. "And there definitely is no romance."

"However"—he leaned closer—"since we are to be wed—"

"We are not going to be wed!"

"I'm certain it would do no harm to give credit where it is due. Lord Helmsley informed me of the details of your dowry."

"Lord Helmsley?" *Thomas?*

"Indeed." Moxley nodded his head eagerly. "He also pointed out the benefits socially and politically of a liaison between my family and yours."

"Did he?" She chose her words carefully. "And precisely how did this discussion of my relative merits as a match come about? Late at night over spirits at his club, I suppose."

"Not at all." Moxley waved off her question, apparently oblivious to her rising anger. "He sent me a note."

"A note?" She struggled to keep her voice level. "He sent you a note?"

"Indeed he did. And I must tell you, I was most surprised and delighted to receive it. I did not know Lord Helmsley thought so highly of me. I was honored to be one of such a select group."

"A group?" She could barely choke out the words.

"Oh, my, yes. At first I was most annoyed to discover I was not alone in the encouragement of my attentions. Then I realized in this day and age one cannot be too careful when it comes to a match."

"One can never be too careful." She clenched her teeth to bite back a more scathing comment. Surely Moxley wasn't saying what she thought he was saying? In spite of Thomas's plan to marry her off, he would never go so far as to peddle her like a plot of land he wished to dispose of. Why, they were at the very least friends. And recently, she'd begun to suspect, quite a bit more.

"And to be included in such an distinguished assembly was an honor, I assure you. Why, I have scarce noted a selection of finer, like-minded gentlemen."

"Dull, boring and tedious," she said under her breath. At once the quality of her admirers made sense.

"However, at this point I can afford to be magnanimous." He grinned or leered, it was difficult to determine. "Since obviously I have won your heart.

She stared at him in disbelief. She was far too angry with Thomas to waste any serious venom on Moxley. Still, he was here and Thomas was not. "What is obvious is that you have not taken seriously one word I have said." She stepped closer and leaned toward him to place her nose at a level with his. "I am not marrying you or anyone. Not now. Not ever."

"Helmsley indicated you would be coy." Moxley cast her a superior smile.

"I am not being coy!" She resisted the urge to scream. Why wouldn't this little man understand? "I am being honest. I do not wish to marry!"

"Are you certain?" Moxley's forehead furrowed. "I was given the distinct impression you were looking for a husband."

"I assure you, it was a most inaccurate impression."

"Really?" He thought for a moment, his face scrunching as he tried to digest this turn of events. "I have wasted my time, then?"

"Yes." She blew a relieved breath. "I do apologize for that. Lord Helmsley had no right to encourage you. I assure you, had I the slightest inkling that you, or anyone else, were under the belief that I was looking for a husband, I would have set you straight without hesitation."

"Quite all right. Not your fault, I suppose. I would have a word with Lord Helmsley about this, but we've never been particularly friendly. Don't run in the same circles, you know. There's every possibility I misunderstood."

"You and a dozen others," she muttered.

"I do think, at this juncture, it is I who owe you an apology." He looked up at her and her heart twisted. He might well be extremely dull and the tiniest bit pompous, but he was also rather sweet. "Although I can scarce be faulted for pursuing a lady as lovely as yourself." He grinned.

She laughed. "Think nothing of it." She extended her hand and asked heaven to forgive her lies. "I have quite enjoyed our time together, my lord, and had things been different..."

He took her hand and pressed it his lips. "If only..." He sighed. "May I escort you back inside?"

"No, thank you. I'd like to remain here for a moment. I quite relish the breeze and the opportunity for a bit of solitude."

"Very well, then."

"My lord"—she laid a hand on his sleeve—"I am confident that you will find an excellent match. A woman to whom you will be"—she forced the words to her lips—"the moon and the stars."

"Do you really think so?" He stood a bit straighter.

"I do indeed, and she will be an extremely fortunate lady." Marianne favored him with her brightest smile.

"Thank you." He started toward the doors, then turned back to her, a hopeful expression on his face. "I don't suppose your sisters..."

"I think not," she said gently.

"I suspected as much." He shrugged and strode off toward the ballroom.

She turned away, rested her hands on the terrace balustrade and stared unseeing into the night.

So Thomas had gone so far in his quest as to solicit suitors for her. And in writing. How could he? This was far and away too much. She was willing to put up with his introductions to the Lord Moxleys of the ton, but this was unconscionable.

Well, it was going to stop right now.

And to think she had begun to believe... She squared her shoulders. It scarcely mattered what she had begun to believe.

She resisted the urge to glance at the doorway where he'd been standing. He'd probably abandoned his guardian post, knowing full well she was as safe on the terrace with Moxley as she'd be with Aunt Louella.

Her fists clenched on the cold stone. She was tired of his nonsense. His protectiveness, coupled with his arrogant belief that he knew what was best for her. If she could, she'd have it out with him right here and now. But a confrontation in public would be far too scandalous and she did have her sisters' reputations to think of, even if she had little concern for her own. No, she'd face the lion in his own den, and when she was done, there wouldn't be enough left of his hide for a decent rug.

"I would wager you are having as good a time as I am." A rueful Lord Berkley stepped to her side.

She glanced at him. He did indeed look unhappy and obviously mistook her anger for misery. "And what is your problem, my lord?"

He rested back against the balustrade and crossed his arms over his chest. "The same as yours, I suspect. The odd and confusing aspects of the relationships between men and women."

She snorted in a most unladylike manner. "They would not be odd and confusing were it not for the arrogant nature of men."

He raised an offended brow. "Am I included in that indictment?"

"Possibly." She studied him. "Have you done anything that I would consider rude and offensive and overbearing and presumptuous?"

"I can't think of anything at the moment.... But on further consideration"— he grinned—"probably."

She smiled. "At least you're honest." She paused and considered him. "Tell me, my lord, what has you so melancholy on this fine spring evening?"

"Love." He sighed deeply. "I fear, like you, I have fallen in love."

"Like me?" She straightened and stared at him. "I am not in love."

"Come, now," he scoffed. "Why else would a beautiful lady be alone on a shadowed terrace, instead of inside enjoying a festive occasion, if she were not considering the desolate repercussions of love?"

"Piffle. There are any number of reasons why a woman would chose a moment of solitude away from a crowded ballroom. Fresh air prime among them."

"If that's what you wish me to believe." He shrugged, obviously not believing her for a moment.

"Lord Berkley." She turned toward him, her tone firm. "If love exists at all, it is nothing more than a tool to bind women to men in a manner that causes them nothing but pain." She hesitated. Did she really want to tell this relative stranger of her past? She drew a deep breath and threw caution aside. "My mother had what was laughingly called a love match. It brought her little more than a handful of children, and weakened her body and her spirit.

"She died when I was quite young, and I cannot recall ever seeing true affection between my parents. It is possible, I suppose, that such expressions of fondness between them were private, but still..." She shrugged as if it didn't matter.

"Surely you cannot rely on the memories of a child."

"But I do." She fell silent, her thoughts going back through the long years. Her beautiful mother. Her indifferent father. She had long ago forgiven, or at least accepted, her father's apathy toward his children. But she could never, would never, understand what she plainly saw as an unfeeling attitude toward his wife. "My lord, do you recall your mother's smile?"

"Saw it just the other day." He chuckled. "Of course, she only favors me with it when she isn't chastising me for one offense or another."

She ignored his attempt to lighten her mood. "I remember my mother's smile vividly. Sweet, but also sad and wistful." She shook her head. "If that is love, I want no part of it. It is an emotion to be found in stories and books and has little to do with the world we live in."

He frowned. "But what of your brother and Helmsley's sister? I understood theirs was a love match."

She waved away his comment. "An exception. Rare as a fine diamond, and all the more precious for it."

"Then you are one of those women who will marry for reasons other than love?" His dry tone told her more than mere words that he had encountered such women before.

"Certainly not. I have no intention of marrying."

"But all women wish to marry."

"If I hear that once more, I shall scream," she snapped.

"Ah, have I hit a nerve?" His teasing grin was infectious and she smiled reluctantly.

"It is a subject that seems prevalent in my life these days." She tilted her head and gazed at him thoughtfully. "Why is it so hard to understand why a woman would not wish to have her life, her future, her finances dependent on the whim of a man?"

"Because that, too, is as rare as your diamond. Whether that makes it precious or just unusual..." He shook his head. "It is not the way of the world, my dear."

"But it is to be my way," she said with a confidence she didn't quite feel.

She'd never before questioned her desire for independence, her need to rely only on herself. No, she had blindly plunged ahead with her *Country Miss* stories, her means to an end, her plan for her life. But lately, in those odd moments of the day, or more often the night, when her mind was not occupied with more pressing matters, she found herself examining why she didn't want to depend on a husband.

Her reasons were still sound. Men, with very rare exceptions, were not especially dependable. Besides, how could she have grand adventures if she was shackled to a man?

But why couldn't she have both? Why

couldn't she find a man to have adventures with? To travel with her to exotic places like Italy and Egypt. A man who wouldn't dominate her life but share it. Who would value her opinion on literature and art and everything else, even, or especially, when it clashed with his own. Who would laugh with her and be her dearest friend. And share her bed.

A man to whom she would be the moon and the stars.

"You do realize the path you've chosen is not an easy one?" Berkley said.

"And yours is easier?"

"Love, my lady, is the most difficult path of all."

"I gather, then, that the object of your affections does not return your feelings?"

"She doesn't know." He sighed dramatically. "We have never met, but she has stolen not merely my heart but my very soul."

"My, that is a difficult path." Marianne bit back a smile.

His forehead furrowed. "Are you teasing me?"

"Not at all. Granted, I am not one to give advice in such circumstances, but it does seem to me that perhaps you should meet before you declare your undying love."

"You are teasing me." He sighed, then smiled. "Although your suggestion has a great deal of merit. And I am doing what I can to accomplish just that."

"I wish you luck on your path. Someday you shall have to explain to me precisely how one falls in love with someone you've never met."

"When I understand that myself, I shall eagerly share it." He laughed and shook his head. "You are indeed an unusual female, and I suspect you might well be able to achieve the independence you crave."

A wave of pleasure washed through her. "That's the nicest thing anyone has ever said to me. Thank you, my lord."

"No, thank you. You have quite lightened my mood." He straightened and offered his arm. "Would you do me the great favor of allowing me to escort you back inside?"

She placed her hand in the crook of his arm. "Only if you will then be so kind as to honor me with a dance."

He tucked her arm close to his side. "You do realize Helmsley will not fail to notice our return together?"

"I do indeed." They started toward the ballroom.

"Nor will he miss our dance."

"Or two. Or the one I plan to share with Pennington immediately following."

Berkley raised a brow. "Helmsley won't like it."

She flashed him a blinding smile. "That, my dear Lord Berkley, is the precisely the idea."

Chapter 11

...for Lord W is actively seeking a suitor for my hand. I know it is his duty as my guardian, but oh, dear cousin, it dismays me to no end.

I cannot allow his efforts to continue. I shall confront him as soon as possible, although I admit the prospect is daunting. It is conceivable he will disregard my objections along with my heart.

Yet how can I bear the prospect of being in the arms of any man save him?...

The Absolutely True Adventures
of a Country Miss in London

Thomas peered cautiously around the library. The last person he wanted to run into was Marianne. The room appeared empty and he stepped inside, wondering if he should check the sofa in front of the fire for hidden sleepers.

He strode across the library to the cabinet housing the brandy and poured a full glass.

Marianne was furious and he wasn't entirely certain why. Oh, he had an inkling—no, more than an inkling—but hoped against hope that wasn't it.

She'd left the ballroom tonight on Moxley's

arm and returned on Berkley's. How that had happened he had no idea, but from the moment she'd rejoined the festivities she'd refused to cast him so much as a casual glance. There was something different in the determined set of her chin and the gleam in her eye, apparent even from across the room. In addition, she'd made it a point to dance with Berkley, twice, and Pennington, also twice, and several other of his friends. And not once did he see her with any of the gentlemen he approved of.

He propped his hip on the desk and sipped thoughtfully.

They'd left tonight's festivities earlier than usual and she'd been pleasant enough to him on the ride home. Unfailingly pleasant. Annoyingly pleasant. Pleasant to the point where he had to fight the urge to squirm in his seat and Becky and Jocelyn had traded wary glances. Only Lady Louella had seemed oblivious to the underlying tension in the carriage.

Thomas had always considered himself a man of both honor and courage. However, tonight discretion seemed wise, and if it was cowardly to avoid Marianne, well, he could live with that. He'd vanished the moment they'd arrived home and headed for his club to wait until it was safe to return. He hoped Marianne was fast asleep by now.

He started for the door, taking his glass with him. If his luck held, he could avoid her until late in the morning or, even better, late in the day. By then she would be calm and rational and more than willing to listen to his explanation and, yes, his apology.

He heaved a resigned sigh and headed up the stairs. If she knew what he suspected she knew—and frankly he couldn't think of anything else he might have done—there was little chance any amount of time would assuage her ire unless, of course, he could put off speaking to her for weeks, maybe even months. No, in this instance years would not be long enough.

He needed a plan. And it had better be smarter than his last plan. At the very least, he needed an idea of what he would say to her. A sound defense of his actions. Oh, certainly he'd already recognized that he had no legitimate defense. Still, he'd done what he thought was best. For him if not necessarily for her. Not that she'd accept that kind of thinking. Perhaps he'd grovel and beg her forgiveness.

His mood brightened. He'd never yet met a woman who did not respond well to abject apologies and sincere groveling. And if he went so far as to admit he had, perhaps, been wrong... The very thought made him cringe—not merely at the idea of saying the words but at his suspicion that she'd never let him forget this little mistake.

Still, he did realize he deserved whatever it was he got.

He simply hoped he survived it.

Marianne awoke with a start. For a moment she couldn't remember why she was sleeping in the chair in her room, or why there was a candle still burning. Of course. She narrowed her eyes. She'd been waiting for Thomas to return home.

She had hoped to meet him in the library, but his valet informed her, in response to as casual an inquiry as she could muster, that His Lordship was out for the remainder of the evening. No doubt with the express purpose of consuming a great deal of liquor. Good. He would need the false courage.

She slid her glasses back up to the bridge of her nose and got to her feet. In truth she could use a bit of false courage herself. It was a long way from her chamber to Thomas's and there were far too many unknowns that could be flitting through the halls of an old house. At least in the mind of an imaginative woman. She pulled her robe tighter around her, grabbed the candlestick and headed for the door.

Thomas knew she was angry. She'd seen it in the wary look in his eye. She doubted he knew precisely what she had discovered, or perhaps he realized full well his crime. Or possibly there was something besides attempting to market her to the most tedious men in society he was guilty of.

She quietly opened her door and glanced up

and down the hall. Starlight glowed through tall windows at either ends of the long passageway.

Marianne crept down the hall carefully and cringed with each step on a creaking floorboard. No one was about at this hour and the chances of someone waking were slim. Still, she had no desire to encounter anyone who might demand to know what she was about.

She was fairly certain she knew which rooms were Thomas's. She'd seen his valet enter and leave any number of times during her stay. He was in the wing opposite hers, down the enclosed corridor, past the staircases that flanked the open gallery overlooking the first floor and nearly at the end of the hall.

With each step down the dark passageway her anger dimmed, replaced by unease. The candle threw shadows that swelled and menaced. She drew a breath for courage and refused to consider how eerie Effington House was at night. She firmly ignored the thought in the back of her mind as to how many Effingtons, the very ones peering down at her from paintings lining the walls, had through the years died here. Peacefully and in their beds of old age, she hoped. And she absolutely refused to entertain the idea that some of them might linger still.

Her heart thudded in her chest and by the time she reached Thomas's door she was certain something unseen was following her. She yanked opened his door without knocking, stepped inside and barely had the presence of mind not to slam it behind her. She leaned back against it and breathed hard, fighting the unreasonable terror that had gripped her in the last endless stretch of the corridor.

When her heart had finally slowed to a more natural rhythm, she glanced around. Thomas's room was overly large, as befitted a future duke. Large, dark furnishings threw equally large, dark shadows. A huge bed dominated the space. Carved posters climbed upward to meet an ornate cornice. The bed hangings were left open. It was, as best she could tell with the light from the candle and the low glow from the fireplace, an exceedingly exotic room. No. An exceedingly *male* room.

An odd sort of snorting sound emanated from the vicinity of the bed. Cautiously, she stepped closer.

Thomas lay sprawled on his stomach, stretched diagonally across the bed. His face was turned toward her, one arm dangling over the edge of the bed. The bedclothes were pushed down to his waist, exposing a firmly muscled back. She swallowed hard. The future duke apparently saw no need for extensive night-clothes.

"Thomas," she said tentatively.

He blew out a long breath in response.

She studied him with detached curiosity. He was the first practically naked man she'd ever seen. And definitely the first man, with clothes or without, she'd ever seen in a bed. Even with her lack of experience, she could certainly see he was a fine specimen of the male gender. The candlelight played across the hard lines of his back and she had the most ridiculous urge to run her fingers over his skin. Her hand reached out on its own accord. His flesh would be warm and smooth and inviting and—

She jerked back and heat flushed up her face. This was not her purpose here! At least, she amended, not tonight.

"Thomas," she said in a low, sharp voice.

He snorted.

She stepped closer and shoved tentatively at his shoulder. "Thomas."

He murmured.

This was not working. She'd already raised her voice as much as she thought prudent. After all, Thomas was the only one she wanted to awaken. Maybe she hadn't pushed him hard enough? Who would have thought the man would be so obstinate even when he slept?

She set the candle on a table by his bed, next to a nearly full glass of brandy. She sniffed in disdain. No wonder she couldn't wake him.

False courage.

Why not? She shrugged, picked up the glass, took a healthy swallow and replaced it on the table.

She pulled in a deep breath, placed both hands firmly on his shoulder, his flesh every bit as warm as she thought it would be, and pushed hard.

He muttered something unintelligible and rolled onto his back. He flung his forearm over his eyes, the covers slipping lower to hang on his hips.

For a moment she could do nothing more than stare. His shoulders were broader than she'd realized. His chest, an intriguing landscape of firm planes and shallow valleys, glowed in the candlelight. A smattering of dark hair trailed from his chest to disappear beneath the sheets.

She grabbed for the brandy and took a bracing swallow. And one more just for good measure. Regardless of the man's obvious charms—and at this moment they were extremely obvious—she was not in his room for a lesson in life or in anything else. No, he was the one who needed to be taught a lesson. He was the one who needed to learn that even the son of a duke couldn't bend people's lives to suit his own purposes, to make his own life more convenient.

Without a second thought, she stepped closer and upended the glass high over his face. A trickle of brandy, not enough for a decent mouthful, barely more than a few drops, really, splashed on his lips. Damnation. She looked at the goblet. Surely she hadn't drank it all? She shook the glass and another drop fell. His nose wrinkled and his lips smacked.

She'd laugh if she wasn't so vexed with him. Still, she stifled a smile; it was rather amusing. He could drink even in his sleep. There was probably not a great call for a skill like that, yet she supposed it could come in useful. She snickered, then clapped her hand over her mouth.

Stop it this minute!

She had to pull herself together. She was angry with him, deservedly, justifiably angry, and it would not do for him to wake up to find her laughing. If she could get him to wake up at all. There had to be a way short of screaming in his ear and jumping up and down on his bed. And while that had a certain amount of appeal, it probably wasn't the best idea.

If there'd only been more brandy left in the glass. She looked around the room. It was really rather spartan, at least when it came to the kind of decorative bits and pieces found in a woman's room. She spotted several things she could probably drop on his head, but she'd prefer not to seriously injure him. At least not while he slept. There were a couple of books on the dresser—poetry, no doubt—but she'd hate to damage a book, and God knows what a heavy tome would do to the sleeping marquess. There were a few other items—matching silver candlesticks on the mantel, an Argand lamp on the dresser next to a pitcher. None of which she could drop on his head.

Her gaze lingered on the pitcher. Surely it was empty? Unless, of course, a servant had filled it in anticipation of his lordship's late-night return. It was certainly worth investigating.

She strolled over to the dresser in a casual manner, as if to convince anyone who might be watching her intentions were completely innocent, and giggled at the idea. At once it struck her that this really was something of an adventure. Oh, not as grand an adventure as searching for ancient treasure in Egypt or even drifting down a canal in Venice, but a minor adventure nonetheless.

She picked up the pitcher and hefted it in her hand. A respectable amount of water sloshed in a satisfactory manner. She grinned. This would do nicely.

She stepped back to the bed and held the pitcher over Thomas's face. That would wake him. She moved the pitcher to hover over his stomach. That would wake him as well. She shifted the pitcher once again. Of course, if a cool splash of water hit him on that part of his anatomy—from what she'd heard through the years, anyway—he would not only awaken but probably be quite alert. On further thought, she hadn't had that much false courage. She repositioned the pitcher once more, aimed for his head and poured.

Maybe her previous attempts had already partially awakened him. Or perhaps he'd been dreaming of shipwrecks and was primed to struggle for air. Or the water could have been a bit cooler than she'd anticipated, but Thomas came to life with a roar. His arms flailed, striking the pitcher. It flew toward the foot of the bed, effectively dousing him from head to toe. He leapt out of bed, his eyes wide with confusion.

"What...what..." he sputtered.

She stared.

The future duke apparently saw no need for nightclothes at all.

Marianne stammered. "You're...you're..."

"I'm soaked." He glared at her.

"You're naked." She gasped. As much as she knew she shouldn't—and she did try not to, but she'd never seen a naked man before, wet or dry—her gaze slipped lower to take in the full sight of him. And a rather startling, although not unpleasant, sight he was.

"Turn around," he said through clenched teeth.

Her gaze jerked back to his. Heat flushed her cheeks. "Oh. Certainly. Of course."

She didn't move. He grabbed her shoulders and turned her to face away from him. "Stay."

At once the commanding tone of his voice reminded her precisely why she'd come to his room in the middle of the night. "Do not speak to me like that, Thomas. I am not a dog to be ordered about."

"What are you doing here?" She sensed him moving behind her.

"I have a matter of some importance to discuss with you."

"Now?" He paused and she could practically hear him thinking. His tone was guarded and considerably calmer. "It couldn't wait until morning?"

"It most certainly could not." She huffed. "If you have sufficiently recovered your modesty, I should like to turn around now."

"Fine," he snapped.

She turned to face him. He'd donned a dressing gown and stood leaning against one of the bedposts, his arms crossed over his chest.

"Why are you in my rooms?" He wasted no time getting to the point, and neither would she.

"Why have you sent notes to the dullest, stiffest, stodgiest men in London encouraging their pursuit of me?"

"They're respectable, not dull."

"Hah! Even you don't believe that."

"I do." He had the nerve to sound indignant.

"Then name one of them who is not one of the most tedious men on earth."

"Just one?" he said in a haughty manner. "Very well."

A moment passed. Then another. "I'm waiting."

"I'm thinking."

She folded her arms, mimicking his stance. "Well?"

"Give me a moment."

"I have."

"The specific name escapes me, but..." He blew a long breath. "All right. I admit it. They are not perhaps the most exciting—"

"Perhaps?" She glared. "They are dull, stiff and stodgy. But you know full well that's not the worst of it."

"No, I suppose it's not," he muttered.

"You practically hawked me to these men." She stepped to him and poked her finger at his chest. "You might as well have taken out an advertisement in the papers. Or put me on a little cart and gone door to door." She jabbed again.

"Ouch."

"Or set up a stall in the market." She stabbed him hard.

"Stop that." He grabbed her hand. "It hurts."

"Good! I want it to hurt." She turned on her heel and stepped away, then turned back. "Do you have any idea how embarrassing it is to discover your admirers, such as they are, have been prompted to seek out your company?"

"Marianne." He stepped toward her. "I wasn't thinking."

"Or how humiliating it is to realize that it wasn't your particular charms that had enticed them but your dowry and family connections?" Angry tears fogged her eyes.

"It was a horrible mistake on my part."

"Or how painful it is to learn someone you trusted, someone you care for, has so little regard for your own desires he would go to such lengths to get you off his hands?"

"I am truly sorry. It was wrong of me."

She narrowed her eyes. "What?"

"I said I'm sorry."

"No, after that."

He sighed. "I was wrong."

"Say it again."

"I was wrong."

"How wrong?"

"Completely and totally wrong," he said sharply. "Is that good enough?"

"For now," she snapped.

Her gaze met his, and for a long moment they stared in silence.

"I must say, though"—the corners of his lips twitched as if he were holding back a smile—"it was the most amusing thing I've seen in a long time."

"What was?"

"The way all those eminently respectable gentlemen were falling at your feet." He chuckled. "You fended them off beautifully."

"I fail to see the amusement in that," she said loftily.

"Come, now, Marianne, admit it. You can see the humor in the situation."

"I most certainly cannot."

"It was as enjoyable as watching a farce at Covent Garden. Or a comedy by Shakespeare." He stepped closer and pulled her into his arms, deftly turning her to press her back against his chest. Her stomach tensed at the contact. "Surely you can see it?"

"What are you doing?" She struggled to keep her voice level.

"Shh. The play is about to begin." He waved his free hand in a wide gesture at the far wall. "There, on the stage, our heroine enters."

"You're mad, Thomas. I knew it on that first night," she muttered, trying to maintain her annoyance. Nearly impossible, as she was all too aware of his body pressed against hers.

He ignored her. "She is lovely but far too stubborn for her own good, with an insane desire for independence and adventure."

"It's not insane." Her protest was weak.

"And here come the eager suitors." He

waved at the other side of the unseen stage. "Oh, dear."

"What is it?" she asked, intrigued in spite of herself.

"They will never do." He heaved a deep sigh.

"Why not?"

"Well, just look at them." He pointed. "That one is too plump. That one too short. That one has more hair on his knuckles than on his head."

"But surely our heroine is not so shallow as to reject a gentleman simply because of his appearance?"

"Of course not," he said indignantly. "She is a heroine, after all. However, they all have one flaw she cannot abide."

She stifled a smile and relaxed against him. "They are boring?"

"Exactly." She felt him shrug. "There is not an adventurous bone in their collective bodies."

"So what does our heroine do?"

"This is where the amusement begins. Watch."

"What?" His breath was warm against her neck and a shiver ran up her spine.

"Why, she picked up that gentleman and threw him off the stage!"

Marianne laughed. "She did not."

"Indeed she did. And look!"

"What has she done now?"

"She kicked that one. Booted him right on his backside." A grin sounded in his voice. "Surely you saw him fly into the audience?"

"She would never..." She could barely get the words out for her laughter. "Never..."

"And there, she felled two others with a single blow. Two!" He shook with silent laughter. "Damnation, she's magnificent. She's cleared the stage!"

Marianne sagged against him, helpless with laughter.

"The crowd is on its feet, roaring with approval. She bows to the audience, scattering kisses left and right. Flowers are tossed at her feet. The applause is deafening!"

"And what does our heroine do now?" She sniffed back tears of laughter.

"Now?" He stilled behind her. "Why, the play is over."

"But what happens to her?" At once she knew they were no longer speaking of an imaginary production.

"I don't know," he said softly.

"Perhaps, as any good heroine would, she goes off to find adventure."

"Perhaps."

"Although"—she drew a shuddering breath—"it is possible our heroine has realized there may well be a great deal of adventure to be found right here."

"Here?" His voice was quietly intense.

She twisted in his arms and rested her hands on his chest, his muscles solid beneath the silk of his robe. She reached up and brushed her lips across his. "Kiss me, Thomas."

He shook his head but didn't pull away. "I fear, dear heroine, that a single kiss will no longer be enough between us. Not here in my bedchamber. Not now."

"Good." She slipped her hands through the opening of his gown and ran her fingers over his chest. He sucked in a ragged breath and caught her hands.

"Marianne," he said harshly. "I warn you. Do not push me too far."

She pulled her hands from his and slid her arms around his neck. Trepidation mixed with excitement and she pressed her body closer. "Kiss me."

His arms wrapped around her, even as indecision warred with desire in his eyes. "This is madness."

"Is it?" She raised her lips to meet his.

"Yes," he murmured against her mouth. "Sweet, sweet madness."

For a moment his kiss was tentative, gentle, as if he were as cognizant as she as to the import of the moment. She trembled at his touch and a curious yearning swelled within her. A need so great as to steal her breath arched between them.

She slid her hands to his shoulders, marveling at the heat of his skin beneath her touch. His hands caressed her back and slipped lower to cup her buttocks and pull her tighter against him. She could feel the evidence of his arousal low against her stomach. Fear mixed with anticipation and pulsed through her blood and she ached with desire.

He gathered her gown in his hands, raising it higher and higher, until his fingers touched the bare flesh of her legs. She gasped at the intimate contact.

He stepped back and in one swift movement yanked her nightgown over her head and threw it aside. For a moment he stared, as if to memorize every line of her naked body.

"Thomas?" Heat rose in her face, but she resisted the impulse to cover herself with her hands.

"You are as lovely as I'd imagined," he said in a voice low with desire.

Without thinking, she reached out and tugged at the tie of his dressing gown. It came free in her hand, the garment falling open. He shrugged out of it and moved to her, drawing her back into his arms, greeting her lips with his. Her breasts pressed against his chest, his hair rough against her skin, which was at once more sensitive than she'd ever known. Her mouth opened beneath his. His tongue met hers, and all gentleness between them vanished.

He pulled her harder against him, his hands roaming over her back and her buttocks in a trailing path of pleasure. She slid her arms around his neck and twined her hands in his hair, needing him closer yet. He wrenched his mouth free from hers, scooped her into his arms and carried her to his bed.

They tumbled onto the mattress and at once were a tangle of arms and legs, a frenzy of taste and touch. She wanted—no, needed— to know every inch of him. And needed him to know her.

She kissed his mouth, his neck, his shoulders. She ran her hands over his back, his buttocks, his legs. Her hand brushed against his manhood and he gasped. And she explored the hard, velvet length of him.

He feasted on her shoulders and her throat and her breasts. His hand traced circles on her stomach and drifted lower to the curls between her legs. She tensed, for a moment fearful of what she wanted, what she needed. His fingers found her most private places.

She sucked in a hard breath. Sheer pleasure coursed through her. She'd never imagined such a feeling, at once overwhelming and yet not enough. Never enough. His fingers taunted and teased and maddening expectation coiled within her.

She writhed on the bed and moaned his name. She wanted more. Needed more. He slipped a finger inside her, then out and back in again. Her breath caught. All her senses centered on his hand and the amazing enjoyment radiating from his touch. He slid two fingers inside her, his thumb toying with her as his fingers slid in and out in an increasing rhythm.

Her back arched and she pushed herself harder against his hand, crying out in frustration and desire. His lips fastened on hers and his tongue mimicked the motion of his fingers. She was adrift in a storm of spiraling ecstasy, desperate for more. For something indefinable just out of reach.

Without warning, waves of overwhelming sensation rushed through her in a torrent of exquisite release.

Thomas shifted to position himself above her, his hands braced on either side, his legs between hers. He stared into her eyes. "Marianne, are you quite sure...?"

He'd stop now if she asked him. She knew it, and her heart swelled. She rested her hand on the back of his neck, drew him downward and sighed his name. "Thomas."

His manhood prodded at her and he slowly eased himself inside her. With a slow but firm stroke he filled her, an unusual but not unpleasant sensation. He withdrew and again slid deeper, then paused as if he could go no farther. At once, he thrust forward hard and pain shot through her.

She uttered a short scream and he clamped his mouth firmly over hers. Now he could stop! Panic rose within her. It hurt and she'd had quite enough! She tried to escape his grasp, but he wouldn't release her. Wouldn't stop. His movements were slow and deliberate and within moments the pain eased. Tentatively, she matched her movements to his. Discomfort vanished, swept away by growing pleasure. She met his thrusts boldly, eagerly. Again tense anticipation filled her.

They moved together as one. Faster and higher and harder. In a rhythm like no excitement she could ever imagine. No adventure she could ever dream. And when at last she thought she'd surely die from the joy of it all, his body shuddered against hers and she exploded around him and the world itself seemed to pause for one glorious instant of rapture.

For a moment or a lifetime they lay together, wrapped in each other's arms.

And he murmured softly against her ear: "Sweet, sweet madness."

Chapter 12

...and he said it was madness. Sheer madness. And, dear cousin, how soon I realized the truth.

It was indeed madness.

Sweet, sweet madness...

The Absolutely True Adventures
of a Country Miss in London

Marianne had never imagined such peace, such contentment, such joy.

Such love.

She'd suspected it in recent weeks. Suspected love was to blame for her eagerness to be with him, for the newfound, tentative feelings he aroused. Suspected there was more to what they shared than mere friendship, but the very idea was absurd and more than a little frightening. Until now she'd preferred to ignore it altogether.

She snuggled closer to Thomas and his

arms tightened around her. How ironic, that she had found love when all she was looking for was life. And adventure. Ironic as well that she didn't seem to mind.

Oh, certainly her future would be much different than she'd envisioned. But surely her dreams could expand to accommodate two adventurers instead of one. Realistically her adventures could not be quite as extensive as she'd planned—after all, Thomas had responsibilities right here in England—but she was willing to compromise. Still, regardless of anything else she may have believed heretofore, love may well be the grandest adventure of all.

He nuzzled her ear. She sighed with contentment and lifted her face toward his. His lips met hers, and for a long, breathless moment she forgot everything but the joy of being in his arms.

He pulled away and smiled down at her. "You need to return to your room before the servants are about."

She laughed. "If you are concerned about my reputation—"

"I am indeed," he said with mock solemnity. He kissed her once more, slid out of bed, plucked his discarded dressing gown from the floor and slipped into it. "It will not do to have my wife as the subject of idle gossip."

She sat up, pulling the sheets around her. "Your wife?"

He grinned. "I shall make the arrangements today. We can get a special license and be wed before the week is out."

A lovely wave of warmth washed through her. "You want to marry me?"

"Of course." He found her nightgown and handed it to her.

Of course. She should have realized it at once. She wanted nothing more than to spend every moment of every day for the rest of her life with him. Obviously he felt the same. Still, it would be wonderful to hear him say it. "Why?"

"Didn't you have some sort of robe as well?"

She ignored him. "Why do you want to marry me?"

He snorted. "There's little choice now."

Her heart stilled. "Little choice?"

"Certainly." He knelt down to peer under the bed. "Your brother would probably shoot me should he ever learn of our, well, lessons. As for my mother"—he shuddered—"I hazard to think what she would do. It's a question of honor at this point. Mine as well as yours."

"That's why you said there was little choice." She chose her words with care.

He got to his feet, obviously more concerned with finding her robe than with what he was saying. "There is also the distinct possibility you could even now be with child. If we wed at once there will be no idle counting on fingers."

"We wouldn't want that," she murmured. A cold weight settled around her heart. She pulled her gown on over her head.

He spoke absently, as if he was discussing

nothing of any significance, and continued to cast around his room for her wrapper. "Beyond that, to be blunt, it will be quite difficult for you to marry anyone else now."

"I don't plan to marry." The moment she said the words, she knew they'd never been truer. Oh, perhaps for a moment she had thought, had considered, had wanted...

"Well, not anyone else, of course." He shot her a satisfied smile.

"Not anyone at all." She was rather surprised at how calm and pleasant she sounded. She slipped out of bed.

"What do you mean?" For the first time he gave her his full attention.

She picked up her robe, hidden in the shadow of the clothes press. "I have told you over and over again that I have no intention of marrying."

"But everything has changed."

"What, precisely, has changed?" She pulled on the wrapper, her action as deliberate as her words.

"Well, we...that is...you and I..."

"You're sputtering again, Thomas," she said as if she were chastising a young child. "You really should do something about that."

"I should really do something about you," he snapped.

She headed toward the door. "Nothing has changed at all. I still have no desire to wed. I am not especially concerned about virtue or reputation. Beyond that I have no wish to tie myself to a man for whom I am nothing more than an obligation of honor. And I'm certain you have objections as well."

"What objections could I have?" He started toward her. "It was my idea."

She sniffed. "For one thing, I am not the kind of woman you wish to wed."

"You can change."

She whirled back toward him, disbelief widened her eyes. "I can what?"

He cringed. "What I meant to say is that I can change, I can adjust."

"I'm certainly not going to risk my future on the possibility of reforming your nature."

"But we do suit well together." Frustration rang in his voice. "You must admit that much."

"For the moment perhaps." She shrugged. "However, you have made it clear that you wish for a wife much more sedate and biddable than I can ever be. Or that I should ever wish to be. You cannot expect me to become what you want in a wife just as I cannot expect you to be what I want in a husband."

His brows pulled together in anger. "And what exactly do you want?"

"Do you listen to me at all?" Her ire matched his. "I have told you. Were I interested in marriage—and nothing that has happened here has changed my opinion on that subject—I should want a man of adventure. An explorer of jungles or a hunter of treasure or—"

"Or some idiot who has nothing better to do than float down the bloody Amazon! The kind of man you find only in your blasted books." He gritted his teeth. "I thought so the first time you said it and I haven't changed my opinion: That is one of the stupidest things I have ever heard."

"Do you think so?" She fairly spit the words. "Stupider than considering, even for a moment, marrying you?"

"Yes, much stupider! I'll have you know I'm considered quite a catch."

"No doubt you'll do nicely if one is looking for an arrogant, pompous ass. However, I am not." Once again she started to leave.

He grabbed her arm and pulled her back. His voice was a study in barely suppressed outrage. "I thought we rather liked each other."

"I thought we did, too." For a long moment they stared and she could see anger in his eyes. She refused to let anything show in hers.

"Oh, come now, Thomas, do be rational about all this." She softened her tone and stepped into his arms. "I know full well you haven't offered to wed every woman you've bedded, and therefore I am appropriately flattered." She leaned forward and brushed her lips against his. "I'm not going to marry you, but I don't see why our—"

"I've had quite enough of this lesson nonsense," he snapped.

"I wasn't going to say *lesson*. I prefer to think of them now as adventures. Just the beginning of all manner of adventures." She kissed him firmly then pushed away and again headed for the door. "I see no reason why our adventures should not continue."

"I don't want adventures, I want to be married!" Thomas's voice rose.

"And I am certain you will be someday." She opened the door and looked down the corridor. Empty. "To the kind of woman you've always wanted." She stepped into the hall and glanced back at him over her shoulder. "But it shall not be me." She nodded and closed the door firmly behind her.

The half-light of those moments before dawn filtered in the tall windows, painting the hall with a grayish glow. How fitting. She made her way back to her room with a steady step, unconcerned about what ghosts might follow. A peculiar calm enveloped her as if she were in a dream.

Quietly she opened her door and slipped inside. She tossed off her wrapper, lay down on her bed and stared up at the high ceiling.

She would not marry a man who wanted her to satisfy some masculine idea of honor. What true heroine would?

And she would never marry a man who did not love her.

Despair washed through her, pain so intense she wondered that she could bear it. The back of her throat ached and tears fogged her eyes.

How could she have been so foolish? Oh, not to have given her virginity to Thomas. Her attitude about virtue hadn't changed. And hadn't she—in the back of her mind, at least— planned this all along?

But to have believed he shared her feelings and not just her desire...how could she have been so stupid?

She'd been wrong about love as well. Indeed it did exist outside of books and stories and was apparently not all that difficult to find after all. No, love crept up behind you when you least expected it, unwanted and overwhelming.

What was exceedingly rare was being loved in return.

Thomas stared at his closed door in shock.

How could Marianne refuse to marry him? It made no sense whatsoever. Regardless of her totally unrealistic view of the world and her position in it, even she had to understand the necessity of marrying at once. She was, to put it bluntly, ruined. And as he had done the ruining, it was up to him to set things right. And that meant marriage. Nothing less would serve.

He combed his hand through his hair and thought back over the last few minutes. She had really seemed rather amenable to the idea until...

He groaned. Of course. It was when he had started talking about the need to wed, rather than any desire on his part, that she had become so coolly pleasant. Well, what did she want from him, anyway?

There had never been any thought of love between them. Friendship, yes, but love? He snorted. He'd been in love, and this was not

214

it. Love made one feel light-headed and quite giddy.

Marianne questioned every word he said, every action he took. She matched her wits against his unrelentingly and, he had to confess, often bested him. Admittedly, their sparring was as stimulating as anything he'd experienced with his friends. But this was not love.

They would suit well together as man and wife. Certainly she wasn't what he'd originally had in mind, but was that, in truth, so bad? She would at least fit in well with each and every Effington female. Hell, she was cut from the same cloth. And if the marriages in his family were tempestuous, they also seemed remarkably happy.

No, he could do much worse than to wed Marianne Shelton. Indeed, he wanted to marry her. The thought pulled him up short.

When had that happened? Or had the idea hovered unnoticed all the while? Growing as he'd watched her with those suitors she'd never consider or during their late nights together over his poems or when he'd take her in his arms?

It wasn't love, of course, but then love had never played a role when he'd considered taking a wife. And perhaps what he shared with Marianne was better than frivolous emotion, anyway. He truly liked her and he'd never especially liked a woman before.

Marrying her would resolve any questions

of honor. And, as an added bonus, would delight his mother and probably Richard and Gillian as well. A match with Marianne would please everyone.

Except, of course, Marianne herself.

Still, how difficult would it be to convince her?

He might not love her, but he did want her. It was startling to realize just how much he wanted her. In his bed. In his life.

He needed a plan. A good plan. He ignored the realization that his plans had never been especially successful where Marianne was concerned, but there was much more at stake now.

No, he didn't just need a plan.

Perhaps, this time, he needed help.

Chapter 13

...therefore he has asked for my hand, yet I am reluctant.

In spite of my fallen state, do I truly wish to tie myself to a man for whom I am nothing more than an obligation of honor? Do I wish to spend my life in a match that is nothing more than a fulfillment of responsibility?

I know full well the prospects for my future are bleak without marriage. Still, regardless of what lies ahead, I cannot agree to wed without affection on his part. I cannot condemn myself to such a fate.

And I cannot do it to him....

The Absolutely True Adventures
of a Country Miss in London

"I've asked you to meet privately with me this morning because I have a matter of some importance to discuss." Thomas firmly closed the doors of the parlor and turned toward the girls. It was time to admit defeat and accept the inevitable. He couldn't succeed on his own.

It had been eight days, and eight glorious nights, since Marianne had first shared his bed, and Thomas hadn't managed to drag her one inch closer to the altar. She acted as if the passion they shared under the covers had nothing whatsoever to do with the rest of their lives. As if they could go on night after night... He steeled himself against the too delightful thought and forced a cool note to his voice. "And I need your assistance."

Becky and Jocelyn sat on the sofa regarding him with similar expressions of guarded interest. Even Henry, lying at Becky's feet, stared with a look of idle curiosity.

He drew a deep breath. "I wish to marry your sister."

"Marianne?" Jocelyn's voice was skeptical.

"Why?" Becky said bluntly.

"Because I think we will suit well together."
His words were short and clipped.

The girls traded glances.

"We thought you wanted someone rather less outspoken than Marianne," Becky said. "Someone a bit more biddable and reserved."

"I have changed my mind."

Jocelyn's eyes narrowed. "Why?"

"I like your sister a great deal. We are well suited to one another."

"You said that before," Becky pointed out.

"It bears repeating."

"It bears scrutiny." Jocelyn studied him curiously. "Marianne doesn't want to marry."

"I know that." He huffed in frustration. "That is why I need help to convince her."

Jocelyn shrugged. "Perhaps in time, if you are indeed as charming as your reputation, you can convince her, but I certainly wouldn't wager on it."

"I would prefer not to wait."

Becky shook her head. "Marianne is not particularly interested in marriage. We love her dearly, but she is rather odd in that respect. No, she plans to travel the world and have interesting experiences—"

"And adventures," he said sharply, waving away her comment. "Yes, yes, I know all that. I intend to change her plans. And you both should want it, too. Since you vow you won't marry before her."

"You seem rather more desperate than most men who simply wish to marry." Becky studied him carefully, then her eyes widened

218

and she jumped to her feet. "Good Lord!" She pointed an accusing finger. "You've—you've..."

"I've what?" A sinking feeling settled in his stomach.

"He's what?" Jocelyn said curiously, rising to join Becky.

Becky grabbed Jocelyn's shoulders and turned her sister to face her. Her voice was low but he could still make out the words. "Think for a moment, Jocelyn. What is the latest development in the *Country Miss* stories?"

Jocelyn frowned. "Why, Lord W has..." She sucked in a shocked breath. She turned a scathing glare on him. "You beast!"

"You fiend!" Becky's contemptuous look mirrored her sister's. "You've ruined her, haven't you?"

Henry growled.

"I daresay, this is not the kind of thing one usually discusses candidly. Especially not with the sisters of the—"

"Ruined?" Jocelyn shot.

"Fallen?" Becky snapped.

"I was going to say bride," he replied dryly.

Jocelyn collapsed onto the sofa and pressed the back of her hand to her forehead dramatically. "I cannot believe this. I knew her strange views about marriage and virtue and what women can and cannot do in this world would bring nothing but disaster."

"That's not the worst of it," Becky said to her sister. "You do realize, if this gets out, she's not the only one whose reputation will be shattered? Her actions will reflect on us as well."

"And we'll all be as good as ruined. Damnation." Jocelyn leapt to her feet and advanced toward Thomas, fire in her eyes. He prudently backed up. "This is your fault. You ruined her. You have to—"

"Fix her." Becky moved toward him in a threatening manner. "I mean fix this." He took another step backward and smacked into the mantel. "Marry her, Helmsley. Now!"

They pinned him with twin accusing glares. At once he realized how a fox felt when trapped by menacing hounds.

"I want nothing more than to marry her." He glared back. "*She* will not marry *me*."

"That is a problem." Becky crossed her arms and paced. "But it shouldn't be insurmountable."

"She can be extremely stubborn." Jocelyn mimicked her sister's pose and paced in the opposite direction. "And she's adamant on this particular subject."

"What would make her wish to marry?" Becky's forehead furrowed.

"If she was sensible, a great deal of money and a lofty title would do it." Jocelyn gave him an assessing look. "At least you have that in your favor."

"Thank you," he murmured, wondering why wealth and a respectable title abruptly sounded less than admirable.

"If there were a child involved..." Becky stopped and looked at him. "She isn't—"

"No," he said quickly, although that was certainly within the realm of possibility. "Not... now."

"However," Jocelyn said thoughtfully, "if you were to get her with child, even Marianne would accept that she had no other choice but to wed."

For a moment, no one spoke. It was definitely a plan, although, like any of his other plans regarding Marianne, not a very good one.

"I don't believe—" he started.

"Probably not." Jocelyn sighed.

"Definitely not." Becky nodded firmly. "We have to think of something else.

The girls continued pacing. Thomas watched them warily. He did hope they could come up with something, because he hadn't been able to thus far.

Abruptly Jocelyn stopped and clapped her hands together. "I've got it. What does Marianne want more than anything?"

"Blasted adventures," he muttered.

"And excitement and travel to interesting places." Becky blew an impatient breath. "We already know that."

"Of course we do, but what makes her want that?" Jocelyn paused, waiting for an answer.

Becky and Thomas exchanged puzzled glances.

Jocelyn grinned. "She wants all that because that's what she's filled her life with. Stories. Books."

Thomas shook his head. "I still don't see—"

"I didn't think you would." Jocelyn rolled her eyes toward the ceiling.

"I do," Becky said slowly. "The way to

capture Marianne's hand is to make what she's only read about come true."

"Not what she's read about, exactly." Excitement colored Jocelyn's voice. "But *who* she's read about."

He narrowed his eyes in confusion. "What?"

"Not what, who! You have to be a hero from a book."

"Exactly." Becky took her place beside her sister. "You have to be the kind of man she's always dreamed of. The kind of romantic, adventurous man she wants. It's an excellent idea."

"And it could actually work." Jocelyn looked at him as if judging him and finding him wanting. "If he can do it, of course."

"He's not terribly imaginative." Becky shook her head.

Jocelyn shrugged. "Well, he will probably need help."

"Would you stop speaking of me as if I were not in the room?" He'd had quite enough. "You have given me an idea and I think I can take it from here."

The girls cast him identical looks of doubt.

"You needn't stare at me like that," he said indignantly. "I am not perhaps the kind of adventurer that fills her books, but I have certain skills."

Jocelyn snorted.

"Oh?" Becky scoffed. "What?"

"I realize you have no confidence in me whatsoever, but I assure you..." He clenched his jaw. "Answer me this: In addition to explorers and the like who people her stories, are there not heroes who are simply dashing and romantic?"

"Of course," Becky said.

"I can be dashing and romantic."

"Really?" Jocelyn snickered. "We've only seen you stuffy and overprotective."

"I have another side," he said loftily.

"You'd better," Becky muttered.

At once confidence filled him. He might not be precisely what Marianne thought she wanted, but when it came to the arts of seduction, and indeed romance, he was second to no man. He had won far harder hearts than hers.

He started to leave, then turned back. Something they'd said earlier stuck in his mind. "By the way, I am curious: Why did you mention the *Country Miss* stories?"

"No reason, really," Becky said quickly.

"None at all," Jocelyn chimed in, her expression innocent. "It just seemed similar." Overly innocent.

He studied them carefully. He'd read the latest installment, of course, and had wondered idly how much wagered money had exchanged hands with the revelation of the innocent's ruin. Now the ridiculous chit was refusing to wed Lord W, and it seemed to him...

Sweet, sweet madness.

He sucked in a hard breath. It couldn't be.

Do I truly wish to bind myself to a man for whom I am nothing more than an obligation of honor?

No, surely he was wrong.

I've written a bit myself.

Becky and Jocelyn bolted toward the door, Henry right at their heels.

A journal of sorts.

"Stop right there." His command echoed in the room.

All three skidded to a halt.

"We really should go," Becky said.

"We have any number of things to take care of," Jocelyn added. "You wouldn't want us to keep Aunt Louella waiting." They inched toward the door.

"Not another step!"

He'd never seen two females, and even the dog, look quite so guilty.

"I have a terrible suspicion you know something I should know." His gaze slid from Becky to Jocelyn and back. "Please, please tell me Marianne is not the author of the *Country Miss* adventures."

"Very well." Becky smiled weakly. "She's not the author."

"I want the truth," he roared.

"Make up your mind," Jocelyn snapped. "Either you want the truth or you don't. And I very much suspect you don't. So why not leave it at that and we shall all be much happier?"

"I don't want to be happy!" What had he done, to be saddled with a house full of irritating women? "I want the truth!"

Jocelyn pulled in a deep breath. "We thought she was going to make it all up."

"We thought she *had* made it all up," Becky added.

"At least the parts about the kisses," Jocelyn said.

"And the, well, rest of it," Becky murmured.

Jocelyn shrugged. "Of course, we did help her with *Country Miss* a bit. And Lord W."

"It was my idea to make her an orphan," Becky offered. "And him a rake."

Jocelyn shook her head. "No, those were my ideas. *You* suggested he ruin her."

"Oh, dear, you're right." Becky winced. "How was I to know she'd actually do it rather than simply write about it?"

"She did want it to be accurate." Jocelyn sighed.

"It appears she based her *Absolutely True Adventures*, at least loosely, on her absolutely true adventures." Thomas paced the room. "Bloody hell, how could she? How could you let her?"

"We had little to say about it," Becky said.

"You should have stopped her."

"Come, now, my lord," Jocelyn said, "do you really think we could have stopped Marianne from doing exactly what she pleased?"

"Still—"

"And furthermore, you needn't blame us. Her *Absolutely True Adventures* wouldn't be so absolutely true if you had kept your head about you," Jocelyn snapped. "In point of fact, this is more your fault than anyone else's."

"What?" This was his fault? "I don't... I can't..."

"Look." Jocelyn nudged Becky with her elbow. "He's sputtering."

"Marianne mentioned that he sputtered." Becky smirked. "But I don't think it's as endearing as she does."

"No." Jocelyn shook her head thoughtfully. "Although you must admit he does turn an interesting shade of crimson."

"More like a scarlet—"

"Quiet," he bellowed. "Isn't it enough that one of your family is doing all in her power to drive me insane? Must you join her?"

He drew a deep breath and forced a calm note to his voice. "Now, then, aside from the two of you, who else knows of this?"

"No one, as far as we know." Becky paused. "Of course, Mr. Cadwallender does, but—"

"He'd never tell," Jocelyn cut in. "Besides, he doesn't know her real name."

"That's something, at any rate." He blew a long breath. "If her true identity is discovered..."

And I shall not rest until I find her.
Berkley!

The man was determined, and who knew how close he was to the truth. If Berkley found out, all of London would know in no time. Berkley had never been good at keeping his mouth shut. And if Marianne was identified as the country miss, it would be assumed Thomas was Lord W. Which, like it or not, he was.

The scandal would be of epic proportions. Not that the Effingtons hadn't weathered more than their share of scandal through

226

the generations, but the girls would be ruined. Any possibility of decent marriages for Jocelyn or Becky would vanish regardless of their dowries. And it was his responsibility to protect them.

Without doubt the first thing he had to do was cease the publication of Marianne's stories. He couldn't simply ask her to stop, of course; she'd never consent. No, he'd have to approach Cadwallender immediately. Whatever kind of man he was, a man, any man, surely would be more reasonable than Marianne.

"Now that you know everything, I was just wondering..." Jocelyn hesitated.

"What now?" he said.

"This won't affect our plans to attend your grandmother's party in the country, will it?" Jocelyn said hopefully.

"We are quite looking forward to it." Becky's voice was eager. "Even Aunt Louella."

Damnation, he'd quite forgotten about the dowager duchess's party. Only war, death or absence from the country was a legitimate excuse for missing the annual event. Besides, Effington Hall, and its extensive park, was an excellent place for a dashing romantic hero.

"No, of course, we'll go as planned at the end of the week," he said absently, already wondering what he could offer Cadwallender to entice him to stop printing Marianne's work.

He'd contact his solicitor at once to see what could be learned of the printer, and with luck Thomas would be able to call on the

man this afternoon. Thomas would do whatever he had to do.

One way or another, the country miss's
adventures were over.

Marianne finished the last line of the newest
Country Miss adventure with a flourish and set
the pen down. She'd posted the previous
installments, but this one she'd take to Cadwallender in person.

Thus far, the amount she received for each
installment had risen. If gossip alone was any
indicator, the *Country Miss* stories were selling
quite briskly. She could scarcely encounter one
group or another at a soiree or rout where there
was not some discussion about the unknown
author and the still-unidentified Lord W.

She stood and stared down at the paper. Now
it was imperative to speak to Cadwallender
directly, to determine how much she could
expect over the course of the next month.

When the season ended and Jocelyn, Becky
and Aunt Louella returned to the country, Marianne would not be with them.

If she could double what she had to date
received, her funding would take her as far as
Italy. If she lived frugally, she'd be able to
remain there for at least a few months. After
that... She shrugged. Well, uncertainty was the
nature of adventure, wasn't it?

She folded the paper, grabbed her wrap,
peered out of her bedroom door, then slipped
from her room and took the servants' stairs to

avoid any chance encounters with anyone—especially Thomas.

Thomas.

She sighed in spite of herself. How had she been so foolish as to think she could share his bed and not want more? And indeed he did offer more. Or at least marriage. His persistence was unyielding and so was her refusal.

It would be so easy to give in and be his wife. But now that she'd discovered the reality of love, she would not marry a man who did not love her. She would not become her mother. There was nothing more to say.

She left by the servants' door and headed for the corner where the hired carriage she'd arranged for this morning would be waiting.

She was determined to enjoy this time with Thomas. Helping him write his poetry and joining him in his bed. The arguments between them were as enjoyable as the laughter. It really was an adventure, if not one exactly as she'd expected. And she would remember their days together always.

Odd, how an emotion she'd never particularly considered now seemed to fill her every waking thought, ruling her life and her dreams.

Chapter 14

...still, Lord W refuses to believe that I will not marry him. His persistence is at once gratifying and unsettling. But I cannot be the woman he wants. And I shall not settle for a man who does not return my affection. I am well aware of the foolishness of my attitude, given the precarious nature of my future. If I have nothing else left, I have my pride. And my heart...

The Absolutely True Adventures
of a Country Miss in London

"There's a lord to see you." The older man's crusty voice drifted back to Thomas over the noise of the press. Pennington's description was apt. The man did indeed resemble a gnome. He stood in an open doorway a few feet in front of Thomas. "Says his name is Helmsley."

A long moment later the gnome grunted and turned to Thomas. "Don't just stand there, go on in."

The office was small and cluttered. A tall, powerfully built man rose to meet him. "Good afternoon, Your Lordship. I'm Ephraim Cadwallender. Please have a seat." Cadwallender waved at one of two questionable chairs that

230

occupied the tight space. "Pardon the disarray." He shrugged and settled in the other chair. "Now, then, how can I help you?"

Thomas sat on the edge of the chair. His voice was firm. "I wish you to stop publishing *The Absolutely True Adventures of a Country Miss in London.*"

"You do?" Cadwallender laughed. "Why would I want to do that?" He narrowed his eyes. "Or, more to the point, why do you want me to do that?"

Thomas drew a deep breath. "Because I intend to marry the young woman in question."

"The country miss?" Cadwallender studied him for a moment. "Then you are—"

"Lord W? Not precisely, of course, but he is apparently based on me." Thomas paused. "But you knew that, didn't you?"

"I have been corresponding with her. I do know where she lives. The rest I could guess at. It's gratifying to know I was right. I do like to know who I'm dealing with."

Thomas huffed. "You do realize the *Absolutely True Adventures* are not absolutely true, don't you?"

"I'd be surprised if they were." He chuckled and leaned back in his chair. "Miss Smythe—"

"Miss Smythe?"

"That's the name she uses. I didn't think that was absolutely true, either." He picked up a pen and tapped it absently on the desk. "The *Adventures* are boosting my circulation every week they appear. Why should I jeopardize that?"

"I have a proposal for you." Thomas paused to let his words sink in. "A very lucrative proposal."

"Go on. You have my complete attention."

"I have made inquiries and have discovered you lease this building. I have also found it can be purchased for a high—yet, given the circumstances, acceptable—price. I propose to buy it and sell it to you for a nominal amount."

Cadwallender shook his head. "I'm afraid that even at a bargain price I do not have the funding at the moment—"

"Then I will lease it to you and allow the rent to accrue toward purchase. Or"—he leaned forward—"I have a number of other commercial properties in the city. You are welcome to see if there is another building that would suit your purposes even better."

Cadwallender whistled long and low. "That is quite a proposal, my lord."

Thomas considered the other man thoughtfully. His solicitor's report, although admittedly hurried, had been quite flattering. Cadwallender looked like an excellent investment. He'd been in business for about four years. His reputation was honest, his debts minor. Thomas's blood quickened.

"I can make you an even better offer. I'm willing to invest in *Cadwallender's Weekly World Messenger*. The investment to include a better facility and a considerable sum of money."

"And all I have to do in return is stop publishing Miss Smythe?" Cadwallender said slowly.

"I'm talking about a partnership."

Cadwallender opened his mouth.

"A silent partnership," Thomas said quickly. "Indeed my only request in terms of what you print is that regarding Miss Smythe."

"Why would you want a silent partnership with me?

"You're smart. You're ambitious. In short, you're a good investment. We can both profit."

"Let me make certain I understand this. If I continue to publish Miss Smythe, my circulation will continue to grow and I will ultimately be quite successful. If I stop, you will provide the funding and facility." He glanced at Thomas.

Thomas nodded.

"And I will get where I want that much faster. However, my circulation will drop." He considered the proposal, then shrugged. "Therefore..."

"You won't do it, will you?"

Cadwallender reluctantly shook his head.

"Very well." Thomas stood and stepped to the door. "You do know that I could simply purchase this building out from under you?"

"I do. I'm also fairly certain you have more honor than most businessmen of my acquaintance."

"Honor has its price," Thomas said under his breath and turned toward the door, then heaved a resigned sigh. He found few things in life as irresistible as a good investment. "Would you be interested in my proposal if it has nothing to do with Miss Smythe?"

Cadwallender stared at him for a long, considering moment. "Very much so." His gaze shifted to a point behind Thomas. "However, if you wish her opinion on it, she's coming this way."

Thomas turned to see Marianne talking to the gnome.

Without hesitation, he shut the door. "She must not find me here."

"You'll have to hide." Cadwallender's voice was collected, but laughter flashed in his eyes. "I'll open the door and you can hide behind it. Unless you have a better idea?"

"I never seem to have a better idea when it comes to Miss Smythe," Thomas muttered, moving into position.

Cadwallender opened the door and stepped out. "Good day, Miss Smythe."

"Good day, Mr. Cadwallender." She favored him with her most pleasant smile. "I trust you are well."

"I daresay I have never been better." He chuckled and his blue eyes twinkled. "What brings you here today?"

"I brought you the latest adventure." She handed him the pages. "I should also like to discuss how they are selling. I plan to travel in the immediate future and I should like to know what recompense I can expect in—"

"Blast it all." Cadwallender frowned, yanked her toward him and quickly changed places.

"Mr. Cadwallender! I daresay, I—"

"Quiet." He nodded toward the door. "Be careful, but look around me and tell me if you know those two gentlemen who just came in."

Cadwallender's body effectively hid her from view. She craned her neck and peered around him.

Pennington and Berkley stood talking to Cadwallender's elf.

She jerked back behind him. "Good Lord! What are they doing here? If they find me—"

"You'll have to hide," he said quickly. "In the office—now."

"Where?" She stepped inside. "Behind the door?"

She started toward it, but he grabbed her elbow and turned her away. "No." He shook his head. "That's the first place they'd look."

"Nonsense, they don't even know I'm here."

"And we shall keep it that way," he said firmly. "Under the desk is the best spot."

She looked at the grubby floor skeptically. "I really don't think—"

"They're coming this way," he warned.

She had no choice. She dropped to her knees and crawled under the desk, refusing to consider what she might encounter there. She pulled her skirts in after her, taking care to make certain nothing showed, and looked up at Cadwallender.

He grinned down at her.

"I do not find this one bit amusing," she snapped.

"Maybe not for you, although it is something

of an adventure, isn't it? Perhaps you can write about it." With that he moved a chair in front of her to help conceal her hiding place.

A moment later she heard him greet the newcomers. "Good day, my lords. How may I help you?"

Someone cleared his throat. Pennington?

"I need to reach the country miss," a firm voice said. Definitely Berkley. "It is urgent that I speak with her."

"I'm afraid that is impossible," Cadwallender said coolly. "She is adamant about remaining anonymous."

"Nonetheless, I need her name." It was definitely Berkley.

"I fear I can't help you."

"He is willing to pay a great deal of money for the information." That dry tone must be Pennington. "You see, this is not a question of idle curiosity; it has become a matter of the heart."

"Oh?" Cadwallender's voice was skeptical.

"I must find her," Berkley said urgently.

There was a pause. "My lord, your words have touched me deeply. I would help you if I could, but in truth I do not know her name, nor where she resides. She visits me here."

"That's that, then," Pennington said.

Berkley ignored him. "Could you at least pass on a letter to her? I have it here."

"Certainly, my lord."

There were a few more cursory comments, then Marianne heard footsteps leading away from the office. Long moments later, the chair was removed and Cadwallender's strong hand reached down to her. "You can come out now."

She grabbed his hand and he pulled her out of her hiding place and to her feet. She dusted off her skirts. "Well, that was certainly interesting."

"It appears you have an admirer." He handed her the letter.

"Oh, dear," she murmured. How had this happened? She was the object of Berkley's affections. The dear man would be devastated when he found out. Or would he? Regardless, it was an impossible situation. She glanced up at Cadwallender. "You will keep my secret, won't you?"

"Until death," he said solemnly.

"Excellent." She smiled, all the while wondering how life had become so complicated.

Cadwallender escorted her out of the office, shutting the door behind them. They crossed the shop, heading toward the front door, and discussed what payment she could expect and how soon. It was better than she'd hoped.

"I was wondering," Cadwallender began, "have you given any further thought to the possibility of including a good murder in your stories? Sales would increase dramatically should that happen."

She laughed. "As much as there are any number of people I should like to do in on paper, I don't think that's possible. Besides, it would not be absolutely true."

"And we can't have that."

"Although, I must admit, you have aroused my interest." She looked up at him curiously. "What, precisely, is a *good* murder?"

"Oh, something gruesome, I should think," he said in a matter-of-fact manner. "Dismemberment is always appreciated by the public."

"Of course," she murmured, a queasy feeling in her stomach.

They reached the door and Cadwallender turned to her. "What about another suitor, then?"

"To dismember?"

"No." He laughed. "To serve as nothing more sinister than a rival for Lord W."

"Another suitor?"

He tapped Berkley's letter in her hand. "It would be absolutely true."

"It would, wouldn't it?" What an extraordinary idea.

"But give this one a name; an additional initial will just confuse readers. Call him something exotic." He thought for a moment. "The name of an animal, perhaps. Fox or Wolf or Lion or Tiger."

"Perhaps," she said thoughtfully. "I shall certainly give it due consideration. Good day, Mr. Cadwallender."

She took her leave, her head filled with the tempting idea of introducing another character. A man dashing and romantic to counter the brooding nature of Lord W.

If nothing else, creating such a man would get her mind off the one man who dominated her every thought. And if a second suitor indeed increased sales, she'd be on her way to a new life, and out of Thomas's, sooner than she'd expected. Exactly as she wanted. As she'd always wanted.

And she firmly ignored a tiny stab of pain at the thought.

The door opened and Cadwallender stepped into the office. "She's gone."

"Thank God." Thomas stepped away from the wall. "I thought I was done for when Pennington and Berkley arrived."

Cadwallender perched on the edge of the desk and folded his arms over his chest. "If you don't mind my asking, how did you get into this situation?"

"I've been wondering that myself," Thomas said with a wry smile.

Cadwallender considered him carefully. "Either Miss Smythe will marry you—"

"She will marry me."

"Or she will travel as she plans—"

"She's not going anywhere," Thomas muttered.

"One way or another, it appears I will not have her *Adventures* for much longer. Your problems will be over and the stories soon forgotten. Therefore, it is in my best interest to accept your proposal." He held out his hand.

Thomas shook it with a firm grasp. "You shall not regret it."

"Not as long as you remain silent." Cadwallender chuckled.

Thomas grinned. "I'll have my solicitor draw up the papers and contact you as soon as it can be arranged."

"In the meantime, if you can convince Miss Smythe to stop writing her stories, I'll not protest or try to change her mind. And I shall do everything in my power to make certain her identity, and yours, are not revealed."

"I should be grateful for that much, I suppose," Thomas said. "Now I simply have to convince her to give up her writing as well as to marry me."

Cadwallender raised a brow. "She has not agreed to marriage, then?"

"I intend to marry her," Thomas said firmly.

"But she doesn't want to marry you?"

Thomas heaved a sigh. "She doesn't want to marry anyone."

"Why doesn't that surprise me?" Cadwallender shook his head.

"Much of this is your fault, you know." Thomas cast him a pointed look.

"Mine?"

"You paid her for those bloody stories, didn't you? You've given her the means for independence."

"Yes, I suppose I have." Cadwallender chuckled. "God save us from independent women."

"I very much fear, in this case, God has left us on our own."

Thomas exchanged a few more comments with the printer, then took his leave. This hadn't turned out quite as he had expected;

nonetheless, Cadwallender was an excellent investment and the day was not a complete loss.

He strode down the street and around the corner, where he'd told his driver to wait for him. Wisely, as it turned out. And he considered once again how to lure Marianne into wedded bliss. Her sisters were right. He had to become the kind of man she'd always dreamed of.

Not an easy task. For one thing, he couldn't explore Africa, he had no desire to navigate the Amazon and Egyptian treasure was too far away.

He had no illusions about who and what he was. He had a good head for business, wrote terrible poetry but was persistent about it and was obviously a failure at the guardian-ship of young women. His finest honed skills—perhaps due to practice—were drinking, seducing women and having a great deal of fun.

He couldn't be one of her blasted heroes from one of her damnable books, but he could be what he was.

A damned fine, respectable rake.

...yet Lord W's insistence on marriage has, if anything, grown stronger. He is an obstinate man determined to have his own way. In that alone we are well matched.

I am turning my attention toward my future and whatever it may hold. I must accept the fact that it will be a future without him in it. It is exceedingly difficult when all I long for is his embrace and his affections.

If he would but say the right words...

The Absolutely True Adventures of a Country Miss in London

If Effington House in London was grand, even it paled in comparison with Effington Hall in the country. Inside and out.

Marianne stood on the terrace and gazed over Effington Park. It was nearly a full day's carriage ride from London and they'd arrived yesterday well after dark, far too late to see anything at all. Now she drank in the sight.

The grounds went on past the rolling hills of the horizon, well manicured and perfectly attended. At the foot of the terrace stairs a gravel pathway led across a short stretch of lawn to a formal garden encompassing an ornate fountain. High boxwood mazes—one square, the other round—flanked the garden.

Did one ever feel as alive as one did in the country? She breathed deeply of the fresh air and marveled at the sheer wealth that made all this possible.

She and her sisters had grown up at Shelbrooke Manor, the Earl of Shelbrooke's ancestral home. Ancient and sprawling, the place was well loved but had little else to recommend it. The old house had been falling in around their ears, until the past year when her brother had at last gained funding for repairs and renovation.

"Do you like it?" Thomas's voice sounded beside her.

Her heart fluttered and she steeled herself against the effect he had on her. "It's beautiful."

He gazed over the grounds with a look of loving pride. "When I was a child, I thought it was all quite magical." He chuckled. "I still do, I suppose."

She smiled at the fanciful notion. "I had no idea you believed in magic."

"It must be the poet in me," he said with mock solemnity, then grinned. "So I daresay the magic probably isn't quite up to scratch, either."

"Nonsense, Thomas. Even a bit of magic is better than none." She laughed and turned her gaze back to the gardens. "This is the kind of place where fairies dance in the moonlight. I doubt there is any magic better than that."

"They've been dancing for a very long time." He gestured at the boxwood hedges. "The mazes were planted more than a century ago by a previous Duke of Roxborough for his new bride. The square one is for family, because its corners are aligned with points of the compass and therefore no matter where Effingtons may scatter, they are still within reach of home."

She stared at him, fascinated by his tale. "And the round one?"

"Ah, the round one is very special. The circle signifies love, eternal and never-ending."

She shook her head. "But a circle is unbroken. Surely there must be a way in?"

"Of course. Even symbolism does need to bow to practicalities now and again." He smiled. "Also, in the center of the maze is a circular area we treat as a room. Each spring, the servants furnish it. For those few who know the secret of the maze, it becomes a private, secluded place. It even has a gate."

"My, you Effingtons do think of everything."

"Indeed we do. Once safely in the maze, you're in the center of everything on the estate yet completely alone."

"Really?" She raised a brow. "Doesn't that depend on how many people know the secret?"

"Indeed it does. But only a few Effingtons know how to navigate the maze. Or rather, only a few of us manage to remember. And the gate can lock...from the inside."

"What of the servants?"

"That is a problem." He shook his head sadly.

"I can't tell you the number of servants we've lost in there. I suspect someday we'll stumble over their bodies—or their skeletons, more than likely."

She stared at him with dismay. "You're not serious?"

"Of course I'm not." He grinned. "We remove the bodies long before they become skeletons."

"Thomas!" She laughed.

"In truth, only a handful of servants know the route by heart, although a map is kept somewhere. Those who are charged with bringing in the furniture routinely tie a string at the entrance to ensure their safe exit.

"At any rate, according to the family legend, the duke vowed the Effington family would prosper as long as the mazes grew."

"Like the ravens at the Tower of London?" she said. "England will stand as long as the ravens remain?"

"Something like that." He cast her a sideways glance. "I never said my ancestors were above adapting an already acknowledged legend to suit their own purposes."

She laughed again. It seemed his presence made her laugh quite a lot. When she didn't want to smack him.

"You might not realize it, but I have any number of ancestors who did not hesitate to bend facts to suit their purposes." He turned toward her, rested his elbow on the balustrade and considered her thoughtfully. "Not all the family skeletons are in the maze."

"What a relief."

"No, no, we trot them out periodically. Usually to make a point but sometimes simply for entertainment. Let me think." He furrowed his forehead in an exaggerated manner. "Just off the top of my head, mind you, it seems to me any number of remote cousins have been jailed for sheep-stealing. There's the distant aunt who married an Italian. Not scandalous in and of itself, but she was considered to be quite mad. Used to run about the countryside stark-naked.

"There was a pirate in there somewhere, although I believe we prefer the more respectable term of *privateer*. And a smuggler or two. Indeed, my family tree is fraught with scandal and unscrupulous branches," he said loftily.

"And to think that I considered you, the heir to all this scandalous behavior, stuffy and rather pompous."

He leaned toward her confidentially. "It was an act."

"And now?"

"I am the unrepentant rake you see before you." He straightened and swept a theatrical bow. "As determined as any Effington before me to get exactly what I want." He grabbed her hand and drew it to his lips. His midnight eyes sparkled in the sunlight. "And what I want, my dear Marianne, is you."

"Stop it, Thomas." She pulled her hand from his. "I will not discuss this now." She turned away pointedly and nodded at the scenery. "Tell me about the garden between the mazes."

"That is the duchess's garden. It's routinely dug up and redesigned with every new Duchess of Roxborough. My mother has done it any number of times." He pointed to the fountain. "She had that put in just last year, shortly after this annual house party, I believe. Do you like it?"

"It's lovely."

He leaned close and nuzzled her ear. "You can certainly change it to suit your preferences when you're my duchess."

She jerked back. "I am not going to be your duchess."

He shrugged, obviously not believing her for a moment. "You'll change your mind before we return to London."

"You are amazingly arrogant, Thomas." She stared in disbelief. "What makes you think I will agree to marry you here when I would not agree in London?"

"Because here you will not be able to resist the lure of adventures only I can offer you."

"What adventures?" she asked with suspicion.

"If I told you, it would spoil the surprise. And I should think one of the key elements of adventure is surprise." He cupped her chin in his hand. "I intend to prove to you that life with me will be as adventurous as anything you've ever read in a book."

"You do?" she said in an altogether too breathless voice.

"I do indeed." He smiled down at her in a most wicked manner. Her heart caught in her throat. "You believe in fairies, my dear, and I believe in magic. You can deny it all you wish, but we are well matched."

"Are we?" she murmured.

Perhaps they were well matched, in all but the one thing that really mattered. The one thing she refused to marry without.

Marianne glanced around the parlor, where those guests in residence at the Hall still lingered. It was considered a small group, at least in terms of this annual Effington gathering. But at dinner Marianne had counted the number present to be somewhere in the vicinity of forty.

Thomas had told her more guests would arrive early tomorrow in time for the well-known Roxborough Ride, which he described as a fox hunt without the fox.

Marianne's equestrian skills were limited, but the Ride seemed like something of an adventure and she planned on at least attempting the course. Becky could hardly wait. Even Jocelyn, never especially fond of hours on horseback, was intrigued, although she would only be an observer. It was difficult to navigate over obstacles when you couldn't see significantly farther than the nose of your horse.

The following night was the dowager's ball, and Thomas had said the crush would be as great as anything seen in London. Marianne had briefly met his grandmother, the dowager duchess, upon their arrival. At the moment, the dowager and Aunt Louella sat in a corner of the room deep in conversation. Although there was a span of at least a quarter of a century between their ages, they apparently knew, or had known, many of the same people. Aunt Louella actually seemed to be enjoying herself. It was a side of her aunt Marianne had never seen, and it was as delightful as it was disquieting.

Thomas was nowhere to be found, and that, too, was somewhat disconcerting. What was the man up to? And what were these adventures he'd planned?

Marianne murmured her apologies, pleading the lateness of the hour, and left the parlor. She headed for the chamber assigned her, if, of course, she could remember where it was. The house was intricately designed. The wood paneling glowed with polishing, the sconces shone brightly and dust would not dare to linger anywhere here.

Effington Hall was twice the size of Shelbrooke Manor and she suspected it had never had so much as a moment of disrepair. Thomas could say whatever he wished about the scandalous nature of his ancestors, but apparently once they'd acquired their fortune, they were clever enough to hang on to it.

She climbed the stairs toward the second floor. For some reason her room was not in the same wing as her sisters' and aunt's, nor were they on the same floor. Perhaps placement had something to do with the numbers of guests expected. Or perhaps Thomas had made certain her room was especially private.

She wouldn't put it past him. Nor would she deny him access. The lessons he'd taught her, or rather the lessons they'd shared, were beyond anything she'd ever imagined. Just the thought sent a shiver of delicious anticipation through her.

She pulled open her door, half expecting him to be waiting for her, and suppressed a twinge of disappointment. The bed was turned down, the doors leading to a small balcony open. The maid who'd showed her to the room last night said it was the only balcony on this side of the house. It was barely big enough for two people and surrounded by ivy. Quite enchanting, really.

She sank into a chair and tried to read a book she'd brought with her but couldn't seem to focus on the words. She hadn't read much at all lately. Life itself was filling her time.

After a long while she tossed aside the book. Obviously this was getting her nowhere and obviously Thomas wasn't coming. It was just as well. After he melted every bone in her body and turned her to a quivering mass of sensation, he'd probably badger her about marriage again. He was becoming quite creative in his persistence. She smiled at the thought. Still, she was as stubborn as he.

She changed into her nightclothes, blew out the candle and slipped into bed. And rolled onto her stomach. Then twisted onto her side. Punched the pillows. And sighed. She squeezed her eyes tight and tried to think of things that made her sleepy. Tried to ignore the sounds of the country at night. The rustling of leaves in the breeze. The incessant chirping of insects. The rattle of gravel hitting the floor....

She sat up and listened. There it was again: the clatter of pebbles on the floor. She threw off the covers, slid out of bed, grabbed her glasses and headed toward the open doors. A spray of gravel landed at her feet. The faint glow from the banked fire helped her spot the tiny rocks. Gingerly, she picked her way through the gravel and stepped out onto the balcony.

"Ah, 'tis Juliet."

She put on her glasses and peered over the railing. Starlight lit the night nearly as bright as day. "Thomas?"

Thomas grinned up at her, one hand behind his back. "No, not Juliet. But far, far better. 'Tis the fair Marianne."

"Quiet. Someone will hear you."

"Not on this side of the house." His voice carried a smug note. Just as she suspected, her room was not randomly assigned. The realization was not unpleasant.

"What are you doing?"

"Marianne, my sweet, I feared I should not see you again."

"Not see me again?" She laughed. "You saw me barely an hour ago."

" 'Twas a lifetime." He pulled his hand

from behind his back to reveal a bouquet of flowers tied with a ribbon. "I come straight from the duchess's garden bearing a token of my affection."

She leaned her elbows on the railing and rested her chin in her hands. "And the duchess won't mind?"

"The duchess wants nothing more than to see me wed. She would sacrifice more than a few posies for that."

"And how, pray tell, do you propose to deliver said token?"

"Much as Romeo would."

"Really?" She grinned. "Didn't he end up dead by his own hand?"

"Then I can do no less." He moved closer to the house and out of her sight.

"What do you mean, you can do no less?" she called after him.

No answer.

"Thomas?" Apprehension twinged through her. "What are you up to?"

His voice was muffled. "I'm bringing you your token."

She stepped to the side of the balcony and could see him at the bottom of the wall. He'd tied the ribbon around his neck and the bouquet hung in front of him like a floral medal of valor. "Surely you're not planning on climbing the ivy?"

"Indeed I am." He studied the ivy for a moment, then reached up and grabbed the woody vines.

"Don't be absurd. You'll kill yourself."

"I've done it before." He'd found footholds and was indeed inching his way up the ivy.

"And how long ago was that?"

"I climbed this vine any number of times when I was a boy." His voice was strained. "I can do it now."

"Now you're some twenty years older and I daresay a great deal heavier." He was a good five feet above the ground. "Thomas, please get down."

The only answer was the rustling of the ivy.

"The ivy cannot hold you. You'll fall."

"Nonsense. I can—" The unmistakable sound of vines ripping free interrupted him. For a moment he vanished amid a wave of ivy. Leaves rustled as if moved by a powerful wind. And a solid thunk sounded from the ground below her.

Her heart leapt to her throat. "Thomas?"

"I'm fine." He lay in a heap of ivy at the foot of the wall. "Just a few bruises. Nothing to worry about." He picked himself up off the ground and grinned weakly. "Apparently I over-estimated the strength of the ivy. I simply forgot that the vines are much thicker and more secure on the other side of the balcony."

He disappeared under the balcony. She scurried to the other end and leaned over to find him. "Don't you think you should give up now? I am suitably impressed."

"It's a blasted adventure, Marianne." He rubbed his hands on his pants and drew a deep breath. "One doesn't let a minor mishap stand in the way of an adventure." Once again he started up the wall.

She studied the ivy skeptically. "The vines don't look substantially thicker to me."

"Well, they are," he snapped.

"I do hope so." She stared down at him. "I would hate to see you tumble to your death."

"As would I," he muttered.

He was making better progress on this side. Perhaps he was right. She relaxed a bit, rested her forearms on the stone railing and watched him.

"It would be difficult to explain to your family how the Effington heir had met his demise."

He grunted in response. It was obviously hard work, but he was nearly halfway up the wall.

"What would I say to your grandmother?"

"Tell her I'm insane."

"Don't you think she's already aware of that?" Marianne shrugged. "After all, I haven't known you for very long, yet I knew you were mad the moment I met you."

"Not nearly as mad as you've made me," he said under his breath.

She bit back a laugh. He was climbing a little slower and she noted him testing the vine before putting his full weight on it. Good. She really didn't want to see him plummet to the ground.

"Would you like some help?"

"Not unless you have a rope handy."

"I could get a sheet," she said brightly.

He muttered something she couldn't quite

hear and she suspected that was probably best. Thomas's attempt at providing her with an adventure was obviously more trying than he'd anticipated.

She leaned far over the railing. He was still a good six feet below the balcony.

"What are you doing?" He glared up at her.

She stretched out her hand. "When you're close enough, you can grab my hand."

"Get back," he said sharply. "You'll fall. I'll fall."

The vine beside her—one of the thickest—quivered, and a few of the suckers sprang free from the wall. At once she noticed that it was not the only branch no longer connected to the house.

"Thomas," she said slowly, "I think you need to climb down. Now."

"Don't be absurd." He panted. "I'm almost there."

"I'm serious about this, Thomas. I really think—"

The vine snapped as if cut and collapsed, sliding down the wall, and Thomas with it. It seemed extraordinarily slow, at least to her. Thomas, no doubt, had a different perspective. The vines, branches and leaves crumpled to the ground. A nasty thud echoed in the night, accompanied by an *oof*. She winced in sympathy.

It looked bad, but at least the ivy hadn't fallen away from the building and had probably cushioned his fall. She stared down at a large tangled pile of leaves and vines. "Thomas?"

"I'm...fine," he said in a muffled voice. "Where are you?"

The vines shifted and Thomas clawed his way free. He threw her a less-than-enthusiastic wave. "I'm...fine."

"Thomas?"

He staggered around the corner of the house, his words drifting back to her. "I'm... fine."

No doubt he wasn't fine at all. He was probably quite scratched and scraped and bruised, although it didn't appear that he'd broken any bones or suffered any serious injury. Aside from his pride, of course.

So much for Thomas and adventure.

She smiled into the night. It really was rather sweet of him. Was she being foolish to continue to refuse his offer? Probably. She heaved a heartfelt sigh. Still, he didn't love her and even his gallant attempt at adventure could not make up for that.

A faint tapping sounded from across her room.

Thomas?

She stepped back inside, crossed the room and flung open the door.

Thomas stood before her, his expression somewhat dazed. "I'm...fine."

Even in the faint light from the fire it was apparent he was anything but fine. His shirt was torn, one shoulder was bare and his trousers were ripped.

Her heart twisted at the sight. "Good Lord, Thomas."

He thrust out the bouquet, which was as tattered as he was. "Your token."

"It's, um, lovely." She grabbed what was left of the flowers with one hand, pulled him into the room with the other and closed the door with her foot. "Do sit down." She pushed him to a chair and he sank into it without protest. "Let's see just how fine you are."

She set aside the bedraggled bouquet, lit a candle and placed it on the table beside him. And then wished she hadn't.

He looked much better in the dark. Where the shirt was ripped, long angry scratches marred his arms and chest. His face and neck had fared somewhat better. She picked up his hands and examined them. They were covered with small cuts and scrapes. "You looked like you've been attacked by an angry cat."

"That's the price one pays for adventure." He grinned weakly.

"Oh, Thomas, you are mad."

"Sweet madness," he murmured.

She dropped his hands and stepped to a half-filled pitcher sitting in a bowl on the dresser. She poured water into the bowl, grabbed a washcloth, then returned to kneel before him.

"This might hurt." She dipped the cloth in the water and dabbed it over the scratches on his chest.

"Yow!" he yelled and sat upright. "Stop it!"

"Quiet." She pushed him back. "These need to be attended to."

"But it hurts." He sounded very much like

257

the boy he'd been when he'd last climbed the ivy.

"It's the price you pay for adventure, remember?" She sat back on her heels and frowned. "I can't do anything with that shirt on. Take it off."

"With pleasure." He grinned wickedly, then flinched. With her help, they managed to get the shirt off. He leaned back and studied her. "Now you may have your way with me."

"Oh, I am a lucky woman," she said wryly, starting to clean the wounds on his arms. They weren't as bad as they'd originally looked. Just surface scratches, really, with scarcely any blood, although he'd probably be quite sore in the morning. "What were you thinking, anyway?"

"I was thinking—ouch—only of you—ouch."

"I suppose, then, I should be grateful you weren't thinking more of me." She turned her attention to his chest. "You'd probably be dead."

"Ah, but what a—ouch—delightful way— ouch—to go."

"What? Attacked by ivy? Falling off the side of a building?" She swirled the cloth in the bowl, twisted out the excess water and started on his hands.

"No, trying to—ouch—capture the hand of the fair Lady Marianne."

She sniffed, dipped the cloth and wrung it out. She got up on her knees and washed the cuts on his face. "There are better ways to do it."

He caught her hand, his voice abruptly serious. "For instance?"

"For instance..." Her gaze met his. *You could love me.* She swallowed back the words. "I'm sure I don't know." She pulled her hand from his and dabbed at the scrapes on his neck, avoiding his gaze.

"You're not terribly helpful."

"My apologies." She sat back and studied him. "There, that's better. How do you feel?"

"Like I've been in a brawl." He touched his cheek and winced.

Impulsively, she leaned forward and brushed her lips along the side of his face. "Does that help?"

"Infinitely." He turned his head and pointed to the other side of his face. "It would help there, too."

"Very well." She placed a gentle kiss where he indicated.

"And here." He raised his chin and she obligingly kissed his throat. And his neck.

He ran his hands over her back and drew her closer, settling her between his knees.

"Thomas," she murmured against his shoulder. His flesh was warm against her lips and his scent filled her senses. Desire as only he could provoke washed through her. "I don't think this is a good idea."

"I think it's a very good idea." He pulled her tighter against him and trapped her with his legs. Through the fabric of his trousers she was well aware of just how good an idea he thought it was.

His hands drifted lower to caress her buttocks through the thin fabric of her nightgown. He pushed aside the neck of her gown and nuzzled the sensitive skin at the base of her throat and she shivered with desire. She shifted to press closer to him, rubbing against his hard arousal and meeting his lips with hers.

"Tell me if this hurts," she whispered.

"It hurts." He nibbled at her lower lip and then gently kissed the corners of her mouth. She moved her hands carefully over his shoulders in a light, fluttering caress—the restraint between them heightening the need gathering inside her.

He sighed under her touch. His lips brushed against hers. His hands slipped lower and he gathered her gown in his fists until he could slip his hands under the fabric and run his fingers along her legs and higher.

"Take it off," he growled softly.

"With pleasure," she said with a smile. She leaned away from him, pulled the garment over her head and tossed it aside. He wrapped an arm around her waist and bent forward to take her breast in his mouth.

She moaned with delight and reveled in the sensual indulgence of his touch. She could gladly spend the rest of her days like this. With him.

"Wait." He stood abruptly and pulled her to her feet. Quickly he took off his breeches, then settled back in the chair.

"Thomas." She laughed. "What are you doing?"

"I have paid the price for this adventure." There was that wicked smile of his again. "Now it's your turn."

He pulled her down to straddle his lap and slid easily into her. She welcomed him with a shiver of erotic pleasure, closed her eyes and let her head drop back. Her breasts were on a level with his mouth and he took full advantage of the position, suckling one, then the other.

She hooked her heels around the legs of the chair and pushed against him, needing him buried inside her. He thrust beneath her, the narrow confines of the chair making his movements shorter, deeper, harder. Her excitement rose and she met the drive of his hips with her own. They rocked together in an ever-increasing intensity of pleasure until the chair creaked in protest. In a corner of her mind not fogged with desire she wondered if the chair would splinter beneath them. And didn't care.

She leaned into him and clutched at his back and he held her tighter. They moved in a rhythm at once familiar and always, always thrilling. Delight spiraled within her higher and higher until at last he groaned against her skin and glorious release shook her body.

She clung to him for a long moment and rested her head on his shoulder, trying to catch her breath. His chest rose and fell against her and she could feel the beat of his heart.

She raised her head and smiled down at

him. "I will say one thing for you, my dear Lord Helmsley: You certainly have a way with adventure." She brushed her lips against his. "What have you to say for yourself?"

He reached a finger to slide her glasses back up the length of her nose and grinned wryly. "Ouch."

Chapter 16

...regardless, I am trying to put Lord W from my mind and my heart. The situation between us is impossible and I cannot continue pretending all is well. It is difficult to live in his house and not be with him, yet I know my happiness lies elsewhere. I must do all I can to forget what he has meant to me and go on with my life.

To that end I have made the acquaintance of an intriguing gentleman who seems somewhat taken with me. Lord L is unlike anyone I have ever met and I suspect he can ease the ache in my soul.

Oddly enough, his friends call him Leopard....

The Absolutely True Adventures
of a Country Miss in London

"Grand day for the Ride, eh, Helmsley?" Pennington pulled up beside Thomas and reined his horse to a stop.

"Indeed it is." Thomas repositioned himself in his saddle and tried not to wince. The aftereffects of last night's adventure were rather more painful than he'd expected. Still, if his aches softened Marianne's attitude even a fraction, they were well worth it.

"Bad night, old man?" Pennington said with a raised brow.

"Nothing serious." Thomas shrugged in an offhand manner. "I took a bit of a tumble. That's all."

Pennington and Berkley had arrived within the past hour and would be staying at the hall through tomorrow night. While they had been invited in previous years, and did come more often than not, Thomas had sent them each a note before he left London, encouraging their attendance. It seemed wiser to have them here where he could keep an eye on them rather than allow them free rein in town to ferret out the identity of the country miss.

"Where is Berkley?"

Pennington nodded toward a group of riders. "He spotted the Shelton sisters and insisted on paying his respects."

"And you'd rather not?"

"In good time." Pennington glanced around. "I don't see the lovely Lady Marianne."

"She's here somewhere." Thomas drew his brows together. "Why?"

Pennington looked startled. "Why not?"

"She doesn't strike me as the type of woman you're usually attracted to."

"She isn't. But she is charming and clever and amusing and I quite enjoy her company. It appears my tastes are changing." Pennington chuckled. "I assure you no one is more surprised to discover that than I."

Pennington studied him curiously. "I rather thought you would be encouraging my attention."

"Come, now, Pennington." Thomas forced a lighthearted laugh. "These girls are under my protection. Why would I encourage the interest of you, of all people?"

"I was given to understand that you wished to find them husbands. First and foremost Lady Marianne. I had also heard you went to the effort of sending—"

"That was a mistake," Thomas said quickly. "You yourself pointed out Marianne would not take kindly to rescue."

Pennington laughed. "I can only imagine how she'd react to the knowledge of your active husband-hunting."

"It is not a pleasant thought." Thomas stifled a grin at the memory of how very pleasant it really was. He forced a casual note to his voice. "Speaking of hunting, how goes Berkley's quest for his mysterious love?"

"Not well." Pennington directed his words to Thomas, but his gaze searched the crowd. Looking for Marianne, no doubt. Thomas brushed aside a stab of annoyance. "Cadwallender says he doesn't know her name or where she lives."

"And you believed him?"

"There was little choice. Short of camping on his doorstep and lying in wait for the lady in question to make an appearance, there was nothing more to be done. Berkley did—" Pennington's eyes lit and he grinned. "I say, Helmsley, do you mind if we continue this discussion later?"

Thomas followed his gaze. Marianne sat perched on an Effington mount, her blond curls escaping from beneath her fashionable hat, too independent to bear confinement. Her manner was relaxed and comfortable, as if she were well used to being on horseback. In her forest-green riding habit she looked like a bespectacled woodland fairy, at once ethereal and earthbound. And eminently desirable. He shifted around uncomfortably.

"Helmsley?" Pennington cast him an assessing gaze. "You don't mind, do you?"

"Not at all," Thomas lied.

"Excellent." Pennington turned his horse in Marianne's direction, then paused. "In case you were wondering, I have no intentions toward the lady at the moment. However, if I did, or should I in the future, I suspect they'd be rather annoyingly honorable." Pennington touched the brim of his hat and grinned, then directed his horse toward Marianne.

She greeted Pennington with an all-too-genuine smile. Thomas tried to ignore a twinge of jealousy. Still, why shouldn't he be jealous? After all, that was his future wife who was far and away too pleased to see another man. The woman who would one day bear his children, laughing with delight at the words of another man. The next Duchess of—

"Don't stare at her." Jocelyn rode up to join him, Becky's horse close beside her. "It's really not becoming."

"Not at all." Becky nodded.

He stifled a sigh. Whatever it was they wanted, now was not the time. He kept his gaze on Marianne but directed his words to her younger sisters. "What do you want?"

"Has she agreed to marry you yet?" Becky asked.

"Not yet."

"Are you at least making some sort of progress?" Hope sounded in Becky's voice.

The thought of Marianne's lips caressing his chest sprung unbidden to his mind. He cleared his throat. "I believe I am."

"Well, you need to work a little faster," Jocelyn said firmly.

He stared at Marianne. Had he ever met a woman who responded so fully to his touch?

"There's someone else," Jocelyn said.

A woman whose eager innocence inflamed his senses...

"Another suitor," Becky added.

A woman who lingered in his mind long after she'd left his bed...

"Helmsley." Jocelyn smacked his shoulder and he jerked his gaze toward her.

"Ouch." He glared. "What is it now?"

"Pay attention, Helmsley. This is important." Jocelyn huffed in annoyance. "There's another man."

"Where's another man?" He narrowed his eyes. "What are you talking about?"

"We're talking about the woman you ruined," Becky snapped.

"The woman you have to marry," Jocelyn said in a fierce whisper.

"Quiet," he said in a low voice. "Do you want everyone to hear? Now explain yourselves."

"Marianne was writing the newest *Country Miss* adventure yesterday," Becky said. "And we just happened to see it."

"Well, actually, we thought it was a good idea to read it." Jocelyn sighed. "Now that we know her adventures aren't quite as fictional as we'd thought."

"It was a simple matter of distracting her." Becky grinned. "Of course, it wasn't quite finished—"

"Would you two get to the point?"

They traded tolerant glances. Becky sighed. "The point, my lord, is that there is someone else."

Jocelyn smirked. "You have a rival."

"A rival?" Thomas drew his brows together. "How can I have a rival?"

"I know it's difficult for you to understand, given your charming manner, but there is another man." Jocelyn's tone was wry.

"When did she find the time?" he said under his breath. He turned his gaze toward

Marianne, who was still chatting with Pennington. *Pennington?*

"It scarcely matters who it is," Jocelyn snapped, apparently reading his mind. "What matters is that there is a *who* and it's the wrong *who*."

"Unless," Becky said slowly, "you've changed your mind about marrying her."

"In which case"—Jocelyn clenched her teeth—"I shall make it my life's purpose to—"

"Threats are not necessary," he said absently. *Pennington?* How could she be interested in Pennington? "I fully intend on wedding Marianne. Even if I have to drag her kicking and screaming to the altar."

"Say, there's an idea," Becky said brightly. "Couldn't you kidnap her and take her to Gretna Green?"

"Oh, that would work nicely." Sarcasm colored Jocelyn's words. "Marianne wouldn't care one whit about the scandalous nature of such an endeavor."

"She'd probably see it as a blasted adventure," he murmured. *Pennington?* What did he have that Thomas didn't?

"On further consideration," Jocelyn said thoughtfully, "she would indeed consider it an adventure, which would be very good—"

Becky grinned. "That's what I thought."

"Although not necessarily one that ends in marriage." Jocelyn shook her head. "You are going to have to come up with something better."

"I will," he said sharply. "Now, then, thank

you both for the information and your suggestions—"

"We are willing to help," Becky said.

"To do whatever is necessary," Jocelyn added. "Goodness knows, you aren't doing all that well on your own."

"Your faith in me is overwhelming." Thomas cast Jocelyn a pointed look. "I am perfectly capable of convincing your sister to be my wife." His gaze shifted to Becky. "Without benefit of kidnapping or other means of force."

"We never doubted it for a minute." Becky's tone was overly sweet.

Jocelyn's manner matched her sister's. "You have our complete confidence."

Thomas didn't believe either of them. In spite of their words, it was clear neither sister thought he could succeed in winning Marianne's hand. At this particular moment, even he had his doubts. Still, her stubbornness was no match for his determination. And he was determined.

He couldn't recall ever having failed to get what he wanted and he refused to consider the possibility of failure now. And no mysterious suitor, be it Pennington or anyone else, would stand in his way.

Who knew adventure could be so terrifying?

Marianne straightened in the saddle and stared at the upcoming course. The Ride was laid out in a series of eight separate courses, each more difficult than the last. This was the third.

269

More than a hundred riders were participating, divided into six teams. The third team was on the course at the moment. Marianne's was next. Pennington was in the group behind hers, but Berkley was on her team.

Thomas and Becky were on the second team and it was already apparent to Marianne their group would surely win the competition. Becky rode with barely controlled abandon, as if she were born on horseback. Thomas handled his horse as if they were of one body, one mind. As confident and compelling as a hero from a book.

She watched him take the jumps and maneuver around the obstacles and her heart leapt with a certain amount of fear and more than a little pride. This was the man she loved. He was magnificent.

"You needn't continue, you know," Berkley said beside her. "There's no shame in quitting at any point. In fact, it's expected that a fair number of riders won't finish." He nodded toward a young man. "The stable master posts someone at the start of each course. All you have to do is indicate to him that you're not going on."

"Yes, well, I am considering it." She grimaced. Still, what would a heroine worth her salt do? She squared her shoulders. "However, not yet."

Berkley frowned. "Are you certain?"

"Not at all." She laughed weakly. "I might more likely end up in the water up ahead than sail over it."

"As many have done before you." Berkley grinned. "I myself have taken a spill or two here in past years."

She studied him carefully. While she was grateful for his encouragement and his company, she found herself a bit uncomfortable in his presence. The declaration of love in his letter was disquieting and she had no idea how to handle the situation. Still, she probably should do something.

Marianne drew a deep breath. "I have given your dilemma a great deal of thought, my lord, and I was wondering if you have come any closer to declaring yourself to the object of your affections."

"From equestrian obstacles to obstacles of the heart?" He raised a brow. "Rather a startling shift of subject, don't you think?"

Heat rushed up her face. "I do apologize. I should never have—"

"Nonsense." He waved away her words. "I did confide in you, after all. To answer your question, I have written her of my feelings, but..." He shrugged as if it didn't matter, but she knew full well it did. "To no avail. She has not seen fit to respond."

"Perhaps," she said gently, "her affections are otherwise engaged."

"Oh, I'm certain they are." His expression darkened. "But he is not the man for her. He will break her heart and leave her alone and ruined."

"Surely he is not that bad." Unease settled in the pit of her stomach.

"He is a black-hearted villain," Berkley said harshly.

She stared in surprise. Were Berkley's feelings coloring his perception? Or had she really portrayed Lord W—Thomas—in such a dastardly way? Certainly she had made him somewhat dark and morose, possibly even threatening, definitely arrogant. With the exception of the arrogance, perhaps, Lord W was more a product of her imagination than anything else.

His exploits—their exploits—had a grain of veracity in them but were only loosely based on her and Thomas's. Still, it was obvious Berkley would never believe that if he knew the truth. Nor, she suspected, would anyone else.

"She must escape from his clutches. I will find her eventually." Berkley's voice was grim. "She needs me."

"My lord"—Marianne laid her hand on his sleeve—"have you considered the possibility that she has not contacted you because she is, well, satisfied with her fate?"

His brow furrowed into a forbidding frown. "I cannot believe that. And I will not until I hear it from her own lips."

She studied him with a sense of helplessness. Poor, sweet man. He'd gotten caught up in her imagination and now fancied himself in love with a woman who bore only a vague resemblance to reality. This was her fault entirely and it was up to her to do something about it.

"My dear Lord Berkley," she said slowly,

removing her hand. "I fear you are some-thing of a fool."

"How can you…" He drew himself up and glared. "I thought you understood. I thought—"

"Piffle." She waved off his comment. "What I understand is that you are pining after a woman you admit you have never met. There-fore, whatever you know of her, or think you know, is incomplete. You have built her out of your own desires and needs. You do not know her at all."

"I daresay, I—"

"You are in love with a dream. A fantasy, with no more substance than the story in a book. Fiction, my lord"—she shook her head—"is not, nor shall it ever be, real."

"My lady, I—"

"Look around you." Marianne gestured at the crowd. "There are several lovely young ladies here. Real women, and I suspect there are any number who could care for you deeply."

He studied her intently. "Do you think so?"

"I do indeed." She laughed with relief. "Why, you are quite charming and more than a little handsome. Any woman—any real woman, that is—would be flattered to be the object of your attentions. And I would suspect more than one would return your affection."

"Really?" A slow, pleased smile spread across his face.

"Really." Satisfaction spread through her. With luck, Berkley would forget all about the country miss now and turn his interest elsewhere. "Now, then, it appears our team is about to begin, whether I am ready or not."

"Never fear. I shall be beside you," he said staunchly. "Should you need my assistance."

She studied the course with reluctance. "It is good to know there will be someone close at hand to help me up should this creature and I part company."

"You may count on me." An odd light shone in Berkley's eye. "I shall remain by your side every minute."

"Thank you," she murmured and directed her attention toward the obstacles ahead, pushing aside the uneasy feeling that while she might have deflected Berkley's affections from the country miss, she might also have pointed them in a new and unforeseen direction.

Or could it be Berkley?

Thomas watched Marianne's team progress through the course. Berkley, usually an excellent rider, hung back from the others to keep pace with Marianne. Her ability on horseback was adequate at best. Thomas was at once grateful for and annoyed at Berkley's attention. Surely she didn't need that much assistance?

He did have to admit, though, she had a fair amount of courage. Misplaced, perhaps, but there nonetheless. She tried to hide her apprehension, but he, and possibly he alone, could see it in the line of her mouth and set of her chin. At least she was smart enough to be concerned, given the increasing difficulty of the courses and her limited skills. But she'd yet to give up. He smiled in spite of himself and noted a surprising touch of pride. She was most impressive, every inch a future duchess. *His* future duchess. And just as obstinate as every duchess who'd come before her.

She made it over a moderately tricky jump but landed hard. He couldn't help but wince in sympathy.

Was Berkley's attention to her simply a coincidence or had he somehow discovered she was the woman he claimed to have fallen in love with? Or worse, had Marianne confessed all to him? After his appearance at Cadwallender's she was well aware of his feelings. No, Pennington would know if that were true. Unless Berkley hadn't told him? Nonsense, Berkley would have told Pennington; indeed, Berkley would have told everyone everything. Besides, if Berkley knew the truth, he would have confronted Thomas at once.

Marianne approached a water obstacle and Thomas held his breath. Her horse was well trained and took the jump with an ease that belied the flash of fear on her face.

Was Berkley the new suitor in the country miss's life? Or was it Pennington? He dismissed the unsettling thought that perhaps it was someone else altogether.

Bloody hell, who could determine anything when it came to Marianne? Why couldn't she be a...well, typical female? Someone who wanted nothing more than marriage and a husband whose desires and needs she would lovingly see to? A woman who would never question the decisions or actions of a spouse?

He blew a long, frustrated breath, knowing the answer at once.

If Marianne were such a woman, then she wouldn't be the one woman who tied his insides in knots and drove him stark-raving mad and ruled his mind as well as his loins.

Thomas watched until she had made it safely through the course, and released a relieved breath. Surely she'd give up now, but who knew what she'd do? She was obstinate enough to continue until she landed flat on her adorable backside. She probably saw the Ride as an adventure: dangerous and exciting.

Perhaps a bit of danger was precisely what he needed to add to his attempts at amorous adventure. Obviously, falling to his death was not dangerous enough for her. And why should it be? She was not the one in jeopardy.

She joined Berkley at the end of the course, her laughter floating in the slight breeze. Thomas narrowed his eyes.

Danger. Adventure. Seduction. Romance.

The words pulsed in his head, the answer teasing just out of reach. Where was the danger in romance? The adventure in seduction?

It was so simple he should have realized it long ago. He smiled slowly. Danger and adventure went hand in hand with the lure of the forbidden and the threat of discovery.

And he whispered a silent prayer to long-dead Effington ancestors for their forethought in fashioning the one place that could provide exactly that.

Chapter 17

...that Leopard is indeed as cunning and clever as his namesake. He is, as well, charming and exciting and far too enticing. I am drawn toward him like a leaf in a current. There is something in his nature that is both frightening and irresistible.

He is not the kind of man one considers for a match and perhaps that is the strength of his appeal. Still, if I am not to wed, then would it be so wrong to taste the forbidden fruits he offers?

As for Lord W, in spite of my efforts, he is always in my thoughts. And in my dreams...

The Absolutely True Adventures
of a Country Miss in London

Marianne plucked the note from its perch in the branches of the round boxwood maze and smiled. What kind of adventure did Thomas have in mind now?

After the Ride, she'd returned to her room, bathed and napped, to awaken to find a note slipped under her door. It was unsigned, but there was no question as to who it was from. Who but Thomas would couch an invitation in such poetic terms? At least *treasure* and *pleasure* rhymed.

"Thomas?" she called, unfolding the note. It contained nothing more than the drawing of an arrow. Obviously, she was to enter the maze. The adventure had begun.

She drew a deep breath and stepped inside. To her right was a solid hedge wall. She turned to the left and followed the greenery to a bend to the right and back to the left. Again there was no choice. She continued through the tall leafy passageway and her confidence built. The maze wasn't nearly as difficult as Thomas had said. Why, she doubted she'd run across even one body. She ignored an entry leading deeper into the structure and continued forward until the corridor ended at a wall.

She swiveled and retraced her steps, this time taking the entry she'd passed before. She stepped through the next opening, this, too, leading deeper into the maze. Perhaps that was the secret? Simply take whatever route led toward the heart of the puzzle.

She drew a deep breath and continued, rather more cautiously than before. It was a bit unnerving, this not knowing where she was headed. Worse, at the moment, she had no idea how to get out. She hit a wall with walkways branching out in either direction and paused.

"Thomas?"

No answer. What if he wasn't here? If she hadn't gotten his note in time? If he'd waited for her and decided she wasn't coming? The idea of someone lost forever in the high, leafy passages did not seem so far-fetched after all.

She took the turn to the right, then stopped and went back to the left. A few feet from the entry, an ivory ribbon lay in the center of the path, leading farther into the maze.

She laughed with relief and picked it up. She followed it around one curve, then the next, gathering the ribbon in her hand as she went. The rounded walkways grew tighter until she reached a point where the ribbon was tied in a halfhearted bow on an iron gate.

She pushed it open, stepped cautiously into the center of the maze and gasped with delight.

It was indeed a room of sorts, with high boxwood walls and the sky above for a ceiling. Wide benches were evenly spaced around the perimeter. In the middle was a small, wrought-iron, linen-covered table and two chairs. She stepped closer. A vase with freshly cut flowers sat beside an open bottle of champagne and two filled glasses. It was a setting straight from a romantic tale.

A tale of seduction.

The gate clanked shut behind her and she spun around.

Thomas leaned against the gate, a wicked grin on his face. "I thought you'd never get here."

"And now that I am?" Delicious anticipation washed through her.

"Welcome to adventure." He was casually dressed in a soft linen shirt, open at the throat, and well-worn breeches. He looked like she imagined a pirate or a highwayman would appear, right down to the gleam in his eye.

"What if I do not wish to partake of the particular kind of adventure you have in store?"

"You will." He turned the key in the lock on the gate. "Besides, I have no intention of letting you go until you agree to marry me."

Her heart thudded in her chest. "Come, now, Thomas, I cannot—"

Before she could say another word, he pulled her into his arms. His lips met hers and she reveled in his embrace, familiar desire rising up within her. He slanted his mouth over hers and kissed her again and again until she thought she'd swoon from sheer pleasure.

"Say you'll marry me," he whispered against her lips.

Say you love me. "Never," she murmured.

"Very well." Without warning he released her and moved to the table. "Then would you care for some champagne?"

For a moment she could only stare. Frustration gripped her and she struggled to catch her breath. "Why on earth did you stop?"

"I was thirsty." He grinned, waved away a bee hovering over the champagne, picked up a glass and held it out to her.

"You are annoying." It wasn't enough that his merest touch drove her mad with need. No, now he wanted to play some silly game under the guise of adventure. Well, she wasn't in the mood to play.

She snatched the goblet from him. The champagne sloshed onto her hand. She ignored it and drained the wine. "Now—" she set the glass back on the table with a firm smack—"I wish to leave."

"Why?" He sipped thoughtfully. "You've just arrived."

"I find this adventure is not to my liking." Abruptly she realized the idea of adventure of any kind was growing weary.

"But it has only just begun."

"Fine." She huffed a defeated breath. He refilled her glass. She picked it up and took a healthy swallow. She liked champagne nearly as much as she liked brandy. "What do you have in mind?"

"First, I'm going to relieve you of that dress."

"Oh?"

"There is nothing quite like the unconfined feel of being completely undressed out-of-doors." He took another drink and set his glass on the table. "Of making love beneath the heavens." He pulled his shirt over his head and tossed it on a nearby bench.

She narrowed her eyes. "What are you doing?"

"Wait and see." He circled the table to stand behind her, then ran his fingers lightly

281

up and down her arms. "Surprise, my dear Marianne, is the very essence of adventure."

He reached in front of her and deftly removed her spectacles, tossing them lightly onto a chair. He lifted her hand to his mouth and licked the dried champagne. She shivered, all annoyance vanishing with his touch. Perhaps she was in the mood to play after all.

He kissed the back of her neck, trailing his lips to the edge of her gown, then fumbled with the tapes of her dress. It loosened about her.

"Thomas, what if someone happens upon us here?"

He nudged the sleeves down and bared her shoulders. "No one will." He pushed her gown and the shift beneath it lower, and she freed her arms from the sleeves. "Those who take part in the Ride typically spend the hours afterwards recovering in their rooms. Besides, even should someone manage to make their way to the center, the gate is now locked from within and the hedges nicely muffle any voices, making recognition nearly impossible."

A lovely illicit feeling shivered through her. She leaned back against him and closed her eyes, reveling in the warmth of his body behind her. "Are you sure?"

His hands skimmed down her sides, gown and shift falling to a puddle at her feet, leaving her clad only in stockings and shoes. "Almost positive."

He was right about being unclothed out-of-doors. Surrounded by the hedges, with only the vast blue sky overhead and the cool air teasing her skin, she'd never felt as free and unfettered, like a woodland sprite dancing in the fields. Of course, she wasn't quite dancing. Yet.

"The danger of discovery, Marianne—it's part and parcel of adventure."

His hands trailed over her stomach and pulled her to mold against him. She could feel his arousal, solid and hot, through his breeches, pressing against her backside. His hands moved upward to cup her breasts and she raised her arm to drape it across his neck. His fingers teased her nipples and they hardened beneath his skillful touch. Her breath grew ragged.

"Do you know what I'm doing now?" His lips whispered against her skin.

"I dearly hope so." The words were little more than a sigh.

He nuzzled the curve between neck and shoulder, then gently pushed her head forward to taste the base of her neck. His hands slipped to her sides and his mouth trailed lower, sliding down her spine in a slow, sensuous journey. She held her breath in an agony of waiting.

She heard him drop to his knees. He kissed the small of her back and his hands danced down her hips and her legs to the tops of her stockings, then around and, slowly, agonizingly slowly, crept upward. She arched her back and folded her arms over her head and stared up at the sky. She was moist with wanting and waiting and couldn't so much as breathe.

His hands reached the curls between her thighs and his fingers parted her flesh.

"Thomas." She shuddered, wondering if indeed she would die with yearning.

His fingers grazed over her and she gasped with the exquisite sensation. His lips caressed her backside and his fingers slipped inside her and out in an ever-increasing rhythm and she moaned with the pleasure of it.

Abruptly, he stopped and stood up, quickly turning her around to face him. Impatiently, he swept champagne, glasses and flowers from the tabletop.

"Thomas, what are you—"

"Quiet." His voice was harsh with desire. He met her lips with his and she wrapped her arms around his neck.

He picked her up and set her on the edge of the table, spreading her legs on either side of him, and lowered her backward until she was lying on the white linen. Like a sacrificial offering to the sky above. Or a feast for the gods of the heavens. Or for a man.

Thomas's lips trailed down her neck to the valley between her breasts. He suckled one, then the next. Her hands grabbed at the linen on the table. His mouth moved lower and caressed the flat of her stomach, and lower still. She tensed with apprehension. Or anticipation.

He pushed her legs wider and dipped his head between them and she stilled.

"Thomas?"

"Do you want to know what I'm doing now?" he growled softly.

"I don't think so."

A moment later, she didn't care. He teased and toyed with lips and teeth and tongue, and delight cascaded through her body. Her world narrowed. She existed only in the feel of his mouth on her. In the throbbing pleasure coursing through her. In the ever-tightening spiral of tension within.

She clutched at his shoulders and without warning her body exploded beneath him in a glorious burst of sheer sensation. Her back arched and she jerked and uttered a short scream.

At once he stood and shucked off his breeches.

She panted for breath. "Thomas, you've never...that is, I never...I mean..."

"I love it when you sputter."

He pulled her upright to balance on the edge of the table and wrapped her legs around him. He cupped her buttocks, pulled her tight against him and entered her in one swift, easy thrust. He filled her and she pushed against him, needing him deeper and deeper within her. They moved together faster and faster and the wrought-iron table rocked beneath them. Once more, delirious anticipation built inside her. Growing, yearning toward release.

Until at last, when she thought she could know no greater joy, no greater delirium, her body again erupted in release. He clamped his mouth over hers and she screamed into it and felt his own release throb through her. His groan echoed deep in her throat.

She buried her head in his chest and clung to him for a long moment. Finally, he lowered her back to lie on the table, braced one hand on either side of her and grinned down at her. She gazed up at him with a satisfied smile and traced a line down the center of his chest.

"That was most intriguing, Thomas. You've never done that before."

"I was saving it." He laughed. Then abruptly his eyes widened. He yelped and jerked back. "Yow!"

She propped herself up on her elbows. "Whatever is the matter now?"

"Bloody hell, I've been stung!" He twisted and turned trying to see over his shoulder.

"Stung?" She sat up. "You mean by a bee?"

"No, by a blasted hawk," he snapped. "Of course by a bee."

"Let me see."

"I will not," he said, his level of indignation far more appropriate to a man in formal attire than one completely naked.

"Come, now, Thomas." She stifled a grin. "Turn around."

"Very well." He huffed and presented his backside to her. She'd never seen it in such excellent light before and she couldn't help but admire the firm, well-shaped buttocks. Not unlike the marble statues at the British Museum. Of course, they weren't marred by a large, red welt.

"Oh dear." She prodded the edge of the reddened area gently and he sucked in a sharp breath. She winced in sympathy. "Sorry. It does look rather nasty."

"It feels rather nasty."

"Still, it doesn't seem to be swelling abnormally. All you need is a good poultice..." She slid off the table and looked around for her clothes.

"Oh?" He turned and raised a brow suggestively. "And just who is going to apply it?"

She picked up her dress and shook her shift free. "I'm certain your valet—"

"If I had a wife," he said pointedly.

"If you had a wife, she would probably be a nice, proper woman who would never agree to an adventure like this. Therefore you would not be in this position in the first place and would never have a bee sting on your bottom." She pulled her shift on over her head.

"What are you doing?" He frowned.

"I'm getting dressed." She slipped into her gown, turned her back to him and lifted her hair off her neck. "Would you help me?"

"I most certainly will not."

She glanced at him over her shoulder. "Why not?"

"The adventure isn't over." He wrapped his arms around her, pulling her back against him. She relaxed in the warmth of his embrace. "I have no intention of letting something as minor as a bee sting deter me and no intention of allowing you to leave."

"You are scarcely able to continue."

"Oh, I daresay I can bravely carry on." He

kissed the side of her neck. "I am wounded, not dead."

"I'm well aware of that." A delightful thrill shivered through her. Perhaps he could carry on.

"However, I have heard of people who have perished from bee stings." His lips murmured against the curve between neck and shoulder, the length of his body pressed against her. "If I were dying, you would have to marry me."

"Would I?"

"Indeed. It would be the least you could do for a dying man."

"However, you are very much alive." And obviously growing more alive by the moment. She laughed. "I suspect you have many years ahead of you."

"With you?" His tone was abruptly serious. The question hung in the air.

Yes, with me. Only and always with me. She wanted to say the words aloud. Longed to say exactly how she felt but the words wouldn't come. If he loved her, she wouldn't hesitate for so much as a moment. But honor alone prompted his insistence on marriage. And she refused to build a lifetime from nothing more than obligation. At once the lightness of her mood vanished.

She ignored his question, untangled herself from his arms and stepped away, doing her best to fasten her dress as securely as possible without assistance. "You're not dying. However, this particular adventure is at an end."

"Untimely," he muttered.

288

"Nonetheless," she picked up her glasses and settled them on her nose, "put on your clothes and direct me out of here."

"If you insist. However, this is not the outcome I had in mind." He heaved a resigned sigh, picked up his shirt and put it on. "For one thing, you haven't agreed to marry me. For another—"

"For another, you have a bit of a problem."

"Aside from the fact that I wish to marry you and you want nothing of the sort?" He huffed in frustration. "I am well aware of that problem."

"You have a more immediate difficulty. How do you plan to get back to the house?"

His brows pulled together quizzically. "The same way I came."

"Let me rephrase that." She tried not to smile. "How will you get your breeches on?"

He stared in confusion then grimaced. "Damnation, it's going to hurt like hell."

"I imagine it will."

He looked more vexed at the idea than anything else but just the thought of his forcing his breeches on over his wounds...she winced. "Perhaps I should go ahead and—"

"Why won't you marry me?" he said abruptly.

"We've been over this again and again. I do not wish to marry and I'm not the type of woman you want."

"I want you."

"And?" She couldn't hide the note of hope in her voice.

"And...what?" Frustration rang in his voice.

Her heart sank and she stared at him for a disbelieving moment. "And nothing, I suppose. Nothing at all." She couldn't bear another minute. She stepped away, turned the key in the lock and drew a deep breath. "It's been great fun, Thomas, and I have quite enjoyed every bit of it, but our adventures together are nearly at an end. I have a bit of money set aside and when the season is over I plan to travel to—"

"Marianne." His shocked voice twisted something inside her. "You can't possibly—"

"I can, Thomas. And I shall. It's what I have always wanted and nothing has happened to change my mind." She drew a deep breath, pulled open the gate and glanced back at him. "I shall miss you."

She stepped into the passageway.

"Surely you're not serious? How can you leave now?" he called after her. "Marianne!"

She ignored him, his voice fading with every step.

Marianne made her way back though the maze with surprisingly few false turns. Her success due perhaps to the fact that her mind was occupied with a far more important puzzle.

It was time to accept the reality of her feelings. Whether she liked it or not, she wanted nothing more than to be Thomas's wife. For that she'd give up the life she'd always dreamed of and give it up gladly. And the longer she was with him, the more difficult it was to refuse him.

She found the entry to maze, poked her

head out cautiously and glanced around. Thomas was right: There was no one about. She drew a relieved breath and started toward the hall.

More and more lately she'd accepted what an odd person she was. No woman in her right mind would wish to live her life without a husband, let alone refuse a man like Thomas over something as minor as love. Besides, for any number of people love came not before marriage but only grew after through years together sharing hardship and delights, triumph and tragedy. And it seemed these days she wanted nothing more than to share those years with Thomas.

But to agree to marry him without his love would be a betrayal of her very soul. Of who she was.

She'd give up her dreams for him and she wanted only one thing in return.

The one thing he apparently could not give her.

Blasted woman. Thomas stared after her. What did she want from him? He was giving her the best adventures he could come up with. Granted, they no doubt paled in comparison with the stories she'd grown up with, but damnation, he was doing his best. Didn't that count for something?

He gingerly pulled on his breeches, yelping now and again with the pain of the fabric rubbing across his tender buttocks. He left the

291

breeches loose, with his long shirt hanging free to cover the fact. It would be dark in another few minutes and he hoped he could make his way back to the house unnoticed.

He'd gone to far greater lengths for her than he'd ever so much as considered with another female. And he'd never before asked any woman to be his wife. But apparently that wasn't enough. He ran his hand through his hair and started to pace. Pain shot through him and he groaned. Apparently pacing was out. He dared not attempt to sit.

Not only were these adventures of hers—he ignored the fact that they'd been his own inventions—causing him a great deal of physical pain, but they didn't seem to be doing any good. Blast it all, he was bruised, battered and now bit. Or more accurately stung, but the result was the same. Adding insult to injury, she now had another man in her life. Perhaps more than one.

And worse, he could no longer even conceive of marrying anyone but her. When he looked at his life stretching out before him, it was with Marianne at the center. By his side, bearing his children, growing old with him.

Admittedly the confidence he'd felt when he'd first begun his efforts to win her hand had faded. But he'd no sooner quit than he'd abandon his poetry. Bad as it may be, he'd never give up writing. And he'd never give up Marianne. Whether she wanted him or not.

It was no longer a question of obligation or honor. It was a quest. A mission, driving and unrelenting. He'd pursue her to the ends of the earth, if need be. For the rest of his days, if he had to. Until she wed him or they were both dead in their graves.

He brushed aside the thought that one more adventure could very well kill him.

Chapter 18

...and I have sensed a change in Lord W's attitude toward me of late. He is much more aloof than usual and his offers of marriage have grown fewer. I am at once relieved and disappointed.

Leopard continues to seek my presence. I believe I have misjudged him based on little more than rumor and gossip. He has done nothing that can be considered improper as of yet and is, in fact, amusing company. He distracts my mind from Lord W and fills my empty hours.

Could he fill my heart as well...?

The Absolutely True Adventures
of a Country Miss in London

The dowager's ball was indeed as grand as Marianne had expected. Impeccably attired gentlemen vied for the attention of elegantly dressed ladies. The scene pulsed with vibrant colors and flashing jewels and there was scarcely room to move. The crush in the Effington Hall ballroom was every bit as great as anything she'd seen in London.

She'd already met any number of Effingtons—two sets of aunts and uncles and numerous cousins. And of course the dowager duchess herself, the matriarch of the Effington family.

At the moment the dowager sat at one end of the ballroom, in a small recessed alcove, engaged in conversation with Aunt Louella as well as Thomas's aunts, the Ladies Edward and William. Yet even now, as Marianne moved effortlessly through the steps of a waltz in Pennington's arms, she had the distinctly uneasy feeling that the dowager was watching her every move.

"You seem somewhat pensive tonight," Pennington said when the music ended. "Is something amiss?"

Yes, my lord, I am in love with a man who does not love me and I'm really rather miserable.

"Not at all," she lied, favoring him with a lighthearted smile. "It is a lovely evening, is it not?"

His smile matched hers. "Well said, my dear, but I don't believe you for a moment."

"It *is* a lovely evening."

"Indeed it is. However, what preys on your mind has nothing whatsoever to do with the merits of the night." He studied her carefully. "This is our second dance together and you have scarce said more than three words to me. It is most unusual."

She laughed. "You have my apologies. However, I would think you'd be delighted to have me keep silent for once."

"Not at all." He chuckled and escorted her off the floor. Pennington flagged a passing waiter, handed her a glass of champagne and took one for himself. "Were you aware that Helmsley cannot keep his eyes off us?" He took a sip. "Or rather, you."

"I hadn't noticed." She had, of course, and had taken great pains not to look at him.

"Indeed," he murmured and she realized he didn't believe her now, either. "Although I have noticed Helmsley's attention is no more apparent than Berkley's."

"Berkley?" She widened her eyes in surprise. She'd danced with him but hadn't noted anything out of the ordinary. Still, she'd been preoccupied.

"What did you say to him?"

"Nothing, really." She took a sip and thought for a moment. "Oh, I did encourage him to give up his mad search for this unknown woman he's apparently quite taken with and turn his attentions towards someone who might return his affections."

"That explains it, then," he said thoughtfully.

She frowned. "Explains what?"

"The look in his eye." Pennington's gaze shifted to a point behind her. "You'll see it yourself in a moment."

She turned to see Berkley approaching with a determined step. Unease stabbed her. "Surely you don't think he... I mean, he doesn't—"

"Surely I do, and I am fairly certain he does," Pennington said wryly.

"Good Lord," she said under her breath and quickly swallowed the last of her wine.

"Pennington." Berkley nodded. "Lady Marianne, I believe this next dance is ours."

"I fear not, my lord," a feminine voice sounded and she turned. Ladies William and Edward stood behind her.

"The next dance is mine." Lady Edward smiled brightly.

"I...er..." Berkley's gaze jumped from Lady Edward to Marianne and back. "Delighted, I'm sure," he said, vainly trying to hide his disappointment. He held out his arm and led Lady Edward to the dance floor.

Pennington snorted. "Well done."

"I am glad to find you so appreciative," Lady William said. "As your next dance belongs to me."

Pennington laughed and swept a bow. "At your service."

Lady William leaned toward Marianne and spoke in a low voice. "Her Grace requests that you join her."

"Why?" Marianne blurted, then cringed.

Lady William laughed softly. "My dear, she is not nearly as formidable as you may think. You have nothing to fear."

"No doubt," Marianne said weakly, her stomach churning with apprehension.

Lady William winked, then turned back to Pennington to accompany him to the floor. Marianne drew a breath for courage and walked the endless distance across the room to the dowager. Or to her fate.

"My dear girl," the dowager said with a smile and waved at the chair beside her. "Please join me."

"Your Grace." Marianne bobbed a quick curtsy and sat in the designated seat, noticing Aunt Louella had vanished.

"I've sent your aunt off to flirt with an old friend of mine."

"I didn't know Aunt Louella knew how to flirt," Marianne said without thinking.

"Nonsense." The dowager chuckled. "All women know how to flirt. Some are better skilled at the art than others, but it's little more than a question of practice. Your aunt is simply out of practice. I suspect it will come back to her.

"Your sisters are quite charming. They seem to be having a lovely time this evening. However"—the dowager nodded at a point across the room—"Thomas does not appear to be enjoying himself."

Marianne followed her gaze. Thomas stood off to one side, a glass in his hand, a non-committal expression on his face. A casual observer would not have noticed anything amiss, but there was a look in his eye that Marianne, and apparently his grandmother, could not fail to see. She sighed to herself.

"Do you plan on marrying my grandson?"

Marianne's gaze jerked to meet hers. "I..." She shook her head firmly. "No."

The dowager frowned. "Why on earth not?"

"I don't wish to marry anyone. Besides, we don't suit." Even as she said the words, she knew they were inadequate.

"Piffle." The old woman dismissed her comment with a wave of her hand.

"Piffle?" It sounded so peculiar coming from someone else.

"My dear young woman, I have been around this earth long enough to know when people suit and when they do not." She considered Marianne for a long moment as if determining just how suitable a match she was, and Marianne resisted the urge to squirm in her seat. "Did you know he writes poetry?"

"Yes," Marianne said cautiously.

"Not many do. It is a closely guarded secret. I am surprised and rather pleased that he has shared it with you." The dowager studied her thoughtfully then sighed. "However, I suppose that explains why you would prefer not to marry him. A man who writes that poorly..." She shook her head.

Marianne stared, shocked. "How can you say such a thing?"

"I can say it because it's true. I love the boy dearly, but..." She leaned toward Marianne. "Have you actually read his work?"

"I have."

"Carefully? Each and every word?"

Marianne nodded. "Of course."

"It reeks." The dowager pressed her lips together and settled back in her chair.

"It does not." Indignation swelled within her. "Admittedly, it needs some work. Polishing, perhaps—"

"Polishing?" The elderly woman snorted.

"But with a bit of effort it could be improved and really become—"

"Quite, quite awful."

"Not at all." How could the lady say such a thing about her own grandson? "I grant you the words are not particularly well chosen on occasion, nor do they always rhyme, and indeed, now and again, he has a tendency to make one up, but they are, well..." She searched for the right words. "Fervent. Intense. Passionate.

"And I think they're wonderful," she said staunchly. "Oh, not wonderful poetry, of course, but wonderful... I don't know. Expressions, I suppose, of who he is deep inside. His soul is in his poems. They *are* who he is."

"Who he is?" The dowager frowned in a skeptical manner. "He knows perfectly well who is. He is Thomas Effington, the Marquess of Helmsley, and one day, God willing, he'll be the ninth Duke of Roxborough."

"No, that's what he is. Not *who* he is."

"Then who is he, my dear?"

"He's a man who writes terribly bad poetry and, even though he knows it's bad, refuses to stop because of the pleasure he takes from it." The words poured out. "He's a man who hates to admit he's wrong even when he knows full well he is. He is funny when he wants to be and funnier when he doesn't. He has a quaint stuffy streak when he's trying to be proper and an annoying sense of honor when it suits his purposes. He's quite stubborn and wants what he wants when he wants it. And..."

A knowing smile quirked the corners of the old woman's mouth. "And you are in love with him."

"I'm not." Marianne met the dowager's gaze and helplessness washed through her. "I am."

"Then marry him. I know he wishes to marry you."

Marianne shook her head. "For all the wrong reasons."

"Are you so certain? Men never know their own minds. It's precisely why we marry them."

"I am sure." She hadn't spoken to anyone about Thomas or her feelings, and the kindness in his grandmother's voice threatened to be her undoing. She ignored the ache in the back of her throat and pulled a steadying breath. "He has not said anything to indicate otherwise."

"But what of his actions? Haven't they proved something?"

"Only that he is determined to get his own way." *And so am I.* "Nothing that he has done has dissuaded me from continuing with my plans for my life."

"Ah, yes, a life in pursuit of adventures." The dowager's blue eyes twinkled.

"How did you know that?"

She laid a hand on the younger woman's arm. "My dear Marianne, has no one told you? I know everything."

Marianne swallowed hard. "Everything?"

"Everything I need to know." She smiled in a smug manner and folded her hands in her lap. "And any number of things that are none of my business whatsoever."

"Oh, dear," Marianne murmured, trying not to wince at the thought of precisely what the dowager could know.

"I must confess, I do rather admire you."

"You do?" Marianne stared. "Why?"

"You have the gift of intelligence and a strength of purpose rare in one so young. You will make an excellent duchess one day."

"Your Grace, I—"

The lady quieted her with a wave and nodded at her grandson. "Thomas, too, has never allowed obstacles to deter him from his chosen path."

Marianne's gaze slid to Thomas. "He is determined."

"As are you." His grandmother chuckled. "You make an interesting pair." She paused, then leaned forward. "May I give you some advice?"

"Please do." Marianne smiled. "I could certainly use it."

"Adventure, my dear, is as much a state of mind as anything else. One can travel the world and never find the excitement to be found within arm's reach.

"Remain true to yourself, but understand happiness may not always be found in the plans we have laid out for ourselves but rather in the unforeseen turns life take us. Do not close your mind, or your heart, to the unexpected twists of life. It is those unsuspected paths that could well lead to the greatest adventures of all." She settled back in her chair. "There, now, wasn't that wise?"

Marianne laughed. "Indeed it was."

"I thought it would be. And now, if you would be so kind as to do me a favor?"

"Of course. Anything."

"Anything?" The dowager raised a brow. "Including marrying my grandson?"

"Your Grace, I—"

"Never mind." She waved away Marianne's protest. "That was not entirely fair of me, although I have never hesitated to disregard fairness when it serves my purposes. And I, too, ignore obstacles in my way. It is a family trait. I will simply ask that you consider his suit with an eye as much toward what he cannot bring himself to say as what he can. And one more thing."

"Yes?"

"Do try, dear girl, to keep him out of the ivy. It quite upsets the gardeners."

"It's about time you came to chat with me." His grandmother gazed up at him with a twinkle in her eye that belied the chastising note in her voice.

"I did not want to intrude." Thomas leaned forward and brushed a kiss on her cheek. "I do hope you were telling Lady Marianne what a good catch I am."

"My lord," Marianne said, a warning in her voice.

"I have been doing nothing of the sort," the dowager said primly. "I have been telling her what a scandalous, stubborn scoundrel you are."

He raised a brow. "That should further my cause."

"I had hoped she would take pity on you, or at the very least see you as ripe for reforming and rise to the challenge."

"Your Grace—" Marianne started.

Thomas chuckled. "And has it worked?"

His grandmother sighed. "I fear not."

"Pity." He studied Marianne thoughtfully. "I had thought to announce my betrothal tonight."

"Did you? To whom?" Marianne asked in a casual manner.

"To the only woman to whom I have ever issued a proposal."

"You wouldn't dare." Her voice was cool in contrast with the spark in her eyes.

"I would indeed." He met her gaze squarely but directed his words to his grandmother. "She would be hard-pressed to cry off after a public announcement. While she is not concerned about gossip in regards to herself, such an incident would reflect poorly on her sisters, and I suspect she would prefer to avoid that."

Disbelief washed across Marianne's face, followed by anger. She rose to her feet. "Why, you arrogant, pompous—"

"I daresay, Thomas," the dowager interrupted, "that is perhaps not the best idea you've had today."

He glanced at his grandmother. "Do you have a better idea?"

"Yes. Take her off and waltz with her." The dowager waved at the dance floor. "Or better yet, take her into the garden and convince her that there is much to be said for an arrogant, pompous ass if he is the right arrogant, pompous ass."

"Your Grace, I'd really rather—"

"Excellent suggestion, Grandmother." He gripped Marianne's elbow and started toward the terrace, ignoring the stiffness and twinges of pain that accompanied every step.

"The mazes are even lovelier at night..." The dowager's voice trailed after them.

"What do you think you're doing?" Marianne said through clenched teeth.

"Smile, my dear. We wouldn't want to attract attention." Thomas steered her through the open doors.

"Very well." A forced smile lifted her lips. "I'm smiling. Now, what are you doing?"

"Taking my grandmother's advice." They crossed the terrace, down the steps to the path to the garden. He stopped at the fountain and released her. "This should do."

"Well?" She folded her arms over her chest. "What do you have to say?"

"Who is he?"

She frowned in confusion. "Who is who?"

"It's Pennington, isn't it?"

"What's Pennington?"

"Or is it Berkley?"

She glared. "What are you talking about?"

"The other man in your life!"

"What other man?" she said slowly.

He stepped toward her. "I know, Marianne."

"You know what?" Her voice was cautious.

He gritted his teeth. "I know you have another suitor."

She backed away. "What makes you think so?"

He hesitated. He could tell her he knew all about her *Country Miss* adventures and the suitor she'd written into her stories. But that secret knowledge gave him the least bit of an upper hand, and with Marianne, he needed every advantage. At least for now. "It scarcely matters how I know, but I do. Now, who is he?"

She stared at him for a long moment, then a pleased grin spread across her face. "You're jealous."

"I am not," he snapped.

She laughed. "You are. How delightful."

"Delightful?" He pulled his brows together and scowled. "It's anything but delightful. I will not have the woman I intend to marry courted by another man. Now tell me who it is."

She hesitated, then shook her head. "No."

The dim hope in the back of his mind that

perhaps she had invented this new suitor vanished with her words. Anger and the oddest touch of pain surged through him.

"Why do you want to know, anyway?"

Why did he want to know? Wasn't it enough to know there was someone else? No. He had to know who. He clenched his fists at his side. "I want to know who my competition is."

"Competition? There is no competition. I am not some sort of prize you can win as easily as you won the Ride today."

"I did do a fine job." He grinned in spite of himself. "But it certainly wasn't easy." He narrowed his eyes. "Nor is this. Now, who is he?"

"I shan't tell you." She turned and started around the perimeter of the fountain. "It's really none of your business."

"It is my business." He fought to keep his voice under control. "You are my business."

"Hah! I am your obligation." She fairly spat the words at him.

"Do you really think so?" An idea took shape in the back of his mind.

"What else am I to think?"

An idea that probably was as ill-conceived as anything else when it came to Marianne. "Very well."

She stared suspiciously. "Very well what?"

"I have done all in my power to discharge that obligation and I shall do no more."

"What are you saying?"

"It's simple, my dear. I told you once I know precisely when to walk away from a game. I rescind my offer of marriage."

"Thomas!" Shock colored her face. "I don't...you can't..."

"You are sputtering, Marianne." He shook his head. "And once again I was wrong and you were right: It's not at all charming."

"I'm just trying to find the right words." She paused.

Her gaze met his and they stared at each other for an endless moment. He would have given his entire fortune to know exactly what she was thinking.

She squared her shoulders. "If that's what you want."

"It isn't at all what I want. However, it is what you want, isn't it? What you have always wanted?" He circled the fountain.

"Yes, of course."

"Then I concede defeat."

"Good."

He jerked her into his arms. "However, there is no reason why we cannot continue to have our private adventures."

"None at all." She stared up at him, challenge in her eyes.

"Although now that I am no longer trying to convince you to marry me, I will no longer risk my neck in my attempt to emulate the romantic heroes in your books."

"Is that what you were doing?" she said under her breath.

"For whatever good it did me, yes." He brushed his lips across hers. "I nearly killed myself for you."

"That would indeed have been a shame."

She slid her arms around his neck. "Although I do appreciate the effort." She brought her lips back to his and he savored the feel of her mouth on his and her body molded against him.

He pulled away and stared down at her. "When the time comes, I shall miss you."

Her gaze searched his face. "Yes, well..."

He tightened his grasp and kissed her again. A no-nonsense kiss with all the skill he possessed and all the passion she alone could trigger in him. At long last he drew back and stared into her brown eyes, glazed with desire and perhaps a bit of confusion. Good. He wanted her confused and off balance. It was her turn. He'd wager no other man could leave her in such a state. And regardless of what he said aloud, he'd allow no other man to try. "Now, then, we should return to the ball."

"Of course," she murmured.

He escorted her back inside and made it a point to stay by her side for the remainder of the evening. Let Pennington and Berkley or whoever else might be in her life try to get close to her. Not tonight. And not ever.

Marianne was remarkably quiet. Oh, she smiled politely and made idle conversation, but if he knew nothing else about her, he knew her well enough to know when there was something on her mind. And with luck, that something was him. It was all he could do not to chortle with delight.

She could make all the plans she wanted for

her future, but her future would be with him and no one else. He had no intention of allowing her to go off in search of adventure. No intention of allowing her out of his life.

And no intention of allowing any other man to take his place.

The evening stretched on endlessly and Marianne counted the minutes until she could escape. She was hard-pressed to appear light-hearted, but she refused to let anyone, particularly Thomas, know of the ache that had settled around her heart.

She should be pleased. After all, she'd gotten exactly what she wanted. Or perhaps, an annoying voice muttered in the back of her head, it was what she deserved.

Thomas was charming and attentive and never let her out of his sight. Even during those few dances she'd shared with someone else, she was all too aware of his gaze on her every minute. Neither Pennington nor Berkley approached her. She wondered if Thomas had said something or simply made it clear with his unspoken vigilance that their attentions were not welcome tonight.

Not that she really cared. His jealousy was gratifying, yet it was born of a sense of possession no greater than if she'd been a prime bit of cattle. If he truly cared for her, she would have relished evoking such a response in him. As it was, it simply didn't signify.

She moved through the remainder of the

evening as if in a waking dream. Why was she so overset about all this? Shouldn't she be relieved that Thomas was abandoning his quest for her hand? She'd never been interested in marriage.

Until she fell in love.

Had she, somewhere in the shadows of her mind or the recesses of her heart, been at least a tiny bit confident that he shared her feelings? Or perhaps it was nothing more than hope. A hope as unrealistic as any fiction she'd ever read. And what had come of it? Nothing save a pain far more real than anything she could have imagined.

She was getting exactly what she wanted. Then why was she so very unhappy?

Chapter 19

...so am I indeed a fool, dear cousin? More and more, I enjoy Leopard's flirtatious manner. And worse, respond in kind.

Still, he is not the kind of man considered fit to share the company of respectable, unmarried women. While I have seen nothing to bear out his reputation, there is, on occasion, a gleam in his eye that gives me pause. Perhaps it would be wise to follow the whispers of advice directed toward me and avoid him. Yet I have not been wise up till now, and for the moment I will do nothing to dissuade him.

Where is the harm? He could not possibly ruin my life more than I have done so already....

The Absolutely True Adventures
of a Country Miss in London

Cadwallender was his last resort. Thomas hated having to ask the printer for help almost as much as he hated having to admit to the man his failure with Marianne.

It had been three weeks since his grandmother's house party and Thomas still had no idea who the mysterious suitor in Marianne's life was.

Both Pennington and Berkley paid calls, more often than not together. Thomas made certain Marianne was never alone with either, and as far as he could determine, she was never really alone at all. But she was a clever bit of baggage and he couldn't be with her every minute of every day, although he was doing his best.

Becky and Jocelyn reported nothing untoward, either. He wasn't sure he could entirely trust them, but they were the only allies he had. They claimed Marianne refused to discuss the suitor she wrote about. Leopard, she'd called him in her stories. An absurd name and obviously made up.

Still, regardless of what his name was, he was a dashing, romantic figure and, according to the *Adventures,* quite compelling and possibly even dangerous. Not that Thomas believed everything she wrote. He knew better than that. But not knowing the suitor's identity was driving Thomas mad. He was no closer to discovering the identity of this Leopard than he was to wedding Marianne.

He'd been confident Marianne would change her mind about marriage when it was no longer offered. It was human nature to disdain what was within reach and long for what one couldn't have. She should be falling into his arms begging for him to make an honest woman of her by now.

Instead, whenever the subject came up—and he made certain it was brought up as often as possible—she dismissed it without hesitation.

Blasted woman.

He pushed open Cadwallender's door, bracing himself for the fumes of oil and ink that assailed his nostrils.

"Good day, my lord." Cadwallender strode toward him, wiping his hands on a greasy cloth.

"Cadwallender." Thomas nodded in greeting and glanced at the cloth in his hand. "Problems?"

"Always." The printer laughed and jerked his head toward the press. "She's a temperamental witch."

"Aren't they all," Thomas muttered. The

312

gnome poked his head out from behind the machine and eyed him with suspicion. "Could we speak in your office?"

Cadwallender led him toward the small room in the back of the shop and waved for Thomas to go ahead and take a seat. "What brings you here today?" The printer raised a curious brow. "Is there some problem with our arrangement? Your solicitor assured me—"

"No, nothing of the kind," Thomas said quickly. "In that, if in no other aspect of my life, all is proceeding smoothly."

"I see." Cadwallender settled on the edge of the desk. "Then it must be the independent Miss Smythe who brings you here." He leaned forward, opened a deep, bottom drawer and pulled out a bottle. "It's probably not the quality you're used to—"

"Quality is relative," Thomas said wryly. "There are moments when quantity alone matters."

Cadwallender chuckled and fished around in the drawer, withdrawing two mismatched, and not overly clean, glasses. He poured a hefty portion in one, handed it to Thomas and filled his own glass.

Thomas took a cautious sip and glanced up in surprise. "Damned good whiskey, Cadwallender."

Cadwallender raised his glass. "If one is going to have a vice, one should enjoy it."

A companionable silence, the kind known only by men who share, however briefly, the appreciation of fine spirits or excellent horse-flesh or a pretty girl, fell between them.

"I gather from your expression and your presence that you are no closer to matrimony today than a month ago," Cadwallender said.

Thomas sighed. "You read her bloody stories. What do you think?"

"I have no idea what to think. They've always had an element of dangerous excitement to them. You know, the sweet innocent and the depraved lord—"

"Depraved." Thomas snorted in disdain.

"—but in recent weeks they seem to have a touch of something else. They're a bit wistful, I think, or perhaps resigned." He paused and studied Thomas. "The curious thing is what I'm hearing from readers."

"Oh?"

"They've begun pulling for Lord W."

"Really?" Thomas said with surprise. "Why?"

Cadwallender shrugged. "I'm not entirely sure. I suspect it might be because this new suitor she's introduced—"

"Leopard," Thomas said darkly. "Ridiculous name."

"Indeed." Cadwallender cleared his throat. "Regardless, he seems like much more of a scoundrel than Lord W. A man who will truly ruin the girl's life. Lord W, on the other hand, is brooding and a bit melancholy, almost a tragic figure. The kind of man who needs a good woman to save him from himself. Readers, particularly female readers, love men like that."

Thomas eyed him over the rim of his glass. "I am neither brooding nor melancholy."

"No doubt. However, the depiction of Lord W is as much fantasy as fact. It's not absolutely true, is it?"

"Hardly."

"Then perhaps Leopard is not absolutely true, either," Cadwallender said slowly.

"True enough to drive me insane." Thomas drew a deep swallow and savored the taste of the whiskey in the back of his throat. "How can I compete with a man I know nothing about save what she chooses to write?"

"You know, my lord, the public is quite taken with the *Country Miss* adventures." Cadwallender chose his words with care. "But readers are fickle and what they like one day does not necessarily keep their interest the next. I have suggested to Miss Smythe she consider the benefits of a good murder to spur readership."

"I suppose I can be grateful, then, that she did not take such a suggestion to heart." Thomas shook his head. "Given her attitude toward me on occasion, Lord W would no doubt be dead by now."

"Barring that"—Cadwallender drew a deep breath—"strictly to keep up interest, you understand, it was my idea to add another suitor to the stories."

"*Your* idea?" Thomas narrowed his eyes. "What are you saying?"

"I..." Cadwallender grinned. "There is no other man."

"No other man?" It took a moment for Cadwallender's words to sink in.

"None at all."

"Then...there is no Leopard?"

"Not on the streets of London." The printer chuckled. "Actually, I suggested Lion or Tiger. Leopard was her idea." He took a sip. "It is a wonderful name, though. Dark and seductive. Readers love it."

"No Leopard," Thomas said slowly. There was no other man vying for Marianne's affections? Relief rushed through him, followed at once by annoyance. "Bloody hell."

"I thought you'd be pleased." Cadwallender paused. "I do hope this little deception of mine is not going to affect our arrangement."

"It isn't. That's business and I can't fault you for wanting to increase business. And yes, I am pleased." He drained the last of his whiskey. "Which does not negate the fact that I have been going to extreme efforts to discover the identity of this nonexistent suitor. She's had me running around like a man possessed, convinced I was about to lose her to some overly romantic rogue. It has distracted me from my efforts to win her hand and made me crazed in the process."

"What are you going to do?"

"I suppose the intelligent course of action would be to confront her and tell her I know she's this country miss." Thomas blew a long breath. "Yet knowing Miss Smythe, I cannot believe that is the best route to take. She is the most obstinate woman I have ever met and she's more than likely to bolt if I am not careful."

Thomas got to his feet and paced the small room. "She is a unique woman who refuses to see the world as it is and insists on viewing life as an adventure in a book. It is time she realizes the difference between what is real and what is fiction. She needs to be taught a lesson."

"What kind of lesson?"

"A lesson about what happens when you twist people's lives to suit your own purposes as she has twisted mine. A lesson about the difference between storybook tales and flesh-and-blood life and precisely what can happen when such stories come true." An idea flashed through his mind. "A lesson she will never forget."

Cadwallender grimaced. "Are you sure that's wise?"

"Probably not." Thomas held out his glass and the other man refilled it. "But it would serve her right."

"Pardon me for pointing out the obvious," Cadwallender said slowly, "but if your lesson miscarries, won't your situation in regard to the young woman be even more precarious than it is now?"

"I could scarcely be worse off." Thomas shrugged and pulled a deep swallow. "And should I succeed..."

"Here's to success, then." Cadwallender raised his glass.

"To success." Thomas clinked his glass

with the printer's. "And to hoping that for once my plans in regards to Miss Smythe actually bear fruit."

Marianne set her pen down, pushed back from the desk in her room and sighed. She couldn't concentrate on exciting adventures and mysterious men when only one man lingered in her mind.

Thomas.

He'd been unusually secretive all day. When he'd returned home briefly from an errand this morning, Marianne had caught his eye and noticed a gleam of triumph that did not bode well.

He'd left the house again shortly thereafter. For the first time since their return from the country, he was not plaguing her with his constant company. Company admittedly she quite enjoyed. However, his lack of attention today was extremely disquieting. What was the man up to?

She'd shared his bed more often than not in these past weeks and still marveled that they'd managed to keep the rest of the household from knowing of their liaison. If anyone, especially Aunt Louella, discovered their true relationship, or worse, she became pregnant, she'd be forced into a loveless union.

Thomas was true to his word and no longer pressed her for marriage, although the topic did rear its head on a regular basis. No, now the man was actually helping her plan her travel with advice on routes and passages.

Oddly, though, she no longer looked forward with the same enthusiasm to the future she had dreamed of. As the time drew closer to leave, the practicalities of the life she'd always wanted grew daunting. More and more she realized Berkley was right: The path she'd chosen for herself was not an easy one. For a woman alone it might well be impossible. It was disheartening to realize her dreams might not be as fulfilling as she'd always assumed. And worse to accept the real possibility that the years ahead might be filled less with adventure and more with loneliness. How could she live the rest of her days without Thomas?

It would be so very easy to tell him she had changed her mind about marriage. Regardless of the retraction of his proposal, she suspected, or perhaps simply hoped, he would still be amenable to wedding her. Yet, had anything really changed in that regard?

She heaved a heartfelt sigh. No, nothing had changed at all. She loved him. He felt only friendship and duty toward her. Up till now, she'd viewed affairs of love in her books with a practical eye. The emotion was little more than a pleasant fiction and had nothing to do with reality. In truth, love was not pleasant at all.

A knock sounded at the door and a maid she'd never seen before popped her head in. "My lady, you have a caller."

Marianne hesitated. Aunt Louella and her sisters had gone to the park and Thomas had vanished. It would be the height of impropriety to see whoever it was alone. "Who is it?"

"He didn't give his name, but he's waiting in the parlor." The girl grinned. "And he's quite dashing, my lady."

"Strange. But I suppose I should at least see him." Marianne smiled. "I'll be right down."

She got to her feet and headed downstairs. Whoever it was, she was in no mood for idle pleasantries. She'd spend a few brief moments with him and send him on his way.

She plastered a pleasant smile on her face and stepped into the parlor. It was empty.

Where on earth did the man go? She retraced her steps and noticed the doors leading into the library were open. She frowned. How annoying of him not to stay put.

She straightened her shoulders, smiled once more and walked into the library.

A stranger stood by the duke's desk paging through a book and looked up at her approach.

"Lady Marianne Shelton, I presume?" He closed the book and tossed it on the desk.

"Yes," she said cautiously and stepped farther into the room. "You have the advantage of me, my lord. I don't believe we've met."

"Ah, but the rest of the world is certain we have." He moved to her, took her hand and brought it to his lips. "I am Lord Beaumont."

"I'm honored, my lord," she said carefully. The maid was right. He was exceedingly handsome. Tall, with hair that was nearly black and eyes almost as dark. Eyes that gleamed dangerously. Unease trickled through her.

"But perhaps you know me better by another name."

"Oh?" She was certain she'd never so much as seen him. She would definitely remember a man who looked like this.

"Indeed. My friends have long referred to me as"—he paused and trapped her gaze with his—"Leopard."

Chapter 20

...still I wonder if I have made a grave mistake. The question preys on my mind. Regardless of his feelings, should I indeed have accepted Lord W's offer of marriage?

And is it now too late?

I must confess, the dangerous nature of Leopard is no longer as exciting as it once was. In truth, he frightens me, and I fear I have encouraged him far too much....

The Absolutely True Adventures
of a Country Miss in London

"What?" Shock swept through her and she snatched her hand away. "Who?"

"Leopard." He wagged his brows in a decidedly wicked manner.

"But I made you up," Marianne blurted.

"Ah-ha." He grinned triumphantly. "Then you are indeed the country miss."

"I'm..." How could she deny it? This man, whoever he was, obviously knew her secret. "How did you—"

"Find you?" He shrugged. "It was not difficult, for a man of my abilities."

"Your abilities?" Her stomach lurched. "What abilities are those?"

"Come, now, my dear, you detailed them yourself in your stories." He stepped closer. "Like my namesake, I am cunning and clever and shrewd." He yanked her into his arms and bent her backward. She stared up into deep, glittering eyes. "And irresistible."

She gasped. "But you're not real!"

"I assure you," his voice was sultry and a shiver of fear raced up her spine, "I am very real." He lowered his lips to hers.

She shrieked and struggled out of his grasp, scrambling across the room. "Who are you?"

"I told you." He huffed in annoyance. "I am Leopard."

"You can't be." She shook her head in disbelief. "You don't even look like a leopard."

"Well, you don't especially look like a country miss." He frowned. "How should I look?"

"I don't know." She waved vaguely. "More like a cat, I should think. Wiry and definitely leaner."

He looked down at himself. "You think I'm heavy?"

"I didn't say that." She huffed. He did indeed appear quite fit. "I just don't think you look much like a leopard. You look more like a..." She said the first thing that popped into her head. "A badger."

"A badger?" He glared. "I hardly think so. Short, fat, bothersome little beasts. I'm scarcely the stuff badgers are made of. A fox, perhaps, I could live with, but a badger—"

"Yes, well, possibly I misspoke. It was simply the first thing that came to mind."

"A badger," he muttered. "Insults on top of everything else."

"Forgive me for insulting you." Indignation surged through her. "I'm a bit flustered at meeting a man I invented."

"I can well imagine. I accept your apology." He studied her in a lofty manner. "Perhaps if you would stop screeching and took a deep breath—"

"I am not screeching!" Although, in fact, she was. Still, if any situation called for screeching, this was definitely it.

"Screeching will not help."

"I daresay it won't hurt." She planted her hands on her hips and glared. "And I'll thank you not to tell me what will or will not help. You certainly have a great deal of nerve, for a man who doesn't exist."

"Ah, compliments at last." He swept a dramatic bow. "I am nothing more than the man you so perfectly described."

"Created, not described."

"Described," he said firmly.

"You"—she aimed an accusing finger—"are nothing more than a figment of my imagination. A creatively turned phrase. A sentence well written."

"Extremely well written." He spread his arms wide in an expansive gesture. "You captured me perfectly."

She shook her head. "I did not capture you at all."

"Oh, but you did, my lady." He moved toward her.

She moved back and thrust out her hands. "Don't come near me."

"I simply want to prove to you how very real I am. That I am, in fact, flesh and blood."

"It's not necessary."

"Oh, but indeed it is." He took another step and again she stepped back. "In spite of the proof of your own eyes, you question my very existence." He clapped his hand over his heart. "You wound me deeply."

She darted out of his reach to put the solid protection of the desk between them and grabbed the book he'd been looking at, substantial enough to serve her purposes. She hefted it in both hands. "Not as deeply as I shall if you come any closer."

He shrugged as if it didn't matter and strolled toward the cabinet where the brandy was kept.

"Given that you are flesh and blood..."

He raised a brow. She could scarcely deny

it at this point. Whoever he was, he was very real.

"What are you doing here?" she said in the most demanding manner she could muster. "What do you want?"

"A brandy, at the moment, I should think." He opened the cabinet doors and poured a glass. "Would you care for some?"

"No," she snapped. The last thing she needed was the too-pleasant and overly relaxed feeling brandy gave her. She suspected with Leopard—and for the first time she acknowledged how silly a name that was—she needed to be fully alert. "I don't mean what do you want right now, I mean what do you want here!"

He glanced at her; his voice was mild. "You are screeching again."

She gripped the book tighter and forced a calm note to her voice. "Forgive me. Now, then... Lord Beaumont, was it?"

"Yes, but you may call me Leopard."

"I most certainly will not!" She absolutely refused to compound the bizarre dilemma facing her with too much familiarity. "How on earth did you get such an absurd name, anyway?"

"I was a spy," he said in an offhand manner. "We all might well be speaking French today were it not for the information I supplied Wellington."

"A spy?" She gasped and circled the desk, keeping the book in hand just in case. He did indeed look exactly like she'd always imagined a spy to look. Dark and handsome, with an amused twinkle in his eye. Far too amused. "I don't believe you."

He sipped his brandy. "I suspected you wouldn't."

"And I don't believe that's your name, either."

"Believe as you will." He shrugged. "The fact remains that it is indeed my name and you have used it in your stories." He studied her over the rim of his glass. "In truth, you have used me."

"I never intended—"

"Regardless of your intentions, you have portrayed me in a less-than-favorable light."

"I said you were clever," she said uneasily.

"You have also depicted me as a scoundrel. A despoiler of innocents." He shook his head in a mournful manner. "It is not a pretty picture."

"I never imagined—"

"It is your imagining that has quite ruined my reputation." He swallowed the last of his brandy and set down the glass.

"Your reputation?"

"Indeed. You see, by this point I should have seduced the country miss. However, in your *Adventures* I have failed to do so. It is not what people expect of me. My reputation is—"

"Ruined." She swallowed hard. "But you said yourself I painted you as a despoiler of innocents."

He waved off her objection. "And that was

entirely too much. You should be ashamed of yourself."

"Well, I suppose—"

"However, my dear, according to your stories"—he grinned wickedly—"you are no innocent. And I should have succeeded with you long ago. It's what people expect of me." He stepped closer. "And I have come to rectify the matter."

"Rectify the matter?" Her voice rose. "Exactly how do you plan to rectify the matter?"

"It's not what I shall do, but rather what we shall do."

"We?" Good Lord, what was he saying?

"Since you have seen fit to tell the world of our relationship—"

"We have no relationship!"

"Not in reality, perhaps, but on paper. And, my dear young woman, people always believe what they read in the papers."

He moved toward her. She stepped to the side. He countered her move, stalking her like a jungle beast. God help her, like a leopard.

"I simply want in truth what everyone believes we already have."

She dove for the door, but he blocked her way, pulling her hard against him and holding her wrist behind her back with one hand. The book fell from her grasp.

"Unhand me at once," she demanded, her voice much shakier than she would have liked.

"Never." He grinned down at her. "You were far too difficult to capture."

She struggled against him, panic rising within her. "Let me go!"

"I don't think so. However, you should probably scream now." Laughter flashed in his eyes.

"Should I?" Her gaze frantically searched the room for a weapon to use against him. Not that she could reach anything at the moment. "Why?"

"Aside from the fact that there are few things more exciting than a screaming woman?"

"Yes!"

"Because I am planning on living up to the reputation you provided me with."

"Really?" Abruptly, and perhaps unwisely, her fear subsided, replaced by curiosity. This stranger might well be irritating, but was he indeed dangerous? Wouldn't a truly dangerous man want to keep her from screaming, not encourage it? She stopped struggling and stared at him. "How?"

"I am going to spirit you away and have my way with you."

"That sounds like something you'd read in a book." She studied him suspiciously. This was getting odder by the moment.

"Yes, well, I'm usually more original than that," he said under his breath. "Now, then, should you scream, I'm sure someone would come to your rescue."

"Do I need rescuing then? You scarcely seem to be making much progress." Oh certainly he had her trapped in his arms, but it was going to be damned difficult to get her out of the house this way. "You don't do this kind of thing often, do you?"

"Are you going to scream or not?" He blew a frustrated breath.

"No. I rather think *you* should do that." She summoned all her strength, wrenched free of his grasp and scooped up the book from the floor. Without hesitation, she gripped it in both hands and swung it as hard as she could against his midsection.

His loud *oof* echoed in the room. It wasn't exactly a scream, but by God, he was right. It was exciting. He grasped his stomach and doubled over.

"Release her at once, you brute!" Thomas's voice thundered from the doorway.

Marianne whirled around. Thomas strode toward them, a picture of gallant indignation. Her heart skipped a beat at the sight.

"I *have* released her." Leopard gasped and straightened slowly, a grimace of pain on his face. He pressed his hands against his stomach and glared at her. "You hit me!"

"Of course I hit you." She folded her arms over her chest. "What did you expect me to do?"

"I didn't expect you to hit me," he snapped. "Damned inconsiderate of you."

Something about his words struck a familiar chord, but she discarded it for the moment. "You threatened to have your way with me."

Thomas sucked in a sharp breath. "How dare you!"

"I'm wondering that myself," Leopard muttered.

"You have impugned the honor of the woman I love." Thomas drew himself up and stepped to Leopard. "I demand satisfaction."

The woman I love?

"I thought you would," Leopard said.

He loved her?

The two men stood toe to toe, nose to nose.

"Pistols, then," Leopard said. "At dawn."

"This cannot wait until dawn." Thomas's voice rang in the room. "Dusk. Today."

"Dusk it is." Leopard nodded. "Newcombe's Hill should serve our purposes."

"A duel?" Marianne's heart leapt. "Are you talking about a duel?"

"Indeed we are." Thomas's gaze never left Leopard.

"You cannot be serious." She looked from one man to the other. "Duels are illegal."

"Affairs of honor supersede the laws of man." Thomas's tone was lofty. "I shall see you at dusk." He stepped away from Leopard and gestured toward the door. "Now get out."

"Gladly." Leopard turned to Marianne and bowed. "And I shall see you again."

"Not while there is breath left in my body." Thomas's declaration sent a shiver of fear up her spine.

"That is precisely the idea." Leopard nodded and strode from the room.

"Thomas." At once she was in his arms. "You can't do this. You'll be killed."

"Hardly, my dear." He gazed down at her with a slight smile. "I have no doubt of my success."

"But even if you win..." Her voice caught.

"It could mean prison, or worse, I shall have to leave the country."

A vice tightened around her chest. "I shall go with you."

"I cannot allow that." Sadness colored his voice. "Regardless of your desire for adventure, exile is not the life I would wish for you."

"But I am to blame for this." It was indeed her fault. If she hadn't foolishly insisted on pursuing the future she wanted, she wouldn't have written the *Country Miss* stories for funding. And would never have provoked a man as dangerous as Leopard, silly name or not. And Thomas's very life would not now be at risk.

"Blame scarcely matters at the moment. What is done is done." He tilted her head back and met her lips with his in a kiss gentle and sweet and...final.

"Thomas." His name was little more than a cry or a prayer on her lips.

He released her and stepped away. "I must go now. There are a but a few hours until dusk and there are arrangements to be made."

"Thomas, don't...." The words choked in her throat.

"I must." He took her hands and brought them to his lips. His gaze never left hers. "Regardless of what the future holds, you will remain in my heart forever." He nodded, turned and strode from the room, never looking back.

Tears stung her eyes. This was like any story of star-crossed love she'd ever read. But it was real and the consequences would be devastating. Whatever happened, Thomas's life was ruined. She'd destroyed it with her foolish desire for adventure.

She sniffed back her tears. She had to stop him. She couldn't allow such a sacrifice from the man she loved.

The man who loved her.

She sucked in a sharp breath. He'd said it aloud and possibly didn't even realize he'd done so. He loved her, and it might well be too late. If she'd married him when she'd had the chance...

What was she going to do? How could she save him?

She paced the room and tried to think. She needed help. Her sisters would be of no use. Besides, this situation was fraught with potential scandal and it was best to keep them out of it altogether.

Pennington would help. He was, after all, Thomas's friend. Surely he'd know what to do. How to stop this madness. She'd send him a note at once.

She stepped to the desk and pulled open the drawer, looking for paper. She brushed aside a set of legal documents. A name on the papers stared up at her.

Ephraim Cadwallender?

A knock sounded at the open door.

"My lady." The butler stood in the doorway. "You have two more callers."

"Tell them I can't be bothered at the moment." She picked up the documents. What kind of dealings could Thomas have with Mr. Cadwallender?

"Nonsense." Pennington's voice sounded in the foyer. "She will see us." He brushed past the butler, followed closely by Berkley.

"My lord," Marianne said with relief and dropped the documents on the desk. She stepped toward him. "I cannot tell you how glad I am to see you. I need your help desperately."

"Do you?" Pennington's brow raised. "First we have a matter of some importance to discuss."

"It can't possibly be more urgent...." The look on their faces pulled her up short. "What on earth is the matter?"

Pennington and Berkley traded glances. Berkley drew a deep breath. "It has come to our attention...that is, we have learned...what I mean to say..."

"Blast it all, man," Pennington snapped. "Spit it out."

"Are you the country miss?" Berkley blurted.

Shock stole her breath. "Me?"

"Yes, you," Pennington said.

"Why would you think such a thing?" she said weakly.

"We saw Helmsley coming out of Cadwallender's shop," Pennington said.

"That scarcely means—"

"It was not difficult at that point to put the pieces of this puzzle together." Pennington studied her intently. "You are, aren't you?"

"And Helmsley, then, is Lord W?" Berkley said.

"Yes." She blew a long breath. "Although the adventures are not absolutely true."

"What did I tell you?" Pennington nudged his friend. "I told you not to believe everything you read."

"Regardless." Berkley squared his shoulders and stepped forward. "Would you do me the honor of becoming my wife?"

"Your wife?" She stared in disbelief. "I thought you had given up the idea of pursuing a woman you did not know."

"How could I, with that villainous Leopard on the scene? And now that the truth has been revealed, you cannot deny that I know you." He took her hand. "And I care for you as Marianne and as the country miss."

"That's very nice and I am truly flattered, but"—she gently withdrew her hand—"marriage between us is not—"

"She's in love with Helmsley," Pennington said flatly.

Marianne's gaze met his. "Why do you say that?"

"It's obvious, my dear, once you know who the players really are in those adventures of yours." He shrugged. "You are, aren't you?"

"Yes...yes, I am." She wrung her hands together helplessly. "And everything has become a terrible mess because of those foolish stories. Thomas could well be killed."

"Killed?" Pennington's tone sobered.

"What do you mean?" Berkley asked.

She brushed her hair away from her face. "He's going to duel Leopard."

Pennington raised a brow. "So Leopard is real?"

"I knew it," Berkley huffed.

"No, he's not real. Or rather, apparently, he is. But I didn't know that." She turned on her heel and paced back and forth. "I thought I had made him up. You know, to add interest to the stories. I never dreamed he actually existed."

"It certainly piqued *my* interest," Berkley murmured.

She paused and stared at the men. "But surely you know him?"

"Don't know anyone named Leopard." Berkley shrugged.

"Rather silly name, I always thought," Pennington added.

"I'm sorry you don't approve," she said sharply. "I was looking for something that no one would actually use, to avoid precisely this problem."

"Still, doesn't he have a real name?" Pennington asked.

"Of course. It's Beaumont."

"Beaumont? Viscount Beaumont?" Pennington frowned. "Tall, dark hair, arrogant—"

"Aren't you all," she muttered.

"Of course we know him. Hasn't been in town much lately." Berkley shook his head. "Never heard him called Leopard, though."

"Never?" How was that possible? If indeed they knew him, surely they knew his absurd name?

"Helmsley has known him for years," Pennington said pointedly.

She stilled and studied him. "You must be mistaken. That makes no sense whatever. I can't believe..." Of course, Leopard, or rather Beaumont, knew exactly where to find—"The brandy!"

She smacked her hand against her forehead. "He knew where the brandy is kept. He's obviously been here before. I should have noticed it at once."

Outrage rushed through her. "Thomas acted like they'd never met."

"Perhaps, my dear," Pennington said mildly. "*Act* is the key word."

"Isn't it, though?" She wanted to scream in frustration. "How could I have been so easily taken in? How could I have believed all that nonsense? *Have my way with you*—hah!"

The men traded uneasy glances.

"They certainly make a convincing pair: a badger in leopard's clothing and a...a..."

"Rat?" Berkley suggested.

"That's it exactly. A rat. A nasty, vile rat. But why?" She paced once again, trying to sort it all out in her mind. "Why would they—why would Thomas—do such a thing?"

She swiveled toward them. "You saw him coming out of Cadwallender's, you say?"

"That's what brought us here," Berkley said.

"Of course." She groaned. "Then he knows I've been writing the *Adventures*. I'd wager he wanted to teach me some sort of lesson." She narrowed her eyes. "He's very fond of lessons."

"And, no doubt, wanted to stop you as well." Pennington studied her cautiously. "I can't say I blame him. The longer the stories are published, the more likely it is that someone will discover the true identity of the author. And her Lord W. The scandal would be—"

"Enormous." She huffed an impatient sigh. "I know that. And I admit, I have made a mess of things." Still... She stepped to the desk and snatched up the legal papers and handed them to Pennington. "What are these?"

Pennington scanned the documents. "They appear to be some sort of business arrangement. It looks as though Helmsley has made an investment in Cadwallender's enterprise." Pennington let out a long whistle. "A very sizable investment. Given these"—his gaze met hers—"one has to wonder, why didn't he stop Cadwallender from printing your work? Obviously, he has the financial leverage."

"He's far too smart for that. He knows full well, given the success of the *Adventures*, I could have easily sold them to another paper. This was probably his way of keeping an eye on me." She stared at Pennington. "When did—"

Pennington studied the papers. "It's dated approximately three weeks ago." He glanced up at her. "Does it matter?"

"Oh, indeed it does. It matters very much." Three weeks ago coincided with the dowager's house party and Thomas's increased efforts to lure her into marriage. Obviously, efforts spurred by his discovery of her writing and a desire to head off scandal.

And nothing more.

And what of his words today? Were they part and parcel of the act he'd concocted with his friend? Another aspect of teaching her some absurd lesson?

"My lady?" Pennington's voice jerked her back to the present. His concerned gaze met hers. "Are you all right?"

"I'm fine." She drew a deep breath and squared her shoulders. "Do you know where Newcombe's Hill is?"

Berkley nodded. "It's just north of the city."

"Would you be so kind as to accompany me there?"

"Why? The only reason anyone goes there is..." Berkley cringed. "Oh."

"I gather that's where the final curtain on this farce of Helmsley's will ring down." Pennington studied her. "Am I right?"

"Indeed you are, my lord. I strongly suspect my presence is expected. After all, how can there be a final act without all the players? It should be extremely interesting."

She favored the men with her brightest smile, disregarding the anger seething within her. And the pain.

"Besides, what farce is complete without a surprise ending?"

Chapter 21

...indeed have learned a great lesson in these past months, cousin. You would do well to heed my words.

Regardless of their station in life, no matter if they are respected or despised, men are vile, treacherous beasts and are not to be trusted. I believe it is a flaw in their nature.

If women were wise, we would cut it out of them at the point of a sword for the sake of all of us. In truth, for the sake of the world itself.

Certainly there would be some loss of life, but sacrifices must be made....

The Absolutely True Adventures
of a Country Miss in London

"I think it went well." Thomas grinned. "In spite of the fact that I kept waiting for her to scream for help to make my entrance."

"I suspect she is not the type of woman who calls for assistance, judging by the way she hit me," Rand muttered. "You never said she'd hit me."

The two men sat in the grass on Newcombe's Hill—more of a rise rather than a true hill, yet high enough to overlook the road from the city.

"I should have expected as much." Thomas chuckled.

"You think she'll come?"

"Of course she'll come," Thomas said confidently. "It's all part of my plan."

"Ah, yes, the plan." Rand eyed him skeptically. "When you asked for my assistance this morning, you explained little beyond the point where I pretend to be this Leopard person—ridiculous name, by the way—you challenge me and...now what?"

"It's quite simple. When we see her carriage round the bend, we'll get into position."

"The duel having already taken place, I gather."

Thomas nodded. "She'll arrive to see you grievously wounded, of course—"

"Of course," he said wryly.

"—and being carried into the carriage." Thomas nodded toward the waiting vehicle and the four men he'd hired to act as seconds and interested parties. It wouldn't do to involve anyone of his acquaintance beyond Rand in this endeavor. No one else he knew could be counted on to keep his mouth shut.

"Whereupon I will give another outstanding performance as to how I shall have to leave England forever to avoid prison. She will realize there is a great price to pay for adventures and will further realize what happens when one bases fictions on real people." He grinned in triumph.

Rand studied him curiously. "That's it, then?"

"Brilliant, isn't it?"

340

"There's nothing more to it than that?"

"Well, yes. Actually, at that point she throws herself into my arms and admits that this is indeed all her fault. And further confesses about her stories and vows that she would do anything to change what has happened." He leaned back on his elbows, gazed out over the countryside and blew a long satisfied breath.

"And?"

"And...nothing. Well, she will agree to marry me and we will then spend the rest of our lives together."

Rand studied him, his eyes narrowed. "You don't see a flaw there? Some, oh, insignificant detail you might have overlooked?"

"No. None at all." In fact, all was truly right with Thomas's world at the moment. He'd get a special license and they could be married within the week.

"You don't know this woman very well, do you?"

"I know her quite well."

"Really?" Rand raised a brow. "Then tell me how she will react when she discovers all this is some kind of ruse to teach her a lesson."

"She'll be so grateful that it's all an act..." What if she wasn't? His confidence dimmed.

"Will she?"

"Of course." He brushed aside the uneasy suspicion that she might not be grateful at all. "Why, we'll probably laugh about it someday."

"I do hope you're right, for your sake. But it seems to me, any woman who could handle the kind of rogue this Leopard was supposed to be"—Rand rubbed his stomach and winced—"and handle him quite well, mind you, will not see any humor in this whatsoever. When do you plan on telling her the truth?"

"I don't know." In point of fact, now that he thought about it, he had no idea when he'd confess all.

Rand snorted and shook his head.

Thomas pulled his brows together in a frown. "What is so amusing?"

"I'm simply recalling the last time we spoke, before I left London. If I remember correctly, your plan then was to find husbands for these sisters and get them off your hands so you could concentrate on finding the type of paragon you wished for a wife." He chuckled. "It appears you failed miserably."

"Marianne is the woman I want for a wife," he said staunchly, knowing he had never spoken truer words.

"Rather ironic, isn't it?"

Thomas cast him a wry grin.

Three riders turned the bend and headed toward them.

Rand squinted in the deepening dusk. "Is that her?"

"Couldn't be." Thomas shook his head. "She'll take the carriage. Marianne isn't an accomplished rider and she'd never come out from the city on horseback. Besides, she'll be alone and there are three of them."

The riders grew closer. Rand got to his feet. "Could you be wrong?" He nodded at the approaching trio. "One of them is definitely a woman. Or a man riding sidesaddle."

Thomas stared for a moment.

"Bloody hell," he muttered and scrambled to his feet. It was indeed Marianne, accompanied by Pennington and Berkley. He should have known she'd get them involved. "She's not supposed to be on horseback. It's too late to get into position."

"Then what do we do?"

"I don't know!"

The horses halted a few yards away.

"Thomas!" Marianne slid off her mount and ran to him, throwing herself into his arms. "Thank God we're not too late."

Perhaps he could salvage this after all.

"You shouldn't be here." He gently set her aside. "I cannot allow you to witness this."

Pennington and Berkley dismounted and strode toward them. There was a peculiar gleam in Pennington's eye, and Berkley's lips twitched as if he were trying to hold back a grin. Surely these old friends of his didn't find this amusing? No, of course not. He must be mistaken. Again. "You shouldn't have brought her here."

"Actually, she brought us," Pennington said mildly. Far too mildly.

"Regardless." Thomas's voice was firm. "She should leave."

"Absolutely not, my lord." Marianne lifted her chin in a courageous manner. "I cannot allow you—"

"Well"—relief rushed through him—"perhaps we can settle this matter without bloodshed."

"—to defend my honor—"

"I am willing to apologize," Rand said quickly.

"—without my presence." She beamed at him.

"Without your presence?" Thomas stared. She wanted him to duel?

"Gentlemen." She turned to her companions. "Where should we stand?" She glanced around. "I do want to make sure I see everything, although I suppose it would be best to stay out of the way."

Pennington nodded. "One can never be too certain of the course of flying bullets."

"Wouldn't want the wrong person shot," Berkley added.

"No, indeed." She placed her hand on Thomas's arm and smiled up at him. "This is so very exciting. Imagine, a duel. A real adventure."

"Marianne," Thomas said slowly. "Perhaps, if Leopard is willing to apologize—"

"I am." Rand nodded vigorously. "I was a cad. A bounder. A beast. And I am truly sorry. I cannot tell you how sorry I am."

"Nonetheless"—she glared at Rand—"Lord Helmsley feels you have impugned my honor and you shall have to pay." She moved back a few paces. Pennington and Berkley joined her. "Now, then, Thomas, shoot him."

"What?" Thomas stared in disbelief. She did want him to duel.

"I said, shoot him." She folded her arms over her chest. "Go ahead. We're waiting."

Rand leaned toward Thomas and spoke in a low voice. "She wants you to shoot me."

"So I hear," Thomas said out of the corner of his mouth.

"Perhaps we could both miss," Rand said.

Thomas scoffed, "And you thought *my* plan was stupid?"

"Well, at least my idea will get us out of this," Rand snapped. "Now, then, where are the pistols?"

Thomas clenched his teeth. "I didn't think we needed them."

"Oh, you are good at plans." Rand rolled his gaze toward the sky.

"Did you forget pistols?" Marianne planted her hands on her hips. "I daresay, my lord, I am disappointed in you. How could you overlook such a thing?"

"The excitement, I suppose." Thomas's voice was weak.

Pennington waved his hand and called to them. "I believe I have pistols."

"Do you really?" Marianne said brightly. "How wonderfully prepared of you."

"Thank you." Pennington smiled in a modest manner.

"I didn't know you carried pistols." Berkley frowned.

"Actually, I only have one." Pennington shrugged. "One never knows when one might be accosted by a highwayman or other brigand."

"That's it, then. One will never do. Besides,

I couldn't possibly duel with weapons I am not familiar with," Rand said loftily.

"Nor could I." Thomas nodded with relief.

"What about fisticuffs?" Berkley suggested. "They could beat each other for a while."

"No." Marianne heaved a sigh. "It's just not the same." She moved toward Thomas. "I gather this means you're not going to save my honor and shoot him?"

Thomas feigned regret. "I'm afraid not."

"And you"—she turned to Rand—"are not going to shoot him so that you may have your way with me?"

"As delightful as the prospect is, on both counts"—he cast Thomas a scathing glare—"I'd say no."

"I see," she said thoughtfully and paused for a long moment. Her brow furrowed in thought. "Lord Pennington?"

"Yes, my lady?" Pennington stepped forward.

"Could I see that pistol of yours?" Her gaze met Thomas's and a heavy weight settled in his stomach.

"Of course." Pennington started toward his horse.

"Wait." Thomas thrust out his hand to stop the man, his gaze never leaving hers. "Why?"

"Because, Thomas Effington, Marquess of Helmsley and future Duke of Roxborough"—her eyes narrowed and fury flared in her gaze—"I want to shoot you myself."

Rand moved away to join Pennington and Berkley. Wise of him, no doubt.

Thomas's heart dropped to his toes. She knew. And she was not amused. "Marianne, I—"

"You what?" She stepped closer and poked her finger at his chest. "You lied to me. You made me think you were in mortal danger. Do you have any idea how distraught I was at the thought that I had destroyed your life?"

"It does sound bad when she puts it that way," Berkley murmured.

It did indeed. Thomas really hadn't considered that aspect. And, in fact, hadn't considered at all what would happen if his plan went awry. "Marianne, if you will—"

"It wasn't bad enough that you wanted to marry us all off without a second thought, offering us to the first man who came along." Realization dawned in her eyes and her gaze jerked to Rand. "That was you in the library that night, wasn't it? The one he said could have his pick of any of us?"

Rand looked like he preferred to be anywhere but here. "Yes, but, to my credit, I did not accept his offer."

"Oh, that *is* to your credit!" she snapped, then turned back to Thomas and poked him again. "Then you had the audacity to attempt to peddle me to the dullest men in all of England."

"It just gets better and better," Pennington said under his breath.

"And all that nonsense about trying to be like a dashing hero from a book." She poked again. "It was an act, wasn't it? Every bit of

347

it. Just to salvage your sense of honor and trap me into marriage."

"Hold on just a minute." At once he was as angry as she. He grabbed her hand. "First, you can stop poking me. I've told you before, I don't like it and it hurts."

"Good!"

"And secondly"—he glared down at her—"I am not the one who courted scandal by putting our entire relationship in the papers for public consumption!"

"You paid Mr. Cadwallender to stop printing my work!"

"I did not," he said indignantly. "I have a legitimate business interest with Cadwallender that has nothing to do with you. Besides, he wouldn't take money to cease publishing those blasted stories of yours. Stories about us!"

"Oh, come, now," she scoffed. "What I wrote bore only the vaguest resemblance to what went on between us. They were not absolutely true, after all."

"True enough that anyone with half a brain could figure out exactly who the country miss was, and Lord W!" He called to Berkley, "Isn't that right?"

"Well, it did take a while," Berkley muttered.

"And that's another thing." He jerked her closer. "Why is it you called me by a mere initial? A *W*, no less—bottom of the barrel, if you ask me—and you give the villain in your piece a dashing, romantic name?"

"I thought it was rather silly," Rand murmured.

"Lord W." He blew a disdainful breath. "What does the *W* stand for, anyway?"

"At the moment, *witless*, I should think," Pennington said.

"Definitely not *wise*," Rand added.

"Well, it certainly isn't *wonderful*." She wrenched out of his grasp and stepped back.

Frustration surged through him. "All I wanted was to marry you!"

"All you wanted was to redeem yourself!"

"There are better ways to do it. I've barely survived." He clenched his jaw. "I have been scraped and scratched and bruised and battered and bit for you!"

"Stung," she said scathingly. "Not bit, stung. And a child would have handled it better!"

"And why did I put myself through all that?"

"I don't know? Why?" Her voice rose.

"Because I want you to be my wife!" he yelled.

"Why?" She shot the word at him.

What did she want him to say? "Because we're bloody perfect together!"

"Why?" she demanded again.

"I don't know." There was a helpless note in his voice. "Fate?"

"Is he really as dim as he seems?" Rand said to Pennington.

Pennington shrugged. "It would appear so."

She stared at him for a long moment. Intensity gleamed in her eyes, but he couldn't find the right answer there. He didn't know what she wanted. "It's not enough." She shook her head, resignation replacing the anger in her voice. "It's not nearly enough." She turned and started toward the horses. "Gentlemen, if you would be so kind as to accompany me back to town."

"Of course." Berkley stepped to her side.

Pennington studied Thomas for a moment with sympathy and disbelief, then shook his head and joined them.

Thomas watched the trio ride off. Rand heaved a sigh beside him. "That didn't go well."

"No, it didn't."

"What are you going to do now?"

"I don't know." What was he going to do? He couldn't let her ride out of his life. He couldn't live his life without her.

"It seems to me, old man, if there was ever a time that called for a good plan, this is it."

"I seem to be out of plans at the moment." Thomas uttered a disparaging laugh. "Good or otherwise."

Never had he felt the kind of despair that now held him in its grip. She detested him, and for good reason. He'd made any number of mistakes with her and now he would have to pay for them. And pay dearly.

And *Lord Witless* seemed entirely appropriate.

Chapter 22

<hr>

...and have at last come to a decision as to my future. It is time to take my fate in my own hands. To that end, I have decided to leave England.

I shall travel in secret—it would not do to let Lord W know my plans. I fear he will not allow me to leave. Or, God help me, in spite of all that has passed between us, I very much fear he will....

The Absolutely True Adventures
of a Country Miss in London

"What are you doing?" Jocelyn said, stepping into Marianne's room.

"What does it look like?" Marianne threw a day dress into the portmanteau on her bed.

"It looks like you're packing," Becky said, a step behind Jocelyn, Henry at her heels.

"You are astute." Marianne moved to the armoire and yanked several gowns free. "That is precisely what I'm doing."

"They'll wrinkle if you don't do it properly." Jocelyn glanced at Becky and jerked her head toward the door.

Becky started to leave.

"Where are you going?" Marianne snapped.

"I thought you could use the help of a

maid." Becky's eyes widened in innocence. "Jocelyn's right, you know, everything will be dreadfully wrinkled, and I thought—"

"You thought you'd fetch Aunt Louella."

Becky and Jocelyn exchanged guilty glances.

"I'd prefer not to deal with her, but I will if need be." Marianne drew a deep breath. "She will not stop me, and neither will you."

"Where exactly are you going?" Jocelyn came closer and sank down on the edge of the bed.

"Italy, eventually." Marianne folded the gowns haphazardly. Her mind was anywhere but on what she was doing. "I shall take a carriage to Dover and a packet to France. It shall be a most adventuresome journey."

"Why?" Becky crossed her arms and leaned against the bedpost. Henry plopped down at her feet.

"Well, there are any number of interesting things that can occur. Just crossing the channel shall be exciting."

"No." Becky heaved an exasperated sigh. "Why are you going?"

Marianne knew full well what she'd meant. "Because I can, and because I want to. I have enough money to get to Paris and, after that, I intend to get my dowry from Richard. This is what I've always wanted and the time is right. And because"—her voice wavered and she ignored it—"there's nothing here for me."

Jocelyn's brow rose. "What about Helmsley?"

Becky studied her. "We thought perhaps you and he..."

"Then you thought wrong." Marianne tossed the clothes in her hand into the case.

Jocelyn drew a deep breath. "But he does want to marry you, doesn't he?"

"So he says." Marianne's gaze met her sister's. "How do you know that?"

"We know everything," Jocelyn said. "All of it."

"And we were rather shocked, too." Becky shook her head. "How could you? We never dreamed you would make your *Country Miss* stories so...so..."

"Authentic." Jocelyn said the word as if it were obscene.

"They weren't absolutely true," Marianne muttered.

Jocelyn narrowed her eyes. "True enough."

"And I shall pay the price for them," Marianne said firmly. A terrible price. A life without Thomas.

Yet what choice did she have? Wouldn't the cost be far greater to live the rest of her days loving a man who did not love her? A cost that would destroy her soul. And the one price she refused to pay.

The back of her throat ached with unshed tears at the thought of the years ahead without him. She ignored it and pulled a steadying breath.

"Now, then, I have a great deal to do, and I could use your assistance. I intend to leave tonight."

"Tonight?" Becky's gaze filled with concern. "So soon?"

"How can you possibly leave tonight?" Jocelyn's voice rose in dismay.

Even Henry stared at her with a mournful look.

"I think it's best." Marianne forced a light note to her voice. "Don't look at me like that. It's not as if we will never see each other again."

"I know this is what you've always wanted, but..." Jocelyn blinked hard in an obvious effort to hold back tears. "We shall miss you."

"And I shall miss you. And who knows? I could be back in no time." Her eyes blurred with tears. "Why, anything could happen. My carriage could break down or my money could be stolen at the point of a pistol or the road could be flooded and I would be forced to come back or I could change my mind—"

"Oh, I do hope so." Becky brushed a tear from her cheek. "Not the carriage or losing your money or floods, of course, but—"

"But you won't change your mind, will you?" Jocelyn's lower lip trembled.

"No." Marianne shook her head. "I won't."

The words hung in the air for a moment and then all three sisters were in each other's arms. They sobbed promises and solemn vows and declarations of what each meant to the other. Marianne knew with a bittersweet surety they would never be this close again. Until now, she hadn't given a moment's thought to how much she'd have to give up to live the life she wished. This, too, had a price.

They'd been through so much together.

Their mother's death. Their father's gambling and the poverty that resulted from it. His demise, and their struggle to make ends meet. But no matter what had happened in their lives, they'd always had each other.

Jocelyn and Becky would be fine, Marianne told herself. Aunt Louella would see to it. They'd no doubt be married within the next few years, with families of their own.

At last, they drew apart.

"Enough of this sentimental nonsense." Marianne pulled off her glasses and wiped her eyes with the back of her hand. "I shall come back for visits and I'll write. Lovely long letters about my...adventures." She was hard-pressed not to choke on the word.

"Of course you'll write," Becky said staunchly.

"Are you hiring a carriage, then?" Jocelyn sniffed and her eyes glittered. "Or taking a public coach?"

"No. I am borrowing an Effington coach and driver. It shall save me a bit of money." She replaced her spectacles and tried to keep her voice level. "I daresay the marquess won't mind. It is the least he can do."

"Why don't you just marry him?" Becky blurted. "Wouldn't it be rather an adventure to make his life miserable? That would serve him right."

"It would certainly teach him a lesson," Jocelyn added.

"There have been one too many lessons already, thank you." She turned back to her bag. "Now, then, if someone would hand me that gown."

Jocelyn passed her the dress. "If you're certain about this—"

"I am."

"Then I suppose the least we can do is offer you some assistance." Jocelyn nodded at Becky. "Why don't you go to the kitchen and see if a basket can be put together for her? It's an exceedingly long way to Dover. I shall go at once and arrange for the carriage."

"Thank you." Marianne forced a smile to her face. If Thomas had not already broken her heart, it would surely break now. Lord, she would miss these two.

Another flurry of hugs ensued, another few tears shed, then sisters, and dog, took their leave.

Marianne's packing was nearly complete. She couldn't possibly take everything; most of the new gowns would be left behind, at least for now. She would send for the rest of her things later.

The girls were right on one count. Thomas did indeed need to be taught a lesson. But Marianne simply didn't have the will for it. The heroines in her books never had this kind of problem. They were always resolute and never gave up. Perhaps Marianne didn't have whatever it took to truly be a heroine? Or, more likely, fictional heroines really had nothing whatsoever to do with the real world she lived in. Pity she didn't realize it sooner. Still, would she have done anything differently?

Probably not.

No, she had no desire to teach Thomas a lesson of any sort. No desire to do anything but turn her attentions toward her future and put Thomas firmly behind her.

And that might be the hardest lesson of all.

Thomas held his glass out silently.

Berkley passed the decanter to Pennington, who refilled his own glass and handed the vessel to Rand, who proceeded to top off his brandy, lean forward and, at last, pour the amber liquid into Thomas's goblet.

He and Rand had scarcely said more than a dozen words since their return to Effington House. Even the arrival of Berkley and Pennington had not stimulated conversation. Now they all sat in the library, furniture haphazardly rearranged to make certain no man had to reach overly far for the liquor. The four men shared the brandy as well as a heavy silence due entirely to the inability of three of them to provide any guidance whatsoever and the realization by the remaining one of how thoroughly he had muddled his life.

"Lord Witless," Thomas muttered.

"Indeed." Pennington snorted. "Admittedly, you haven't handled things in the best possible manner."

"He's been damned stupid, if you ask me," Berkley said.

Thomas narrowed his eyes but held his tongue. He preferred not to hear it but could hardly deny it.

"So." Rand cleared his throat. "What's the plan now?"

"Other than my intention to drain every drop of brandy in London..." Thomas stared into his glass. "Haven't got one."

"That is a bad sign." Rand shook his head. "You always have a plan."

"Not this time." Thomas looked up hopefully. "Maybe she'll forgive me?"

Skeptical silence greeted the question.

"I didn't think so," he muttered and drew a long swallow.

"I do think Beaumont has something there," Pennington said. "I think it's time for some sort of plan."

"Really?" Thomas raised a brow. "Then I hope you can come up with something. All of my plans have been dismal failures thus far." He took another drink. "I even did battle with ivy for her."

"Perhaps we need to look at this in a logical manner." Pennington's voice was thoughtful.

"Hah." Thomas slumped back in his chair. "We are talking about Marianne Shelton. Logic plays no role whatsoever."

"Come, now," Pennington said, "logic always plays a role."

"Not with her. All she's interested in, all she's ever been interested in, are damnable adventures and grand excitement and traveling the world.

Just like her blasted books." Thomas took another sip and wondered why the potent liquor was not making him feel the least bit better. "She's never wanted marriage in and of itself. But if she did, she says she'd want the kind of man she's read about. A jungle explorer or treasure seeker or pirate or some such nonsense."

"That's what comes of allowing women to read." Berkley nodded his head sagely.

The other three men stared at him.

"What did I say?" Berkley's eyes widened.

"Not a bad idea, actually." Thomas raised his glass to Berkley.

Rand chuckled. "Far too late to help you, though."

"Besides," Pennington added, "there is nothing quite as dull as an ignorant woman. Oh, if she's pretty she can be amusing for a time, but after a while one needs more in female companionship than a lovely face."

"Or a well-turned ankle," Berkley said.

"Or a fine figure." Rand nodded.

"Or golden hair that dances around her head like a halo," Thomas murmured.

The other men traded glances.

Pennington drew a deep breath. "She's in love with you, you know."

"She hates me," Thomas muttered.

"Hardly." Berkley huffed. "She loves you. She told us so herself."

"And you, old man"—Rand leaned toward him—"are in love with her."

"Hah. Wouldn't I be the first to know if I were in love?" Thomas's manner was glum.

"She drives me mad. She's not at all the kind of woman I would fall in love with. She's far too independent and stubborn and—"

"And you said it yourself." Rand grinned. "When you were saving her from the clutches of Leopard."

"I would have liked to have seen that," Pennington said to Berkley.

"You said—"

"*You have impugned the honor of the woman I love,*" Thomas murmured without thinking. "Did I say that?"

"You did indeed." Rand nodded. "And with a great deal of enthusiasm."

"Now, the question is"—Pennington studied him—"did you mean it?"

"Did I?" He hadn't really considered it. He'd been so busy trying to talk her into marriage, he hadn't given love more than a passing thought. He'd been so concerned about appealing to her head, he'd paid no attention to her heart. Or to his.

He knew he wanted to share his life with her. Couldn't, in fact, conceive of his life without her. The very thought triggered a heavy weight in the pit of his stomach. It was a miserable feeling. In fact, he was miserable. And what, save love, could do that to a man?

"I am in love with her." His voice held a touch of awe.

"It's about time you realized it." Rand grinned.

"And more to the point," Pennington said, "she's in love with you."

"I'm in love with her," Thomas murmured. "And she's in love with me." The truth struck him like a slap across the face. "Bloody hell." He bolted upright and clapped his hand to his forehead. "That's what she wanted to hear, wasn't it? When she kept asking why I wanted to marry her? She wanted me to tell her I loved her."

"I believe you said *fate,* at that moment," Rand said wryly.

Pennington chuckled. "*Lord Witless* does seem more and more appropriate."

Thomas groaned. "I have made a mess of it all."

"It's probably not too late to fix things." Pennington sipped his drink. "She might well be amenable to listening to your abject apologies—"

"And declaration of love," Rand said.

"And don't forget groveling," Berkley threw in. "Women love groveling."

"In the morning," Pennington continued. "After she's had a chance to sleep on it. Life always looks better at the start of a new day."

Thomas wasn't entirely certain he could wait until tomorrow. Still, Pennington was probably right.

Thomas's spirits lifted. He would go to her first thing in the morning. No. He would awaken her at dawn. He'd tell her what an idiot he'd been and swear his undying love and, yes, grovel as much as was needed. And surely she'd forgive him for being such a fool. After all, she loved him.

Thomas grinned. "Now, that sounds like a plan."

The door to the library slammed open.

"Helmsley?" Jocelyn's voice rang in the room. "Are you in here?"

The men sprang unsteadily to their feet.

Jocelyn and Becky swept toward them, followed by Henry.

"What are you still doing here?" Jocelyn planted her hands on her hips.

Becky copied her sister's stance and tone. "You should be gone by now."

The dog growled.

"Gone?" Thomas drew his brows together. "Where would I go?"

"After Marianne, of course," Jocelyn said.

"And where, pray tell, has she gone?" Pennington asked.

Jocelyn squinted into the shadows and Pennington stepped forward. "My Lord Pennington." Jocelyn cast Pennington a delighted smile and offered her hand. "I didn't see you. And Lord Berkley as well." Her gaze settled on Rand. "I don't believe we've met."

"Now is not the time for introductions," Thomas snapped. "What are you talking about?"

Jocelyn withdrew her hand reluctantly and glanced at Becky. "Didn't you tell him?"

"I wasn't supposed to tell him." Becky shook her head. "I was supposed to arrange for food. You were supposed to tell him."

"No." Jocelyn shook her head. "I was talking to the driver. You were the one who—"

"Tell me now!" he roared.

"You needn't take that tone with us," Becky said in a huff.

"This is not our fault." Jocelyn's eyes narrowed in an accusing manner. "If you'd done your part, she'd be married by now."

"Regardless," Thomas clenched his fists, "where is she going?"

"Italy," Becky said with a sigh. "But Paris first, and—"

"Dover," Jocelyn cut in. "She's on her way to Dover and then to France. I did tell the driver...what was his name?"

"Greggs?" Thomas said.

"I told him to drive as slow as possible. They probably haven't gone far." Jocelyn's eyes narrowed in a threatening manner. "You have to stop her."

"Of course I'll stop her. I'll leave at once." He started toward the door.

Rand grabbed his arm. "I think, at this point, you do indeed need some sort of plan."

"And it had better be more successful than anything else you've tried," Jocelyn said. "You can't simply *ask* her to return. She's hiding it well, but she's angry and hurt and not at all her usual self. I've never seen her like this." She studied him suspiciously. "What did you do to her?"

Guilt surged through him. "We had a bit of a misunderstanding."

Berkley choked. Pennington coughed. Rand cleared his throat.

Becky stepped toward him. "She said she wouldn't change her mind. She said nothing short of accidents or floods or being robbed of her money would make her come back."

"Robbery, eh?" Rand said and looked at Pennington.

"It's ridiculous, of course. Still..." Pennington nodded thoughtfully. "It might well work."

Thomas's gaze slid from one man to the next. "What might work?"

Pennington grasped the elbow of both girls and steered them to the door. "If you would be so kind as to make certain our horses are made ready."

"What are you going to do?" Becky asked.

"We have a few items to discuss, preparations of our own, then we shall be off to recover your sister." Pennington eased them out the door and closed it firmly behind them.

"What preparations?" Thomas shook his head in confusion. "What are you talking about?"

"Damned if I know," Berkley muttered, obviously as lost as Thomas.

"Helmsley, old chap." Pennington chuckled. "In times of trouble a man should always be able to depend on his friends for help. And you are about to receive just that."

Apparently, the brandy had affected Thomas far more than he'd suspected. None of this made the slightest sense. "What kind of help?"

"Come, now, Helmsley, think for a moment. For a woman whose view of the world, and the men in it, is colored by fiction, what kind of man—in a fictitious sense, at any rate—is every bit as exciting as an explorer or pirate or..." Pennington paused significantly.

"Or?" Rand prompted.

"Or..." At once the answer popped into Thomas's mind. "Oh, no. I daresay that's...well, it's..." Absurd? Ridiculous? Mad? "Inspired." Thomas laughed. "I couldn't have done better myself."

"Then I do believe, gentlemen"—Rand raised his glass in a toast—"we have a plan."

Chapter 23

...for I do not know what will happen next, dear cousin, or worse, whom I can trust.

Will my story end well? Or will tragedy and despair be my fate? Was it not Shakespeare who spoke of loving not wisely but too well? I fear I have done neither.

It is as if I am trapped in a carriage, its horses careening out of control, its speed growing faster and faster.

A cliff drawing ever closer...

The Absolutely True Adventures
of a Country Miss in London

It seemed as though Marianne had been in the coach forever, although it was probably not much more than an hour. An endless hour in the darkened confines, with nothing to do but think. And Thomas was the only thing on her mind.

But thinking was getting her nowhere she hadn't been over and over again. It was an unending circle. Her love for him. His sense of obligation toward her. It was past time to put away all thoughts of him and what might have been and look toward the future. If she worked very hard, she might well be able to summon up some enthusiasm for at last living her dream.

Perhaps she should try to get some rest. It had been a very long, and very strange, day and she hadn't realized until now how exhausted she was. She closed her eyes and rested her head back against the leather squabs. The noise of the wheels against the road faded, the clop of the horses' hooves dimmed and the steady rhythm of the coach lulled her. She dozed somewhere between waking and sleep and barely noted the coach pulling to a stop.

The door jerked open and Greggs poked his head in.

"My lady, I fear we're being robbed."

"Robbed?" She jerked upright, at once fully awake.

He glanced over his shoulder, then turned back to her. "They want you to get out."

"Don't you have a pistol or some kind of weapon?" she said in an urgent whisper, adjusting her glasses. "Aren't you going to fight them off?"

He looked at her as if she were insane.

"Don't seem too smart, my lady. There are four of 'em." An order was barked behind him. Greggs held out his hand to assist her. "You'd best get out. Now."

She scrambled out of the coach.

There were indeed four highwaymen: two still on horseback, the other two having dismounted. They stood just out of the meager circle of light cast by the coach lanterns, one a short distance in front of her, the other next to Greggs beside the coach.

Her heart thudded in her chest. They were a menacing sight and looked exactly as she'd ever imagined highwaymen would look. Exactly like something from a book. All wore long masks that covered their mouths, the eyes nothing more than slits in the fabric. They had on tricorne hats and voluminous capes and might have been quite dashing if they weren't so terrifying. Greggs, however, seemed remarkably calm, as if this sort of thing happened every day.

"Move away from the coach," the leader ordered. At least she assumed he was the leader, judging by the wicked-looking pistol in his hand.

She drew a deep breath and stepped forward. *Dear God, what were they going to do to her?*

"Alone, my lady?" His voice was muffled by the mask. "What is a pretty thing like you doing traveling alone at night?"

"I prefer to travel alone." She ignored the tremor in her voice. It was best not to show fear. That's what a true heroine would do. But it was obviously much easier in a book.

"Not wise." One of the highwaymen on horseback shook his head. "Rather foolish, in fact."

"He's right. The roads are dangerous, especially at night. Why, anything could happen to a woman like you. Anything at all," the leader drawled. Was that a threat in his voice? Of violence? Or worse? She struggled to hold back panic.

"Why would you take such a risk?" he asked.

"It's none of your concern." In fact, she hadn't thought of the dangers of travel at all until now. She forced a calm note to her voice. "If your intent is to take my money, do so and be on your way."

"Not so fast, my lady. You have aroused my curiosity. Gentlemen?" He raised his voice to address his companions. Was it a touch slurred or was it the distortion of the mask? "What do you think? Why does a lady like this travel alone? At this late hour?"

"There's only one reason," one of the mounted men called. "She's running away. Probably from a man."

"I most certainly am not." She raised her chin even as she realized that was exactly what she was doing.

The leader studied her for a long moment. Fear shivered through her. She refused to even consider what his intentions might be. At last he spoke, his voice low and suggestive. "What kind of fool would ever let you go?"

"He is not a fool," she said without thinking.

"Ah, then there is a man?" He laughed in triumph. "I knew it all along."

She clenched her fists but refused to say another word. Why were they, or rather he, baiting her like this? At least the anger he provoked took her mind off her fear. Abruptly she realized that this was her first true adventure and she'd never been so scared in her life. Anything could happen. They could kill her, or worse. For the first time she wondered if perhaps adventure wasn't best left to fiction.

The leader tossed the pistol to the man beside Greggs, then circled her, taking care to stay beyond the perimeter of light. She resisted the urge to turn to follow his progress. Resisted the urge to open her mouth and scream with the terror bubbling inside her.

"And do you love this man?" he said behind her.

"You are extremely impertinent, for a thief," she snapped.

"You are extremely sharp-tongued, for a woman whose life is in my hands." He stepped back into view and returned to his original position.

"Perhaps you don't know to whom you're speaking," the brigand with the pistol said casually. "Before you stands the notorious, the infamous, the—"

"The Poet Highwayman. At your service." The leader, or rather the Poet, swept an overly dramatic bow and his hat tumbled to the ground. He snatched it up and slammed it back on his head before she could so much as see his hair. It would have been comical under other circumstances.

One of the mounted men leaned toward the other and spoke in a low voice. "The Poet Highwayman? I didn't know we called him that."

"Quiet," his companion ordered.

"Well, I've never heard of you. The Poet Highwayman?" she scoffed. It was rather silly. The kind of thing that sounded exciting in a book but in reality was rather ridiculous. "Why, that's as absurd a name as...as... as..." *As Leopard?*

"It's not absurd at all," he said loftily. "I shall take your money, but I leave you with a poem in return."

One of the bandits groaned.

"I'd prefer to keep my money," she said slowly.

Leopard was a silly name and nothing more than a product of her imagination. Was this Poet Highwayman a fiction as well? Oh, certainly there was a real man standing before her. And three others, all equally real, here as well. Still, wouldn't a poet highwayman be subject to ridicule from other robbers? Unless he was so wicked and murderous no one dared to snicker at him.

Her gaze slid carefully around the gathering. Only one pistol was in evidence. Certainly there could be more, but if so, wouldn't this band of thieves be brandishing their weapons? At least a little? However, if they'd forgotten to bring pistols...

There was something extremely odd about all this, and distinctly reminiscent. Why, hadn't she already been confronted once today by a man with a ridiculous name? A man who was not who he claimed to be?

Her fear faded. Was it at all possible? She narrowed her gaze. "And I don't want a poem."

"It is not your choice. Let me think." The Poet tilted his head and folded his arms.

Surely Thomas would never...he wouldn't dare...

"I don't know that a poem is really necessary tonight," the armed robber said pointedly.

"A poem is always necessary," the Poet said firmly. "A poem of love, perhaps."

Of course, she'd never dreamed Thomas would arrange a false duel, either. How much more complicated would it be to devise a feigned robbery?

"Do you love him?" he said abruptly.

And what kind of real highwayman would want to know such a thing?

She crossed her arms over her chest and studied him thoughtfully. He was certainly of Thomas's height and stance. And arrogance. "If I tell you I do, will you let me go?"

"Never." She could hear the grin in his voice.

"I see." She considered him for a moment. "And what if I tell you I don't love him? Will you let me go then?"

He paused for a moment. "No." His voice was a shade less lighthearted than before. "Never."

It was Thomas. She was certain of it. Why

else would Greggs be leaning against the carriage with a stupid grin on his face? She wasn't sure if she should be furious at the terror she'd just tasted at his hands or relieved that it was all a ruse. Or perhaps she should see just how far he was willing to go.

"Very well, then." She heaved an exaggerated sigh. "Since I refuse to answer and you refuse to let me go on my way, I suppose I have no choice but to throw myself at your mercy."

"My mercy?" A distinct note of unease sounded in his voice.

"Yes indeed." She turned her face away, rested the back of one hand on her forehead and reached the other toward him in as dramatic a gesture as she could muster. "Just...be kind."

"What do you mean, *be kind*?" Thomas said cautiously.

She cast him an annoyed glance. "I mean when you ravish me." She resumed her pose. "Be kind."

"I don't want to be kind," he said quickly.

Someone snickered.

"Oh, dear." She sighed again and clasped her hands together under her chin. "I knew it was too much to hope for from a notorious, infamous outlaw such as yourself. I suppose I have no choice but to accept my fate. Do as you will with me."

"No!" He huffed. "What I mean to say is, there is no need to be kind, as I do not intend to ravish you."

Someone snorted.

"You don't?" She planted her hands on her hips. "Why not?"

"Well, I—"

"What kind of notorious, infamous high-wayman are you?"

"The kind that spouts poetry," one of his companions said wryly. She'd wager anything it was Pennington.

"So there will be no ravishing, then?" she asked.

"No!"

"Are you sure?"

"Yes!"

"Well, if poetry is the best I can expect"— she lifted a shoulder in a disdainful manner— "do get on with it."

"Thank you," he muttered. He cleared his throat, paused, drew a breath and began. "For good or ill the night has led us on this grave adventure. With one so fair, the stars do pale in jealousy and censure."

"*Censure?*" a man astride murmured. Berkley, no doubt.

"It rhymes." The other rider shrugged. Definitely Pennington.

The Poet—Thomas—ignored the comment and continued. "Her hair gleams gold, her eyes glow brown with laughter and with life. But stubborn wench, this country miss, will naught be any man's wife."

Any lingering doubts vanished.

"My lady," the man with the pistol called. "If you would like, I'd be happy to shoot him for you right now and put us all out of our misery."

And surely that was Beaumont.

"Not necessary." She waved aside the offer and tried to keep her face composed. "I've become rather fond recently of bad poetry."

"It's not that bad," Thomas said indignantly.

"No? But I thought you said it was a love poem," she said innocently.

"It is." His voice was cautious.

"Thus far you haven't mentioned love. And you've spoken only of the woman. What of the man? If this is indeed a love poem, shouldn't it be his story as well as hers?" With her words she realized it was no longer amusing. No longer a simple jest.

"May I continue?"

"Please do." She held her breath.

He thought for a moment, then began. "He taught her well, she taught him more, still love was never mentioned." A serious note sounded in his voice. "Till he found truth within his heart. 'Tis called the marriage lesson."

She swallowed hard.

For a long moment no one spoke.

"Not bad. Not bad at all," Pennington murmured.

"But what does it mean?" Berkley asked.

"Yes, what does it mean?" Her heart beat faster. "Truth within his heart?"

"It means, my stubborn country miss, he loves her." He stepped to her and swept her into his arms. "I love her. Or rather, you."

She stared up into the slits of his mask. The back of her throat ached and she wasn't sure if she wanted to laugh or cry or both. A faint whiff of brandy tickled her nose. She spoke without thinking. "You're drunk."

"I most certainly am not. I do not get drunk. I occasionally drink a bit more than is wise in an effort to live life to its fullest."

She stared at him for a long moment. A wink of gold at the edge of his mask caught her eye. It was the tiny but distinct Roxborough crest.

She bit back a smile. His mask was nothing more than a cravat, and probably poorly tied, at that. "Did you bring some for me?"

"Some what?"

"Brandy, of course. I am rather fond of it." Her voice lowered. "And rather fond of you as well, my lord highwayman."

"You're more than fond of me. You cannot live without me." He pulled off his hat and mask. "I can tell by the way you're looking at me."

"Oh, and how is that?"

"As if I were the moon and the stars." He gaze meshed with hers and she saw the same look reflected in his eyes.

"And you love me," she said with a soft laugh.

He stared, his gaze searching hers. "I think, now, I've loved you from the beginning."

"It took you long enough to realize it." She wrapped her arms around his neck. "You were too busy thinking of ways to entice me into marriage to consider the only thing I couldn't argue with."

"That's because I am a practical man. You need someone with two feet on the ground," he said firmly. "We are well suited."

"And who would that practical man be? A bad poet? Or someone who can't plan a simple farce? Oh, that is a man with both feet on the ground." He really did see himself as a practical man, but in a few very important ways he was as much a dreamer as she. "You are right, though." She brushed her lips across his. "We are indeed well suited."

"I knew it." He grinned triumphantly.

"However, what I really need much more than a practical man"—she paused—"is someone to share my adventures with."

He studied her for a moment. "Will they kill me?"

She shook her head. "Probably not."

"Very well." He smiled slowly. "Then, once more, my love, will you marry me?"

"Probably."

He lifted a brow.

She laughed and gazed up at him. "Yes, I will marry you."

His lips met hers and she kissed him with all the love within her, knowing, at last, it was returned. He tasted of brandy and promises and all the adventures of tomorrow. She drew back and gazed up at him. "This changes nothing, you know. Wed or not, I still want adventures in my life."

"Well, I did promise." He grinned wickedly. "And it's not too soon to begin." He scooped her into his arms and carried her toward the coach. "Gentlemen, I thank you for your assistance, but I believe I can handle things from here."

"Damned fine plan." Beaumont grinned.

"And not bad poetry," Pennington said.

"I gather this means she's going to marry him?" Berkley said in an aside to Pennington.

"As soon as possible," Thomas said.

"Bad piece of luck there," Berkley muttered.

She laughed. "What are you planning now, Thomas?"

"The infamous highwayman is going to take you into the coach and have his way with you."

"Ah, well, if he must." She nuzzled his ear. "I have always wanted a man of adventure."

And the rocking of the coach all the way home had nothing to do with the quality of the roads and everything to do with lessons learned and adventures just begun.

...and yes, dear cousin, I have at last accepted Lord W's offer of marriage. It came with a declaration from his heart.

It is, as I'd always hoped, a life filled with adventures. Yet, I have found there is more excitement to be had within the embrace of one man's arms than in an entire world. It was a lesson I had to learn. A lesson of life. A lesson of love.

And in the end, a marriage lesson.

The Absolutely True Adventures
of a Country Miss in London